FORBIDDEN FRUIT

Stanley Gazemba

D0061632

THE MANTLE

New York

A version of this text was previously published in Kenya as *The Stone Hills of Maragoli* (Kwani? 2010).

This book is set in Alternate Gothic and Palatino Linotype.

Cover art by Michael Soi of Nairobi (@michaelsoistudio).
Cover design by Charala of Madrid (99designs.com/profiles/charala).
Interior design by Susan Leonard (roseislandbookworks.com).

ISBN 978-0-9986423-0-7

Printed and bound in the United States of America by McNaughton & Gunn, 960 Woodland Drive, Saline, MI 48176.

First edition, 2017

10 9 8 7 6 5 4 3 2 1

THE MANTLE
21-33 36th St.
Astoria, NY 11105
mantlebooks.com | @TheMantle

For Mama, Agnes,
a tireless hard worker—
God bless

FORBIDDEN FRUIT

Chapter One

THE AIR OVER the village that evening was pregnant with tension. A thick dark cloud loomed heavy above the grey colored thatch huts that dotted the steep green hillsides in kindred patches, threatening to cry rain any moment. As thunder boomed in the distant ridges hemming in the village to the west, the villagers became frantic. Young men and boys lost their patience with the stock, trying to herd them out of the rain, while the women hurried down to the river with pots and metal pails on their heads to get water to prepare the evening meal, hoping the rain wouldn't catch them on the way back. The air was damp and charged, the orange-streaked evening sky occasionally rent by a bolt of lightning that lit up the chaos beneath in bright white light for a brief electrifying moment. Night was fast approaching.

Ombima was scared—not of the approaching storm, but of what he was about to do. He ran along a winding path that was covered in fine red dust, which wound its way through the homesteads downhill into the valley separating their village from the next one, Kigama. The two villages were typical of the surrounding villages in that part of Maragoli in Western Kenya: small and inhabited by peasant farmers and petty traders. Above the gently snaking valley, in the midst of which a stream of icy crystalline water swiftly sped over rocks and other impediments, now hung a long thin wisp of mist the color of smoke from burning bone-dry wood. It was getting thicker and denser so in the next moment it would be virtually impossible to see across to Kigama. Then, when the storm struck, it would descend upon the country and shroud it in a thick blanket of fog and driving hail, the strong winds ripping branches out of the tall eucalyptus trees like avenging demons.

But it was not this that Ombima was afraid of. Neither was he scared of being caught out there in the deluge. In these parts, storms were heavy. Stories were told of men struck by lightning and reduced to "dry meatless statues." No one really knew of anyone who had died like this, but these stories were told to warn children, as Ombima's grandmother had once warned him as a boy. No, he was not scared of all these imaginary fears. He was scared of what he was about to do.

All his life into grey sideburned middle age, Ombima had never really stolen from anyone. He had always worked tirelessly for what little he had. Of course there were those petty offenses, like pilfering fruit from a neighbor's tree and things like that that everyone does as a boy and which is not seriously considered as theft. But stealing to satisfy a burning need he had never done. He had always gone out of his way to keep on his cloak of honesty, even after he got married and the hardships of looking after a family pressed.

Today Ombima was going to steal. Not money, not silver. He was going to steal food. Plain, life sustaining food, and it weighed him down with such shame he could hardly keep his head straight.

He left the path as it started to creep into the thorny bushes and made his way across the open field to his left. This field was covered in a thick carpet of coarse tough grass and shrub that the cattle turned to only during the dry season. As he went across, he was careful not to step on thorns with his bare feet. The thong of his *akala* sandals that he always wore around the village evenings and to Mbale on market days had come off, and there was no money to pay for its repair at the local shoe-maker's. He still had not washed from the day's labor for the rich man, Andimi. Grains of red earth still clung to the thin hairs on his muscled legs, which protruded out of the folded ends of

2

his patched trousers. His skin was clammy with the sweat of the fields. Perhaps he would not manage a bath that evening because of the fast-approaching storm and darkness. That is, if he was not caught out on his mission.

At the end of this field was a fence of barbed wire marking the beginning of Andimi's kitchen garden—a "kitchen garden" indeed! It was, in the true sense of the word, really a farm, because it was double the size of Ombima's property. And all that just for a "patch" of kitchen vegetables and bananas! In fact it was said the open field that Ombima was now crossing belonged to Andimi as well, only that he had not developed it yet, which was why the villagers took advantage and grazed their cattle on it as if it were community land.

The barbed wire was rusty and closely stranded, overgrown with grasses and creepers. By now it was favorably dark, but still Ombima was wary. Someone could still be lurking about in the garden even at this hour, and so he had to be watchful. He had thought of an explanation should he be found. He would say he was looking for his stray calf. But at this hour, with the storm coming like this, it was unlikely anyone would be about. He could explain himself outside the fence. But inside the fenced-off garden... that would be another matter.

He peered closely into the darkness of the trees looking for movement. A chill in the raging wind made him clasp himself, and for some reason other than the impending theft, his teeth chattered.

* * *

Andimi's wife, Madam Tabitha, was feeling rather wound up, and not because of the approaching storm. There were things on her mind. Indeed there had been since the noontime break at school. She had had a disagreement with the headmaster about an additional levy he proposed to charge parents for chickens one of the teachers had suggested they rear in the little yard behind the staff kitchen. This was purportedly to help improve the diet at lunch times, where occasionally they were to slaughter one of the birds in the place of the usual *sukuma-wiki* (collards) and pounded *ugali* (maize meal) or maize and beans. It was a fine idea to keep the birds and it would certainly do to boost the morale of the staff. But then the question was: should the parents finance it?

Madam Tabitha had been of the idea that since it was the teachers who would eat the chickens then it should be they to dip into their pockets to pay for the ten pullets that were proposed, and not the parents. But of course not everyone had agreed with her. Someone had even mumbled something that some people could afford to put up an argument for the parents because they knew they were sitting pretty back home. This had not escaped Tabitha's ear.

Kanzika, the games master, had been on her side though, arguing that the chickens would be a burden to the parents. He had gone even further and brought up the matter of pupils being sent on errands other than schoolwork. It was clear he was referring to a recent incident where the entire Class Six had been sent out to carry bricks from the valley in Kegoye all the way to Kiritu where the headmaster was constructing rental houses. One of the parents who had chanced to be passing that way had spotted his son in the work gang and raised a storm over the matter.

Clearly Tabitha had stirred a can of worms, and as the argument progressed, it easily degenerated into a heated exchange. It was not to be a very pleasant lunch break, and by the time she got home that evening Tabitha was dying for her evening cup of tea and some peace of mind.

She had changed into a nightgown and sat with her tea on the back veranda ruminating over the events of the day. But then it was only for a while. Soon one of the workers came up to report some happening in the homestead while she had been away, on top of requesting for a "small" loan to pay the veterinarian man for servicing his new grade heifer. Madam Tabitha went inside for her woolen shawl and, passing round the poultry house, disappeared into the cool breeziness of the swaying banana trees. The garden was the only place where she could get some peace and solitude.

* * *

Ombima stood by the overgrown fence for a while, listening. And then, moving swiftly, noiselessly, flopped down on his belly and crawled like a lizard under the lowest strand of the rusty barbed wire. He flattened his thin form as close to the ground as possible so his nylon shirt would not get caught on the sharp barbs. He got up and crouched close to the fence, watching the long shadows in the swaying trees. There was an open stretch running along the fence, a path really, along which Andimi passed when inspecting the laborers' work. The shrewd businessman unfailingly made this daily walk whenever he was at home, no matter how busy he had been, before paying them their daily pittance. Ombima stayed down, watching and listening. There was only the sound of swaying plants, no footfalls. Then he slowly rose and sprinted in a crouch across the open stretch into the engulfing darkness of the banana plantation.

He made his way through the bananas, ears pricked for the slightest sound, heart hammering in his chest in anticipation. And there before him, flourishing with all sorts of foodstuffs a hungry man could think of, was Andimi's kitchen garden. Of course Ombima had often come here in a group to work. Then, perhaps because of being with the others, and because he had no design upon them, thinking only of the work, the wealth of the garden had not struck him as awesome. But now, all alone in the sprawling garden, it hit him. Everywhere he looked he saw thriving produce: slender banana trees bent over with fruit that was so heavy it was breaking their backs; pawpaw trees with their pumpkin-sized fruit, shiny and engorged, so ripe even the birds could not make up their minds which was the choicest.

He saw cabbages that would make a man break out in a sweat if he were given the punishment of carrying one on his head to Chavakali market. He also saw pumpkins, big and round, sitting squat in their lush green bedding like monarchs of storybook splendor. Even in the dim light of the dying day, Ombima could visualize the richness of color in the skin of every fruit he saw. And the wonders just opened up, spreading far and wide as if one person could not own all of them. It was the Garden of Eden incarnate, and he Adam, sole lord over it all.

For a while Ombima could not make up his mind just what it was he wanted among all that was spread at his feet. He wanted to pick the biggest cabbage in the patch, and at the same time he wanted to uproot some cassava, which would be more filling. He wanted to pluck the fattest of the pumpkins and at the same time he wanted to take off his shirt and spread it on the ground so he could pile on it juicy red tomatoes, like children do when they gather *tsimbulumbutu* berries in the bush. He wanted to take a little bit of everything.

It was the sudden falling of a pawpaw fruit shaken out of the tree by the wind that made up his mind for him. The fruit—huge and ripe—fell like a bomb and struck the ground just short of where he was, startling Ombima. He froze, ears cocked, certain that someone had heard the noise. He was poised to bolt out of there like an arrow the instant the shadows shifted to reveal a presence.

But the wind was whipping the banana trees so noisily no one could possibly have heard. His heart hammered in his chest like a drum. He dashed forth and grabbed the precious fruit off the ground, inspecting it as if it belonged to him. It was slightly squashed—doesn't matter, a pawpaw is still a pawpaw. He was charged now. He dashed from plant to plant, plucking this, snatching that. In the heat of it, a feeling he had never experienced before spread through him. It was thrilling. It was not fear anymore. He could move. He could pick what he wanted.

Soon, there was a huge pile on the ground and when he stopped, he realized he could not carry everything in his arms. But immediately, as if he had been doing this all his life, an idea struck him. Quickly he tore off his shirt and spread it on the ground, heaping on as much as he could. He tied up the tails and sleeves into a thick knot so it formed into a little bundle that he could easily hoist over his shoulder. Then, just as he prepared to take up his load and leave, he remembered bananas. He had not taken any. And yet they were his favorite. How thoughtless one can get some times...

Ombima dropped the bundle on the ground and ran up to a tree he selected at random and hopped onto the soft stem, propelling his lean weight up the tree more like a monkey. As he wrenched the bunch out, the tree trunk suddenly snapped and the next minute he was sitting on his stinging bottom on the hard ground, the crown of the tree together with the bunch all over on his shoulders. It had happened so suddenly.

He wrestled his way out of the entanglement and grabbed at what fruit he could, eyes darting wildly left and right, certain that the next minute he would be caught. Clutching what he could to his bony chest, he grabbed for the bundle. He then dove into the darkening shadows and ran back the way he had come, bare heels tapping the loamy soil like drumsticks on an old skin.

Ombima reached the fence and, throwing himself flat on his bare belly, crawled underneath the lowest strand like some reptile, his loot firmly in his grip. As he pulled himself away his back caught on a sharp barb and it tore through his flesh. But his adrenaline was pumping and so he did not think much of this, rising, running, cutting across the open field like a ghost, clasping the bundle close to his body, the whites of his bare soles flashing in the fleeting illumination from the lightning that suddenly rent the sky.

What Ombima did not know, even as he fled, was that all this time someone had been observing him. As the first heavy raindrops fell, the shadows in the banana grove down the path just yards from where Ombima had snuck through the fence shifted and a figure disentangled itself onto the leaf-strewn path. Madam Tabitha stood wrapping her soft woolen shawl closer to herself, shivering a bit with cold. She stood for a while staring after the fleeing figure, occasionally illuminated by flashes of lightning as it tore across the open field beyond. Then she turned and hurried up the path toward the house, just as the rain started a musical staccato among the swaying banana leaves.

Chapter Two

THE DOWNPOUR FROM the day before had washed the village paths clean of dust and debris. There was a pleasant freshness in the early morning air that was partly the odor of the washed earth. The grass along the paths was green and fresh, sprinkled with clear droplets of the morning dew that scintillated in a bright array of rainbow colors when they were struck by the pearly shafts of the rising sun. The tree leaves were equally fresh, drooping with dew and wetness, succulent and supple with good health. The earth was a deep rich red. Even the tree trunks had shed their rotting slough and were a virgin smooth grey green.

It was a heady day. Ombima was up early. He was to work in Kigama that day, and was afraid that he would report to the farm late because there was quite a distance he had to cover to get there. His wife, Sayo, had made him some *mukenye* mash from the potatoes and beans he had brought the day before and left it by the fire, just the way she knew he liked it. He did not want to bother her that early to get up and make him tea. He secured his work trousers about his loins and pushed aside the huge rock that was usually wedged against the door at night, disturbing the big cock that lay on his belly just next to Aradi's head. He passed into the cool morning, pulling the door shut behind him.

As he urinated into a lantana bush he scratched his flank and whistled softly, watching the steam rise up in curls from the bush. His tiny compound was walled in by tall shaggy cypresses, the drooping branches at the top providing a vantage perch for the valley's hawks and crows as they waited to swoop down on his chickens as they scratched for food in the banana grove. The hills in the distance were shrouded in a thick pink mist. Had the rains truly returned? Last night's might just be one of those surprise *chuvwi* season downpours that deceived the villager into planting a second crop only to disappear shortly after, leaving the ground so hard and dry that the seeds were roasted beneath the surface. Whatever the case, a couple or so similar downpours would certainly do the village farms a lot of good.

The footpaths were busy with people going to work. Ombima went down an incline and stopped at Ang'ote's hut, a reed-thatched hovel that was in bad shape. The roof was pitched, the thatching giving in many places, and Ombima imagined what it would have been like inside there in the rain. Like a home without a woman, it was badly in need of care—the grass had invaded the compound and would soon creep up the eaves.

He called out.

"*Yooo!*" came the hoarse reply. The door creaked and Ango'te bowed out under the low hanging reeds. He was a frail man, whose appearance was no more endearing than his hut. But he was cheerful. His hands were securing his worn trousers about his waist, grimy shirt tucked under his arm. He squinted into the surprisingly bright morning—the sun catching on wet leaves that multiplied its glare.

"The day has broken, my friend, Ombima," he called out in greeting, struggling into his shirt.

"Indeed it has," replied Ombima, slowing a little to allow him to catch up.

"And what a lousy one it is too," Ang'ote said, clearing his throat loudly and spitting a blob of phlegm into the pathside grasses.

"Lousy, you say?" asked Ombima, rather surprised because he thought the morning was beautiful. "I think this morning is wonderful!"

"So you say," said Ang'ote, trotting up to get to Ombima's side, thrusting a last arm into the shirt. "So you say, my friend. And it is good for you to think so, knowing you've got yourself a woman back home."

"*Ohooo*. I sure missed your line of argument there, *bwana*." The two friends hurried on toward the valley. The narrow path they had taken crawled into an entanglement of bush and they had to stoop low. The hoof marks left by the cattle in the soft earth were filled with water, creating tiny puddles that squelched underfoot.

They met a couple of school children going the other way, hurrying to get to their school up in the rocky hills of Kisangula. The students carried their knitted school bags containing their few schoolbooks clutched underneath their arms. The bags were made from scavenged pieces of thread, patiently worked on by a blunt homemade needle. In the other hand they carried little mounds of cow dung on bits of banana bark to smear their classroom floors with. Their scrubbed feet shone pale yellow from the dew, their faces smelling of tallow soap.

"*Vuchee*, Ang'ote!" they called, their faces lighting up. "You are late, you know. Mudeya-Ngoko is already on the farm with his big stick."

"Ang'ote, the cock woke up earlier than you today," said the boy, measuring his step as they approached. "You must have passed by Eregwa's house yesterday," he added, wagging a puny finger in the manner of the schoolmaster. "Look, you didn't even wash your face, *heeei!*"

They liked to speak in jest with Ang'ote, delighting in making fun of his unkempt appearance. Ang'ote made a mock lurch at the boy, pulling a mean face, which made them run, their shrill laughter ringing.

As the two men crept into the valley the grey mist fell about their shoulders and hid them from sight. Ang'ote stopped by the swift stream that passed through the trees to wash his face.

"I was thinking of replacing the old thatch at the apex of my hut. What do you say?" Ang'ote spoke as he swirled the cold water about in his mouth, rubbing his finger against his stained teeth in the motions of his habitual morning act of ablution.

"What do I say?" Ombima watched his friend gurgle the cold water in his mouth. "I think you should build a new hut, Ang'ote. That termite-infested shack you call a house is going to collapse on you one of these days! All it needs is a reasonable downpour."

"Ah," Ang'ote half-rose and seemed to remember something. He dug into the folds of his greasy trousers and took out a little white stick with a splayed end. He chewed and softened the stick for a while before rubbing it vigorously against his yellowed teeth. He then rinsed his mouth thoroughly, spitting into the lush reeds competing for space along the banks of the stream.

"Sure, sure. Some sound piece of advice," he said when he was finished. "As if you live in a mansion of stone yourself."

They walked on up the path, maneuvering through the thick undergrowth, trailing plants coiling around their heels like snakes. The path emerged out of the thick woods and twisted through the maize farms on the steep incline. From this point above the valley the shafts of early morning sun struck right across, filtering through the tall trees in an opalescent wash of gold and silver. On the other side their own village, the hamlet of Ivona, spread far into the sun-washed hills of Kisangula. The numerous little batches of cone-shaped huts were etched like some beadwork pattern in the dappled landscape.

As they crossed the maize fields they saw that most of the crop was damaged following the storm, the supple green stems bent close to the ground.

"I wonder if this season's crop is going to be as good as the last one," said Ombima.

"I don't think so. The beans have been ruined worse than the maize. They will be good only for burning lye, or food for cattle. They will have to raze the maize. Otherwise if the rodents

12

get to the grain first then it too is ruined. And, honestly, just who cares what happens to the crop?"

"Why?"

"Why? Because it's none of my business whether the crop does well or not. To people like Andimi who have many acres of farm under maize, maybe it would matter."

"I see. You are envious because you don't have a crop of your own to look forward to. But, come to think of it, where did you ever have any?"

"I wonder when," mused Ang'ote in surprising acquiescence.

The banana trees showing at the other end of the damaged maize field were mangled, their leaves shredded to strips by the falling hail stones, some of them snapped in two, the tatters fluttering in the light breeze like the old flag that flew outside the government offices at Vihiga on Fridays. The hail must have been heavier on this side of the valley.

"Maybe it's time you found yourself a woman, my friend," Ombima said.

"You think so?" Ang'ote was walking a step behind, his head bent, eyes following Ombima's thick heels, which shone bone-white from the dew of the morning. Talk about women, which at his age he was receiving more of, made him uneasy. Walking ahead, Ombima did not see the effect on his friend.

"Look, Ang'ote." Ombima said, "I'm serious. I think you need to get a little more serious with life. Say, take a look at yourself. I'm your friend, and yet I can still see some of these things. You are dirty every day of the week and always soaked in drink whenever someone in the village brews for the weekend. It is because you don't have anyone to go back to at home. You don't have someone to smear the floor and walls of your hut, and to look after your piece of land. You are going to contract a bad disease from the rats and fleas that infest your hut unless you get someone to look after it. Say, you can't even have warm meals! You are growing a small tummy from eating leftover *ugali*

13

and your face is all wrinkles from loneliness... my friend, I real feel pity..."

"Oh, shut up, Ombima, will you?" Ang'ote suddenly snapped, his eyes flashing. "How many times do I have to tell you to stop poking your nose into my private business? You know, I'm really getting sick of hearing this trash from you. Look, why don't you just mind your own business?"

Ombima missed a step, slackening, but recovered. "And see you waste away your life, is it? No, my friend, Ang'ote. I believe it is my duty to advise you as your friend."

"Sure, sure it is." Ang'ote paused to blow his nose noisily into the bushes. He had heated up suddenly and a film of sweat covered his face despite the chill of the morning. "You purport to be my friend. Indeed all of you do! Fine. But one just can't help wondering: if all you know so well what is good for me, then how come you are still such poor men? Eh? How come you've still got to toil in the hot sun for Andimi almost every other day of the week in order to keep your skin on your miserable bones? How come you travel the same path as I, the failure, eh? Tell me!"

Ang'ote's eyes were flashing in his excitement. He fumbled in his pockets and brought out the stub of a foul smelling cigarette he had rolled out of old newspaper the day before and proceeded to light up in anger. "Eh? How different are you from me, Ombima?" His voice was raised, saliva flaking the corners of his mouth. "How come you are no better than I am?"

"Someone listen to this madness," said Ombima, his eyes rounded in disbelief. "Oh... oh... oh... oh Ang'ote. Are you now comparing yourself to me?" He was clearly surprised at the insinuation in his friend's words.

"*Ehe*? And why can't I?" said Ang'ote, stopping and drawing himself to his full height.

"Look," Ombima started, his tone falling, jaw working as he sought the words. "I mean, just look at yourself, Ang'ote. You never bathe. You eat so badly. You have lice in your clothes... I mean, you live like a hermit!"

"You live like a hermit," Ang'ote mimicked. He looked his friend over, taking in the tattered clothing, weighing him carefully from head to toe. But it had been too much for the two of them. Ombima was his best friend and he knew it. He burst out laughing.

"Listen to you speak, oh... oh...!" Tears came to his eyes as the laughter turned into gasping fits. Ombima, who knew he had crossed a line when he said "you can't compare yourself to me," joined in the laughter, which was mirthless, a forced reconciliatory laugh that fooled neither of them.

"Oh, how you do make me laugh, my friend!"

They emerged out of the maize fields into the tea plantation. Many of the pickers had not yet arrived. The sun had broken over the hills, shining brilliantly on the tea. There was Chabeda, son of Eregwa the brewer, shivering to his chattering teeth in a long, tattered woolen sweater that draped his tall body like a sheath. He was with a tall, bony young man from the Vuyiya hills who had just joined the work gang and whose name Ombima could not remember. The latter was smoking a thin Rooster cigarette in conservative little puffs, needing to save some of it for his friend Chabeda. The two had met at a funeral night dance, and Chabeda had instantly made friends with him and invited him to try his fortune out here.

Other than these two, it was only Mudeya-Ngoko who had arrived, as was usual with him. He was already at work, placing the long reed baskets in every line according to how he wanted the work to be done, whistling as he hobbled about on his duty as if it was the most involving task of all on the field. Mudeya-Ngoko, the overseer of all the other workers, was clad in his usual cigarette-butt-stubbed thin nylon shirt over which he wore the long dirty yellow mackintosh that had been handed to him just the other day by Madam Tabitha. It was hard to believe this man was still a hopelessly poor man, despite all that had been extended his way by the family all the years he had been in their service. Maybe some people just never had the luck.

"Good day to you, Ageng'o!" Ang'ote called, moving carefully into the narrow line so the icy dew on the rich green leaves wouldn't wet his clothes. Ageng'o was Mudeya-Ngoko's real name. But then if you asked any of the workers, almost all of them knew him as Mudeya-Ngoko, which means "chicken thief." Where the name came from no one really knew. It was said it had been baptized by the same jester, Ang'ote, in response to a tale that had gotten to the workers' ears about the young man's early childhood, before his influential "uncle" came into his life and changed it rather dramatically. The young man, growing up in near destitution close to the distant town of Mago in the parentage of two dirt-poor wagers, had oft resorted to the most available option to ease the pangs of hunger that nearly always seemed to assail him. Mudeya-Ngoko was also a voracious eater who could down an amazing portion of *ugali* in one helping, despite his slight build. It was said that when hunger thus struck and it was in the deep of night when he couldn't get to sleep, the young man would sneak out of his father's compound and roam the village in the company of the village mongrels, terrorizing people's chicken houses. No one really knew how true this tale was, but they all liked to assume that it was because it fit well with his character. It also gave him a name.

Whistling and dragging baskets through the tea, Mudeya-Ngoko did not hear Ang'ote's greeting.

"*Eee?* Ageng'o! I was talking to you, young man," called Ang'ote, moving up to where he was. "Or have you gone deaf these days?"

"Oh, sorry. I'm fine." Mudeya-Ngoko had a thin piercing voice that sliced with ease through bargains, sealing a disgruntled worker's fate with a raw finality that not even the employer himself dared raise a finger to. This was just the kind of character who, if he were working in a big state-run company, one might find sitting at the boardroom table acting as the hatchet man of his fat bosses. And he had the face to go with the voice too: pointed and shrew-like, the chin and lips sticking out an inch, bushy eyebrows shading the shifty, beady eyes that missed very little.

"*Oooo*... I see," replied Ang'ote. "It's good to hear you are in good health. What would happen to us if you were to be taken ill, Ageng'o?" Ang'ote said, walking up to him. "We would surely starve! I just thought for a while there that you were turning a deaf ear to an old man, son."

Mudeya-Ngoko failed to catch the thin satire. Like people used to being fawned upon, he failed to tell flatterers apart from the serious.

Mudeya-Ngoko, Ombima, and Ang'ote laughed at what Ang'ote had said, although for different reasons. Ang'ote, right in his element, winked across to Ombima as if to say *get the fellow in a jolly mood and you don't have to carry tea to the buying center afterward.*

The pickers started to arrive. One by one they came up over the lip of the valley, then paused a while at the edge of the expansive tea estate, hands resting on hips as if defeated by the shear expanse of it. It was a familiar pose, the way ants do when they crawl out of the ground and find the hill of sand they were building tiny grain by grain had gotten no bigger than they had left it the day before. This happened with many of the pickers. And then, in acceptance of fate, they—the men—bent over and folded up their trouser cuffs. The women simply hitched up their skirts a bit, as if this made a difference. Looking only at the shrubs ahead of them, the field workers plunged into the green sea.

Rebecca, the elderly woman whom Ang'ote made no secret his affection for, came up out of the maize fields and stood pensively at the edge of the estate. She wore a torn old *lesso* thrown over her shoulder in the fashion of a shawl to keep away the morning chill. She cast an image of strength in her old woolen cardigan that was torn all the way up her sleeves so her elbows poked out, and which sagged permanently to one side, as if she carried something heavy in one pocket. This morning, though, there were deep worry lines etched on her face.

Normally, Rebecca was disposed to be in a playful mood whenever she was among the other workers out in the fields, so much so that sometimes they found it hard to believe that this woman was the persistently struggling personality that they all knew. She was forever bending over backward to eke out an unrelenting hand-to-mouth subsistence for herself and the brood of countless young grandchildren who devoured every morsel that she extended their way. The little ones were like insatiable vermin, left in her charge by her deserting family fleeing to the city, where blinking lights beckoned. One tough old lady who stood up to her call, the strain of her effort rarely showing on a rounded old face that had once, a long time ago, been beautiful, but which was now so ravaged by the hostile sun of the open fields and by life that it looked almost like the skin of a sun-dried pea pod. Etched in these cruel lines, though, was the ever-living promise that molded her sturdy character.

It almost seemed like Ang'ote would walk up to her side as everyone, watching furtively from lowered eyes, anticipated. But then Mudeya-Ngoko spotted her, so she hurried to her work place so as not to risk losing a day's wages.

Aseyo, the wife of the local carpenter, arrived late in the company of her friend Oresha, who was skilled at midwifery and at almost every obstetric mishap a village woman might experience giving birth. These two were known to lag behind mornings so that they might find all the tea baskets assigned. Mudeya-Ngoko would then have no choice but to assign them to hoeing, a task they seemed to enjoy because they worked under little supervision.

Mudeya-Ngoko, who used to think it was punishment, seemed to have realized otherwise of late, when he saw that they hardly ever put up an argument. There was little he could do because the two had a way of shrugging off any reprimand that he, or any other person for that matter, might aim at them that wasn't outright rude—the words seem to go through the right ear and come out the left. Also, it was just the other day that Oresha had helped Mudeya-Ngoko's wife deliver a rather troublesome baby with a shriveled torso for such a big head and the ears of the father, huge and fan-like. And so he really couldn't touch her, not just yet.

He made as if to head toward them and the two pretended to hurry to their assigned workplaces. For these two Mudeya-Ngoko, this little king in a colony of defiant little people, would waive his barrage of the plentiful expletives by which he ruled everyone else. At most, he could only glare at them, conscious of the thin wall of brittle respect that stood between them.

After they had traded news of the day and the latest piece of gossip had done its round, everyone soon got busy. Coarse thick fingers initially stiff from the lull of the night picked up the tempo, flitting in practiced, mechanical rhythm over the low bushes. Conversation gradually stopped as the stained fingers plucked at the juicy tipping shoots, tough thumbnails cutting into the more stubborn twigs. The callused palm, toughened by work, soon filled up and the hand flipped over the shoulder into the sagging basket weighing down the picker's bent back. Washed by the dew covering the luxuriant leaves, the skin of the palms soon turned a corny white color, the joints in the fingers stiffening into their gnarled angles in the plucking "posture" as the frost bit. Their *tap! tap!* was rhythmic, hanging in the thin hilltop air as the huge workforce sped over the first portion of the estate, devouring the soft tender shoots as if they were the money that they sought at the end of it all.

Each of the workers knew only too well the import of the productive early morning hours. They darted their work-honed hands to and fro with deftness, determined to fill the first basket before the sun came up. After that they knew they would have to slow down.

They had successfully pushed the argument that for that day they were to be paid per kilo of what everyone eventually brought in. That way they would be at a slight advantage, given the luxuriant newness of the first tipping crop they were plucking. Everyone knew that this crop was heavier than the more mature crop. Of course Mudeya-Ngoko had put up an argument for his boss as usual, but then the massive voice of the real wage earners overwhelmed him.

Ombima worked alongside Ang'ote who kept up a lively chat with the women. It never ceased to amaze Ombima just how the fellow could talk and work at the same time. He did a good amount of both well, and even spared time to glance back over his shoulder now and then to point out a bad job done by someone else in another line. The fellow, for all his shortcomings, was an invaluable pacemaker whose absence from work wouldn't go unnoticed.

Mudeya-Ngoko kept up his rounds, sneaking up behind those who were either lagging behind or doing a hasty job to remind them to put up a handsome show for their money. They shouldn't forget that it was he who held the purse strings. Other than that, Mudeya-Ngoko beat back into place the side stems that the workers had raised and pulled out any weeds rising above the bushes. That was about all the work he did. One wondered why the fellow had to stick around like gum when at the end of the day it was a man's work that was going to determine his pay anyway.

They said he was a distant relation to the wealthy man. How true this was no one really could tell. But all they knew was that Mudeya-Ngoko was one real powerful chap. He could command Andimi's ear and make it hear what he chose, on top of being in the complete trust of the lady of the house. This meant he had the power to hire and fire a man at a whim, if he so wanted. No one wants to get in the bad books of such a person.

The sun rose up in the clear blue sky and the dew dried off the leaves. The polythene sheets they wore around their waists to keep their clothing dry got clammy and moistened inside, and they had to take them off. The baskets got heavier and, one by one, the workers broke off to go empty them in the bigger baskets beneath the old gum tree in the center of the estate where they normally assembled at meal times. Right then, the tea break was never timelier. Some of the women broke off a while to stretch their breaking backs. As for the men, occasionally someone produced a cigarette stub, and then they all stood as if waiting for a smoke, even those who didn't smoke.

They all lowered their loads and made a weary beeline for the huge gum tree, one or two of them pausing to survey the work they had done, as if they were not quite in a hurry for the break. They all assembled in the welcome shade of the gum tree and lowered their heads between their knees, waiting for Mudeya-Ngoko to unveil whatever it was inside the covered *ciondos*. There were huge kettles of tea and *sinias* full of maize and beans, mixed and cooked overnight in a large earthen pot so the beans were engorged and soft and the maize kernels so tender and fat they had burst their skins. This was everyone's favorite. Indeed it was said that if a young man wanted to build a house in a day without having to pay for the labor, all he needed to do was prepare huge quantities of this meal and avail generous quantities of *busaa*, the local brew, as well. With that, all it took was just passing the word around.

Indeed, providing a proper meal was something Andimi was well known for. No one ever had a quarrel with him there. He took good care of his workers, perhaps subscribing to the commonly held adage that the way to a man's heart is through the stomach.

The tea was to take a long time. The workers divided themselves into groups according to who usually joked and chatted with whom, and they sat themselves down on sheaves of leaves they plucked out of the overhanging branches of the shady old gum tree that had been watered over eons on spilled tea and soup.

At the sound of bare feet trampling the earth and the smell of food, the giant ants residing permanently in the scarred bole of the old gum tree crawled out to join their mates, poking blunt shiny heads crowned with giant jaws out of the numerous holes in the ground. They took up ready position, waiting to drag bits of food several times their weight and size to store in their underground cellars.

Ang'ote was bent over a *sinia* of maize and beans, his graying shaggy beard already matted with brown soup. He sat squarely above the humped plate with his legs crossed underneath him as Rebecca poured the steaming tea into mugs. Ombima sat across from him, glad that they had Oresha and Rebecca in their group because, naturally, the women would indulge in that nonsense of removing the skins from the maize grains as they ate, which would allow him and his friend more to eat. Ang'ote gave a loud impatient yawn and said, "Hurry up, woman, will you? Some of us are hungry, you know."

"Indeed," supplied someone from the next group, tongue in cheek. "You know that hunger bites especially deeper in the belly of someone who doesn't have a woman back home to prepare his meals."

Obviously the remark was aimed at Ang'ote. "Yes, you are right," he countered. "So you just shut up and eat. And be grateful to Andimi for keeping the likes of you alive, you ungrateful son of a frog!"

"*Bayaa*! Can't you men have some manners?" said Oresha. "A passerby would easily think it was a party of children eating!"

"And what business would the passerby have here?" asked Ang'ote, glaring at her.

The after-tea stretch was long and dull, punctuated by laziness and much chat and less work. Someone was heard to say that it was actually a mistake for Andimi to feed his workers this well while they were still expected to be productive, even though it was a blessing on the other hand. The workers' stomachs would be stretched so taut they could barely bend over the tea bushes. All they seemed good at doing right then was farting and burping, trying to get some of the gas they had consumed in haste to come out.

Soon the sun climbed up in the sky overhead and it was too hot to work. Mudeya-Ngoko had shouted himself hoarse trying to get everyone serious with what they were doing. Hardly anyone was listening to him. They figured they already had done enough for the day.

It was a welcome relief when the school children started going by on the path across the valley leading from Kisangula, signaling the day was gone. There was nothing left to do but prepare to carry the tea to the weighing center. All at once, Ang'ote developed a splitting headache and went to lie down under the gum tree. As if on cue someone else twisted an ankle on an outcropping root and it was just too painful to walk. This was a game they all knew too well.

Mudeya-Ngoko ceased ranting eventually and, after the baskets had been counted and entered against everyone's name in the dog-eared old notebook he always carried with him despite the fact he was really quite illiterate, the womenfolk—together with the men who did not know how to play sick—hoisted their heavy loads onto their heads and set off for the buying center.

Ang'ote, Ombima, Oresha, Aseyo, and three other villagers set off for Andimi's place to see about their pay. Even then, one of them had other plans for the day.

Chapter Three

OMBIMA WAS TIRED and anxious as he walked down the village path that evening. It was late and there was hardly anyone about, most people having retired to their houses for the night. Walking along the winding path one could see inside the little houses set in the middle of the neatly kept compounds. The flames of the tin lamps hanging from walls or placed atop soot colored tables fashioned out of salvaged wood flickered in the wind, causing the orange tongues to twist grotesquely. The weak light framed the doorways, inviting moths and other night flies to buzz lazily about the flame. Around the low tables sat families, some having their meal and others just idly reliving the day's events. The eyes of the children, in this rare moment of warmth amidst the grown-ups, were aglow.

Ombima carried a bundle of cassava in his arms. The front of his shirt and his arms were covered in dirt. He hurried on through the thickening night, pausing at the bend ahead to ensure the way was clear. If anyone were to run into him he would not say from where he got the cassava.

At the next bend in the path he stopped. A woman was coming from the direction of the village *duka,* humming softly to herself. He ducked into a clump of lantana shrubs and waited. She came closer and he saw that she looked familiar, clad in an old poorly darned woolen sweater with a *lesso* around her waist. She was barefoot. She carried a bag of flour and what looked like a loaf of bread and a packet of tea leaves held close to her bosom.

When she was close enough she stopped. She looked left and right. Then she placed her purchases on the grass by the side of the path and ducked into the unkempt hedgerows close to where Ombima was crouching. A moment later, he heard a hard splashing sound. This stopped and he heard the sound of a tight rubber band drawn then let loose to slap against bare flesh. A moment later the woman reappeared, adjusting her *lesso* and picked up her goods.

When she had walked several paces Ombima edged out of the lantana and followed her as noiselessly as he could, more from curiosity than anything else. She branched onto the narrow path that led to the river, then shortly left it and entered Ang'ote's bushy compound, going straight into the hut. A short while later a light came on inside the hut. From inside the hut Ombima heard soft voices. He wanted to get closer to listen in. He looked at the cassava in his arms and he thought of Ang'ote and the time of day. It would certainly seem odd if his friend were to open the door and find him outside. In the end he decided it was none of his business. Turning, he walked off in the direction of his own compound to mind the business waiting for him there.

The tiny compound was in darkness, save for a faint glow of the evening fire that showed through a gap in the slightly open door. It wasn't a big compound really, but it was well kept. There was the single hut in the middle, underneath the bough of an old mango tree that directly faced the entrance, so that if you sat in the main room you could see the people passing on the path, without them seeing you. Beside the hut was a smaller one set at the edge of the compound next to the hedge, the latrine. Behind the main hut towered banana and pawpaw trees, which at this time of the year did not have much fruit on them. It was off-season for the mangoes, just like it was for the handful of guava trees that dotted the compound. And unlike the wealthy Andimi's pawpaws that were richly fertilized, his had to make do with the little nourishment they could find in the over-farmed earth. The maize in the little patch behind the hut was still green, the crowns just now peeking out of the lush foliage. It was a neat compound, but it supported little to eat.

He went under the low hanging eave and was immediately assailed by the smoke inside. His family was seated around the smoky fire in the tiny cooking area at the back that also housed their cow and a calf and a few chickens that they owned. His wife, Sayo, was adding water to a pot in which she boiled some of the bananas he had brought the day before in their skins. The children, Aradi and his younger sister Saliku, were poking in the fire with long sticks to turn some of the bananas that they were roasting. Aradi's eyes were swollen red and watery from blowing into the glowing embers.

Sayo looked up when Ombima came in and greeted him, her eyes widening in surprise at the cassava he set down. On seeing the cassava, the children sprang to their feet and assailed him, "Ba-ba-ba! Ti-ti-ti!" He snatched up Saliku and ruffled Aradi's woolly head. He could feel their tense excitement in his tired bones. They were gazing down at the load of fat cassava on the floor, and he knew just what they were waiting for. No one in the whole village loved fresh cassava as much as his fourteen-year-old son did.

Sayo stood at the other end of the hut. There was no lamp in the room, but he could see the thankful, slightly reserved look on her face in the orange glow of the fire. She mumbled something, but he didn't quite catch what it was.

As he went into the inner room to change from his work clothes he heard her shout at the children to keep off raw cassava unless they wanted to invite bloated bellies. There was that strained note in her usually mellow voice that told him something: *she knew*. And for that he couldn't bring himself to offer an explanation as to how he had come by the cassava, his courage to lie to her deserting him.

He went about shedding his work clothes in the dark inner room, moving about in the familiar darkness with the aid of his hands and feet, whistling softly to himself. He emerged a moment later stripped down to his brown undershorts, the worn old towel that he shared with Sayo secured around his loins. He went into the bath shelter behind the house still whistling tunelessly.

Shortly he called out, "My water is cold, I say, someone!"

"A moment, *eei!*" he heard Sayo grumble to herself inside the hut. "You always take too long to come home, anyway."

He stood still in the dark listening to the chirping of the crickets and other night creatures, idly scratching at his groin. The dilapidated bath shelter made out of old banana leaves woven around a wooden framework badly needed repairing. He always said he would do it first thing after he came back from work the following day but, characteristic of him, never quite got around to doing it. Maybe it was because it was situated behind the house, out of sight of any visitors.

He could see the night outside through the gaping holes in the thatch, swirling dark movements that concealed children's demons and the village's night witches. He could see the night sky beyond, a pinkish purple streak without birds. Total darkness would come and then stars and glow worms would appear.

Sayo came round with a jug of hot water that she had drawn from the bubbling *sufuria* on the fire. The water had been meant for that evening's *ugali*, but now she would have to add some more and wait for it to simmer, delaying the meal. She poured the steaming water into the broken half of a pot propped up on stones in the corner, which served as a bath. She was humming some tune to herself, like she usually did when lost in her own thoughts. As she made to pass by on her way out, Ombima reached out and caught her by the arm and said, "Wait."

She stopped, stiffening, the empty jug held in front of her.

"What is it?" She was facing the opposite direction, and there was the tightness in her voice that said to him the same thing her silence in the house had. He could feel her closeness in the dark and in the faint evening light her eyeballs shone white like sun-bleached beads floating in oil. This made him feel worse.

"Sayo, there's something I've got to tell you."

"*Ehe?*" she leaned her head to one side, half turning, and he could feel her gaze on him in the dark. "It's not what I suppose it is... I mean..." He drew close to her and could feel her warm breath on the sensitive skin of his throat. He was aware of his callused hand against her smooth skin. Her arm was still warm from the fire.

"Sayo, I..." he started to say, but for some reason, looking at her in the concealing smoky light, he could not bring himself to utter what it was he had intended to say. "No, not now. I'll tell you later." His voice was like coarse sandpaper at the back of his throat. He slowly let go of her quivering arm. There was that unquestioning calm about her, especially this particular evening, which unnerved him.

He watched her go into the hut. When she was gone, he squatted over the bath. The water was warm and, touching his skin, he felt the cuts and bruises open up and begin to ache. But the smell of tallow soap scouring the grime and dirt off his skin was relieving, nearly soothing, but not just because his body was tired.

He put his head into the water and remembered a time in his youth when he had first gone for a swim in the river in the moonlight. The water had been just as warm on his bare skin, the current tickling the hairs at the base of his spine. He splashed water over his back and scrubbed vigorously with a piece of coarse netting that had once served fishermen on the distant lake in Kisumu. He was so refreshed that for a moment he forgot the guilt of what he had done that evening and the other one before. Despite himself, he started to whistle again.

Ombima was feeling clean when he went indoors a short while later. Sayo was ladling out the food into deep enamel bowls using a glowing stick for a torch. She had prepared his fire, really just a pile of red embers shoveled out of the hearth and into an old cooking pan that she no longer used. It now glowed in front of his favorite folding chair in the main room. The chair was propped up at his customary position against the wall directly in the doorway where he could see out to the compound entrance. He sat down to warm his hands and feet as he waited for his meal.

It was dark outside. He could barely see beyond the front door. Hundreds of fireflies trafficked in the open yard. They went in unfixed circles that blurred and shifted, as if the flies were drunk with the warmth of the languid night. Sometimes they did not fly in these random circles. Instead they massed together, the way they usually did in the open field next to the village church just outside the compound of the old lady, Ngayira, who lived alone in a leaning old hut and who, people said, kept a cub leopard on the firewood rack up in the roof of the smoky windowless hut. It was said that the cub assisted her in her sorcery, for which she was famed.

Looking at the fireflies massed thus, Ombima got this odd thought that it was indeed Ngayira's leopard that had been sent by its keeper to stalk his compound for the soul of one of his children. It was a stupid thought but it was the kind that, dropping in at an empty moment like this with his anxiety, could perturb even nonbelievers. He scraped in the glowing coals for a big red one, thinking of throwing it at the phantom creature to scare it out of his compound. But just then, Saliku came into the room bringing his bowl of bananas and a cup of tea. With his scraper in the coals he pretended he was simply fanning the embers.

"Father, are you cold?" his daughter asked as she set the meal on a stool and sat cross-legged on the floor by the fire. "It's a rather warm night to be warming yourself at the fire."

"Yes, my old bones feel the cold, *Bebi*." He addressed her by her pet name deliberately because he knew it irked her. At ten years old she insisted she was no longer a baby, but a grown girl.

"But you are an old man, Father. And old men don't warm themselves at the fire," she said, tucking one leg under the other, that familiar crease of concentration appearing on her brow as she gazed up at him. She had really meant to say a "grown up."

He ruffled her unkempt hair affectionately as he reached for his food. Although darker than her brother Aradi, Saliku's eyes were gleaming white, gazing steadily but intelligently from their depths like a keen puppy waiting for a trick. Her narrow shoulders angled forward slightly, causing her tiny chest to curve inward. There was a grace about her long limbs that reminded Ombima of her mother as a girl. "Who said I am an old man, *Bebi*? Did you see me with my back humped, leaning on a walking stick, eh? Did you?"

She laughed at the mock reprimand.

"But you are just a *bit* older, aren't you, Father?" she persisted, moving up closer to the fire.

"Yes, I am just a *bit* older," he mimicked, talking over a scalding lump of banana. Bananas, like potatoes, burn all the way into the stomach. "But then, don't you heap age on me that is not really mine, hear? I am still a young man in every other right, I believe," he added with a wink.

"But you are just a *bit* older than Aradi and me and Mother," she paused challengingly.

"Think so?" There was a gleam in his eye, and she knew there was something cooking on his mind. "You really think I am that old? Then why don't you dare me to a race tomorrow, and then we'll find out who between the two of us is truly the older?"

"Sure. Where? Just you say it!" Her eyes were shining with excitement. "Say, can you race me down to the river?"

"Why not?" said Ombima, enjoying it.

"Then that is settled! Tomorrow first thing when you get home from work we race." She said it in the manner she might reply to a most thoughtless challenge thrown her way that she was certain to trounce with ease. "I swear you won't catch me! I can run faster than a rabbit—just you wait!"

"Yes, you just said it there, little *Mbenze-henze*. And there's no need to add more. However, I think I should caution you. Do you recall the story of proud Hare who found Tortoise waiting for him on the finishing line at the end of the race? It might just turn out to be your fate!"

"*Ohooo…* That's what you imagine, eh?" she gave him a dismissive look from underneath her eyelids.

"In that case let me not waste my words on such a loud-mouth as you. I bet you'll eat back your own words at the end of the race tomorrow," Ombima said.

In the red glow of the dying embers, Saliku looked gaunt, even while her rounded face bubbled with laughter. He was alarmed at how fast her health was deteriorating of late, troubled day and night by the strange ailment that afflicted her, which the trusted village doctor—who also worked at the government hospital in Mbale—seemed unable to treat properly. A thought had recently occurred to him that he try Oresha and her herbal concoctions to see if they would achieve anything. He would discuss it with Sayo.

Saliku was a lively, cheerful child and it made Ombima sad to watch this strange disease eat away at her. Ombima peeled another banana and bit into its salty flesh, grimacing as the hot steam trapped underneath the brown skin scalded his tongue. Aradi came into the room then, his stuffed belly showing through the torn hole in the front of his old nylon shirt, which their mother had snatched just the other day from the jaws of their black cow.

"Father, you don't know what I learned today!" There was a look of excitement on his face, his dark eyes shining. "I learned to ride a bicycle!" The boy had been fighting to ride a bicycle all year.

"Aradi, you've not been borrowing other people's bicycles again, have you?" Ombima paused, lifting his head. There was a scowl on his face. "I remember I warned you to stay clear of other people's possessions."

"But, Father, I didn't damage it in any way…"

"That doesn't answer the question," said Ombima, glaring at the boy. "You borrowed, didn't you?"

"Yes, Father," said Aradi, his gaze dropping. "I am sorry."

"You didn't listen to me son, did you?"

Aradi was quiet for a while, chewing his lips thoughtfully, waiting for the spanking that would follow. "It is because we do not have one of our own," he said at length. "I am sorry, Father, but I really wanted to learn to ride."

Both father and son were still for a while. Saliku was about to say that Aradi had not "borrowed" the bicycle from Indimuli, the shopkeeper, but that he had actually paid for it. She had seen him sneak into the inner room used by their parents and steal a shilling from the rusty savings tin hidden in the thatch above the bed. And it was with this shilling that he had paid for the ride. But then, when she saw the look Aradi was flashing her, she thought better of it.

"You shouldn't borrow other people's bicycles again, Aradi," Ombima said, lifting his gaze to the squeamish Aradi. "I don't want to have to pay for any damage if you should have an accident. However," he hastened to add in as reassuring a voice as he could, "this is not to say that I am discouraging you from riding. No, I am not. Indeed it is in my plans to acquire a bicycle of our own in the near future."

"Really, Father?" the boy marveled at this, his eyes widening. "Are you, really?"

"That is my plan indeed, son. We will certainly own a bicycle—after we've built a new iron-roofed house, that is. And so you must be patient, son."

A glossy warmth radiated off the faces of the children at the promising words. For a moment, they felt like all their troubles could be wished away at the batting of an eyelid. Ombima ate on in silence, moved by the glimmer of hope that shone on the faces of his children. He told himself silently that he could achieve this at all costs. Looking at them so happy, yet to be tutored in the ways of the world, he silently swore that he would. He thought that for them, he should yet make it in life, that there was still a whole wide future ahead of him and his family, new horizons waiting to be scaled. This thought alone infected him with a strange vigor and an overwhelming jolt of rekindled hope. He was not an old man yet, he told himself. No, not just yet...

The children's talk slowly ambled on to the impending Christmas season, a time of the year that every child, and indeed every villager, looked forward to with anticipation because it was a time of festivity and excitement, a time when there was no rain and the sun was not as strong overhead as it was in the first months of the year, when cool breezes rustled the trees all day and a new moon graced the starry night sky.

A time also for the bigger children, especially those from the few well-to-do families whose parents sent them to schools in distant towns. It was a time for falling in love. Christmas was a long, lazy, vacation when there was hardly any work to do but just beat drums and sing.

"We are going to sing in the church choir this time, aren't we?" Saliku was saying to Aradi.

"Yes, that's right," said Aradi with a thoughtful expression on his face. "Only if *you* just come along to watch, but not to sing." He turned to look at his stunned sister. "I remember last time you accompanied me to the auditions we were not selected."

"How so?" asked Ombima, interested. He had been half listening in on their conversation.

"You don't know, Father?" The boy wore that raised-brow expression that said he was about to tease his sister. "Saliku sings like a frog!" he said it and his eyes widened. "Ask her to sing now. Hear for yourself," he hastened to add when he saw the look that had jumped into his father's eye. "I swear it was her voice that made..."

"Hey! Hey! Don't you say such things about your sister, you!" Sayo was standing in the doorway holding a mug of tea, her face stern. "How many times must I warn you about that dirty language, you scoundrel?"

"Sorry, Mother," Aradi was subdued, not wishing to bring their mother's wrath on himself.

"Yes, go ahead and apologize to her too," Sayo glowered, pointing at him.

Cornered, Aradi turned shamefacedly and made a show of apologizing. But his sister, not quite placated, pinched an inch of his cheek, the way they usually settled their arguments and said, "On top of that you must promise that you will go with me."

The boy's pride could hardly allow that. But then, he saw that clearly no one was on his side, besides the pressure on his cheek was getting unbearable. And so he reluctantly assented with a stiff nod.

"That's better."

Later they went out to see the new moon that had suddenly appeared from behind a thick silver-lined cloud, washing in a dull pearly light the night that had just a moment before been so dark and impenetrable. Fireflies zapped about in tight little spirals, their glowing bottoms blinking on and off, on and off, like drunken men in a pit, foolishly swaying in and out of each other's way.

Occasionally some night bird broke suddenly out of the tall cypress trees marking the hedge of the compound and flitted noisily across the silver-grey sky, the raspy beat of its shaggy wing disturbing the peace. And then it was still again, save for the ceaseless soft rustling of the leaves up in the cypresses, as if in murmured conversation that only they understood. They always did that, especially deep in the still of night, even on a clear night when there was no breeze. It made one wonder.

Back indoors Sayo stacked the few folding chairs in the room into a corner, preparing to bring down the children's mattress from the place where they hang on a string from the rafters. It was not much of a mattress really, just stained old jute bags — the sort used to pack sugar and coffee beans — sewn together and stuffed with old banana leaves and the straw from the fields. As she made the beds, she disturbed the few chickens that usually slept on the chairs in this room, chased away by the dominant chickens from the cozy warmth of the kitchen area. The noises of the chickens and the puff of dust she raised off the smeared floor with her broom disturbed Ombima, but he sat still, hunched over the dying fire.

She made a ruckus of putting the children to bed and banged the front door shut, cutting off the dreamy view of the living night outside. Then Sayo came and took away the fire and Ombima had to get up and go to bed.

In the inner room, Ombima stood by the bed and absent-mindedly unbuttoned his shirt, the buttons popping out of their wide holes with accustomed ease. He could hear Sayo undressing at the other end of the room, her movements graceful in the familiar darkness.

"What is it, Sayo?" he finally asked in that tone his voice usually assumed when they were alone in the dark. "I can tell there's something on your mind."

He lifted the old blanket and slipped into their creaky old bed, its lumpiness all too familiar, like the fit of an old shoe.

"Can you?" Sayo took her time easing her undergarment over her head because the fabric was old and could easily tear. She draped her clothes on the back of a chair by the bedside with the care that people who don't have enough take with the little they have. She then slipped under the blanket on her side of the narrow bed.

"I know when there's something on your mind," said Ombima, stirred by the warmth of her body close to his. "You are forgetting I knew you as a young woman, just a girl really, who couldn't look a man in the eyes when spoken to, and that I've lived with you all this while. So, come on, out with it, woman." He tickled her in the ribs playfully and she sighed, leaning against him. He held her close, shielding her vulnerable softness in his bony embrace, the way she usually liked it.

"Please open the window," she whispered. "I want to look at the night outside."

He leaned across her and twisted the bent nail that secured the tiny window above her side of the bed.

The night sky outside was silvery, dotted with a faint star or two. The immense orange moon hung in the sky above the line of shredded banana leaves like a giant ball of fire in another world. A slim strand of cloud pierced it like a thin blade, coming out the other end. Other than that, there was nothing else in the lambent sky.

For a while Sayo groped about idly with her hand, faintly caressing his wiry body, her silky fingers lingering a while on the spot on his back where the flesh was raw and raised in a thin welt that the sharp barb in Andimi's wire fence had rent. Her face was calm, and her eyes like pits of fire, gazing steadily at the magnificent moon. They stared in silence for a while. Then, suddenly, Sayo said, "Ombima, I want you to tell me something."

Ombima was silent, staring at the lonesome fiery fluorescence, mesmerized beyond words.

"I want you to tell me something, Ombima," she repeated. At the same time she moved lower into the curve of his embrace, so her arched spine was warm against his skin. "I want you to tell me in front of this moon that you don't have another woman."

Ombima went still all of a sudden, as if he had been pricked with a pin. He sucked his breath in and his mouth hung half open.

Chapter Four

THE FOLLOWING DAY there was a surprise twist. Ombima was appointed to work in the compound and not out in the fields with everyone else. This meant he would be working alongside women, weeding the banana and cassava crops. Normally, everyone welcomed the reprieve, and indeed the rest of the workers would go to any length to get to work in the cool shade of the banana trees away from the sunny fields. More than that, as Ang'ote fondly put it, they would be working close to the hearth—meaning they would get their food while it was still warm.

But then it was only to the advantage depending on the circumstances. Take this particular day: Ombima was the only man amidst the chatter of village women. It wasn't very amusing. This was because the women were taking opportunity to throw barbs at him, away from the support of the rest of his male friends. Also, in Ombima's opinion, the women worked less and talked most of the time: Abiri did this and that to his wife of ten years… Aguvasu's wife, who had been heard crying the night before, rebuking her husband for refusing to do this and that "midnight" bidding… Abiri's teenage daughter Mmbone, that conceited high school girl—who in the village doesn't know about her? That she had developed rather a suspect posture of late, hadn't anyone noticed… And Abiri himself, hadn't he failed to make it to Maneno's beer drinking ceremony Sunday? Did anyone ever know why? It went on…

And worst of all, Ombima found that there was very little he could contribute, being uninitiated in their manner of trading gossip. The long hours they wasted just leaning on their hoe handles prompted him to conclude that bunching a number of women together without a few men in their midst was a sure way of inviting trouble.

It was such a relief finally when the sun started to drop out of the clear sky and the tea picking party was heard coming back from the buying center. At the sound of their approach, the women broke from their work and stretched their sore backs. They glanced over their shoulders to survey the work they had done, and one by one they hoisted their hoes to their shoulders, preparing to depart.

That day, a little surprisingly, Andimi himself was there to give them their pay. He had just arrived from his business *safari* as they turned into the compound, and he was in a jovial mood too, as indicated from the loud laughter that rang out of the bowels of the rambling bungalow. Perhaps he had just successfully wrested some prime property away from an equally thrifty real estate mogul after coveting it for sometime. Such were the man's day-to-day activities. The villager who had not had the good fortune to travel beyond the realms of his hill-enclosed home could only speculate.

The laborers assembled on the mown grass in front of the house and waited. From a distance, they looked like a bundle of sweat stained rags left on the expansive manicured grounds by a careless gardener. About them bees and butterflies flitted busily from one flowering bush to another, in the process disturbing the scent enfolded in the petals, so that in a short time the garden was a mixture of the perfume of roses and gardenias surrounding the waiting villagers.

Andimi's house was rather imposing. Set up on slightly raised ground, the rambling wings seemed to simply spread on and on in crafty twists and bends. Maximum sunshine flowed directly into the rooms from many windows, which seemed to have been fitted into every bit of the wall. The walls were painted a brilliant white, almost clinical compared to the smoky grass-thatched hovels of the laborers.

Up these walls scrambled climbers of various types now in bloom—brilliant pinks, reds, yellows, and whites. The bungalow's roof was made of what the villagers jokingly called "baked potlings," bits of pottery shaped in such a way that they overlap one another and baked in a kiln until they were red and hard. This was a completely new way of roofing to the common villager, who knew only the abundant grass of the fields since the days of his forefathers. Or, if the produce of his farm was particularly good, as was the case of Ngoseywe, whose bonus pay for the previous year's tea crop had outdone everyone else's in a highly suspect manner, then they went to Mbale and hired a pickup truck to cart their iron sheets to the village.

At such a rare moment in the life of a villager, a horde descended on his homestead to tear down the smoky thatch from his old hut and pass up the shiny sheets of iron to the *fundi,* who nailed them onto the smoky roof beams using funny looking nails that had caps on them, as if he never intended for them to ever come off. And all this work for close to naught expense on the proud fellow who would be moving up in the world, for the excitement of it all was pay enough to the more-than-willing hands.

Afterward the hut stood like a beacon brightly reflecting in the sun to as far away as Bukulunya and Chugi. But this luster lasted a short while, for soon sun and rain corroded the silvery zinc coat and left dull sheets that in time became rusty, just like the old sheets on the latrine at the buying center in Eruanda that the weighing clerk and the old men of the *kamiti* used.

After fitting such a roof, a man could stand out on the gravel road that passed by the tea buying center and, rubbing his developing paunch the way Andimi sometimes did, would point out his home to a friend he was making an appointment with and say "Thaaat one over theerrre, the one between those tall trees. The one with the *mabati.*"

41

But Andimi's house was in a class of its own. Walking up the crushed limestone drive that snaked up to the solid, lavishly varnished door with a smoked glass plate set in it just at eye level where, the villagers said, it afforded the wealthy man the benefit of scrutinizing his visitors as they came in without them seeing him, many a villager was simply awed.

Sometimes they even forgot what business it was that had brought them there and, when the wealthy man finally opened the door to their timid *tap tap* from the enormous brass knocker, they often broke into incoherent mumbling about things that weren't even within a kilometer of the initial problem. To this the wealthy man laughed, thunderously but with good cheer. Then the over-awed villager was sent on his way with a dismissive promise to "look into that." When Andimi was in a good mood, the visitor might even be allowed to stand in the entrance hall awhile and watch through a window the *televisheni* picture of the president all the way in Nairobi on the seven o'clock news.

This solid front door now opened and Andimi emerged, garbed in a flowing, delicately embroidered *kitenge* robe that he usually wore in the evenings. His plump, rather feminine, pink-soled feet were planted inside soft leather sandals. He stepped down the polished red step and approached the crowd on the front lawn with a wide smile on his round face, flashing teeth that only bit into soft-boiled eggs and other choice foods. He stopped a meter or so away and stood there a while with his hand raised mid-air, a frozen gesture while he worked something out. He clutched a small white khaki moneybag that was fastened with a drawstring. The other hand was buried in the folds of his robe, idly caressing the curly hairs on his stomach. He stood thus, inspecting them a while before he bellowed a general greeting in a rich warm baritone that Ang'ote imagined would give wonderful accompaniment to his old lyre.

He went on to deliver his short customary speech, walking among his employees the way an army officer might do amid a company of fresh recruits, scrutinizing their grime and squalor with spiteful little eyes that pretended to proffer friendliness. He radiated only riches, from his delicate calfskin sandals which, it was said, were made in London to his own specifications, to his stylish hair that gave the impression every one of his curly black hairs had been groomed and brilliantined separately.

They said besides owning an immeasurable tea estate in bits and pieces scattered far and wide within the surrounding villages, the man also owned a string of all sorts of businesses all the way from Kakamega to Kisumu and back again the other side of the road: butcheries, mills, drinking places, and even a pawn business that specialized in recovering (for a fee) money and other goods for creditors from debtors who wouldn't pay. All these together with numerous other petty businesses, like a fleet of handcarts for hire in Kakamega town for instance, could mint money with least investment and hassle. Mind you, all these properties of just *one* man. That, despite his huge mass and rather sluggish predisposition, the fellow was actually a computing wizard who shrewdly kept track of his every cent and what it did at what time. The joke went that you could steal a whole cow and get away with it but not ten shillings from him. He would sniff you out sooner than later. That if you tried to hoodwink him in a transaction, he kept up that chubby smile of his to make you feel like he hadn't sensed a thing, but in reality he was giving you the benefit of the doubt. Indeed he was so wealthy none of his children—incidentally all girls—attended the local schools. They came visiting sometimes once in a year, or not at all, from wherever it was they went to school far away in another country, no one knew where.

Eventually he came to the end of his small talk and started doling out their pay, which the tired laborers right then needed more than words: a speech could not keep a hungry mouth fed until the next day.

They lined up and received their share one by one, thereafter making a beeline for the open gates, wide smiles written on their sunburned, sweaty faces. They were like people coming from Holy Communion, but heading right back to their old sinful ways.

Ombima came up in his turn and basked in the brief instant that the wealthy man's attention was focused on him, a common layabout with not a penny to his name who also happened to bloodlessly rob the same provider to keep himself and his family fed. He lived through a brief moment of near glee there as he made contact with riches and splendor.

It struck him as interesting that Andimi had to actually come out of his "baked potling" palace to give them what was their due, and—Ombima humored himself—actually took the trouble to keep smiling while at it to make sure that his work force would not desert him the following day for another master somewhere else. For a brief moment, Ombima found himself wondering just what it actually felt like to be rich and famous.

As Ombima left the compound, he noticed Madam Tabitha, Andimi's wife, standing in the open doorway, one of her "clan" children playing with a fat white and chestnut colored pussycat at her feet. There was a serene look in Madam Tabitha's eyes, as if her thoughts were focused somewhere distant. He wondered what she was thinking about, or, for that matter, if someone like her had any problems worth giving thought to at all.

The talk of the menfolk as they walked down the village path was of the beer drinking ceremony that was timed for that coming Sunday at Eregwa's, the brewer's. Now that they were rich men with a week's wages in their pockets they could afford talk of drink and merrymaking.

As for the women, it was talk about the market day tomorrow in Mbale and the *mitumba* clothes they would purchase for their children. They talked of purchases of meat and all those coveted condiments for their stew pots which, had they had mouths, would have complained about the watery vegetable soups they had been doling out every other day. One in the group also talked of a new pair of rubber sandals and another of a bottle of orange juice to stow away for the children in early preparations for the approaching Christmas. They all talked of a great deal of things, some they could afford and others well beyond their reach, all in this deceptive, delightful moment for the wage earner. And they could afford to do so: today was payday, the tireless laborer's short-lived reprieve.

Ombima felt it was too early to go home and decided to walk with Ang'ote to his hut for a bit of manly chat to while away the rest of the time before the day died. They passed by Mama Sabeti's compound on their way, where Ang'ote obtained a half pint of milk daily, having no cow of his own, and no children to send for that matter.

Ang'ote's house was always a mess. First, one had to be careful on entering, lest one got himself an army of termites all over his hair. The roof was low, the thatch rotting and overgrown with weeds. A patch of Wandering Jew was ravenously taking over the stripped apex, as if they meant to conceal the naked poles that were now at the mercy of the weather after a storm had ripped off the top thatch. That was on the outside.

Inside was a real hazard because one couldn't really see where he was going. There was no opening other than the single front door that let in God's light and kept much of it out as well.

Stools and implements were strewn all over on the floor. There were old hoes and used tins of cooking fat that Ang'ote meant to clean out and use for drawing water, and which could cause grievous harm to a foreign toe stepping carelessly about. And there were dented old pans that he had inherited from his doting grandmother as a parting gift and a particularly dangerous twisted band of metal that he normally used to lift the *sufuria* off the fire, and which lay on the floor, rusty and weird looking.

"Make yourself comfortable somewhere, *bwana*," Ang'ote said, watching Ombima survey the place, a bemused expression hovering on his face, as if he was wondering what the other man could probably be thinking.

"You are waiting for God's good angel to show you a place to sit?" He groped about for a matchbox, not sure where he had left it, even though he was doubly sure he had one. He soon gave up. Instead he stood on his toes and pulled some dried grass out of the thatch, which he stuffed in the cold fireplace. Using his finger, he groped about in the ashes till he found a live ember.

Dragging up an empty plastic barrel that normally stored water, he sat himself down and went to work fanning the fire, feeding it with broken pieces of twig, as if it was the most delicate task he had ever performed.

There was a little water in the chipped pot in the corner and so it had to be used with utmost care. Washing hands would deplete the supply and Ang'ote did not. All the same, one noticed some recent attempts at cleaning up. The floor was swept and attempts made at ordering things, Ombima noticed. Even the dry maize stalks stacked in the corner stood in some kind of orderly arrangement. But then, it appeared as if whoever had taken the trouble had done so in vain, for everything was quickly reverting back to its old familiar disorder.

"Ang'ote," said Ombima with a twinkle in his eye, "why do I see the hand of a woman in this place? I mean, I hope I'm not mistaken... but certainly...?"

Ang'ote had been piling pieces of wood on the glowering fire and he paused.

"You could at least persuade her to fetch you a jerrycan of water from the river, don't you think?" Ombima went on.

"Yeah? And just how did you know this woman you speak of was here?"

"Now, now, don't you pretend, Ang'ote. Everyone knows that you and Rebecca have got something going, and that there's definitely more than the rest of us are supposed to know going on lately. You know this is true, Ang'ote. As a matter of fact, I happened to see her coming in this direction last evening. She was carrying a packet of flour and some milk, I think..."

he broke off to look at the half-used packet on the rack against the wall. "Now, don't pretend, Ang'ote. The flame that burns between you two is an open secret, however discreet you might try to be."

"I'm not pretending about *anything*, Ombima," Ang'ote suddenly retorted with a flash in his eyes. "Indeed, I'm not pretending in the least that I enjoy being spied on by any of you." He made a grating noise at the back of his throat and spat on the floor, rubbing the spit into the dirt with the heel of his foot. "Tell me, Ombima, just what is it that is your business in whatever might be going on between Rebecca and me?" There was a new tone to his voice, which Ombima had never heard before.

"Look, I sure touched on some tender spot there, my friend," said Ombima, backing down. "I'm sorry."

For a while Ang'ote glowered, something that must have been anger flashing deep in his eyes. And then he shook his head and bent back to the task of lighting fire. He found a *sufuria* and placed it on the roaring fire, pouring in a splash of water, which hissed angrily on contact with the hot metal. He sat back on his haunches and broke dry maize stalks one by one on his knee, feeding them into the fire that now lit up the hut a bright orange. The crack of the dried twigs and the roaring of the ravenous flames were accentuated by the heavy silence that had fallen in the hut. The orange blue flames lapped over the sides of the *sufuria* and soon the heated metal started sizzling, the water erupting into hundreds of air bubbles which rose from the bottom of the pan and broke up on the surface, sending off scalding steam that mingled with the pale blue smoke and rose in a lethargic twist toward the hut's apex.

It was too much. Ang'ote's scowl broke suddenly and before he could stop himself, he burst in a fit of laughter that saw huge tears jump into his eyes. Only he could laugh that way—the way only people like him who've never shouldered any responsibility in their lives are capable of. Ombima just couldn't help joining in.

"You sure feel like a couple of teenagers, the two of you," said Ombima when his laughter subsided. "You are too fidgety all of a sudden."

"And there's reason for it," said Ang'ote, rubbing his stinging eyes which had now gone red from the smoke. He leaned closer to his friend as if he wanted to confide an intimate secret. "There's reason, my friend Ombima. That woman has cast a spell on me. One thing I can say of her, and it isn't a lie," he held up a finger as if speaking in the strictest confidence. "She sure knows how to take care of an old bachelor. I must admit I feel like sunshine whenever she is around. *Aaaah...*" He took in a deep breath, sitting back on his heels, "*that* I must give to her." His eyes glowed briefly in the orange light, as if he was at that moment experiencing a deep inner peace. But a shadow crossed his boyish calm. "Only one thing I wish she would stop though—her ranting." Yet again he and spat into the shadows. "It would get to anyone's nerves the way that woman insists on drumming order in almost everything she touches," he threw his hands in the air as if in exasperation. "Don't do this, Ang'ote. Don't do that... *Ah!*"

"And she's sure got reason to if you ask me. You really can be quite a mess sometimes, Ang'ote." Ombima helped himself to some leftover cold cassava in a bowl on the food shelf, which he well knew had been at the mercy of the rats and roaches the whole day. He speculated a while over a couple of fine groove marks that ran at one end of the cassava and decided they possibly couldn't be poison, put it into his mouth and bit off a large mouthful.

"Why don't you just marry her, Ang'ote?" he said, his mouth full.

"Oh, that," Ang'ote scratched the side of his head. "The woman just wouldn't hear a word of it."

An expression that was almost sorrowful flashed on his face as he spoke, catching Ombima a little by surprise. In all the years he had sat with Ang'ote, he had never known him to express grief or sorrow. Even when his grandmother died, something everyone had expected would affect Ang'ote especially badly, given that she had almost been his entire life, they had been wrong. It had come as a shock, but then Ang'ote hadn't spent his days mooning over it. Instead he surprised everyone when he led the mourners in making merry all through the entire week of mourning, as if it was someone else's burial at which he had been hired to entertain. It was always a flippant sneer that seemed to say "the world for us all, the devil and his own" as he cracked off in his jocular, carefree manner. But now here, gloom showed itself.

"I've lost count, my friend," he said, looking down, his face drawn in. "I've lost count of the times I've tried to persuade that woman to stay over for the night or move in permanently."

Ombima shifted uncomfortably and looked at Ang'ote and thought of something to say. It was hard for him to speak. In the end he managed a stupid question: "Don't tell me you haven't..."

"Haven't what?" Ang'ote glanced up, not certain what his friend could be inferring.

For an answer, Ombima averted his gaze as casually as he could, turning toward the unmade bed on the far side of the hut against the wall. The bed was covered with what looked like the skin of some animal, but which was actually an old blanket, perhaps come down from his doting grandmother too. It was all too obvious what he meant.

"Oh, *that*?" Ang'ote broke off stirring the tea. There was a faraway look in his eyes, which were trained on the floor between his feet. Then he shook his head and said softly, "She is a nice woman."

"Just that?"

"*Huhh*? You want the bare details?" He offered Ombima a boring, owlish look.

"I just imagined, well she might be a bit... er... rusty in the hinges, you know..." Yet again Ombima found amusement in his own words.

"...A bit 'rusty in the hinges,' what a choice of words!" Their laughter was so loud it must have been heard by people passing by outside. "No, my friend, you imagined wrong," Ang'ote finally said when he had regained a bit of his composure. "She does well, yes. You know..."

He was going to elaborate, but then changed his mind. "Some other time, my friend. It is now late, and you can see I don't want to invoke the memories, having to spend the night alone, like my fate is."

The tea was served in chipped old tin mugs that had a grassy smell. The two friends lounged back against the smoke stained walls and sipped in silence. Between them, the fire ate up the bark of the dry maize stalks and leapt out in thin tongues that momentarily threw the hut into orange light, making their faces shine like those of animals caught in a forest fire in the night, enthralled by the savage beauty of it against the dull night sky, not knowing it could spell their own death. It was quite dark by then, and in the cracks in the walls the crickets and other nighttime chirpers had taken up their call. A fat grey rat scuttling up in the roof paused to regard them. In its unhurried pose, the tiny red eyes glowed, shining with unprovoked menace.

"It is wondering who you are," said Ang'ote, following his friend's gaze. "It doesn't know you. Only Rebecca is known to them in this house."

"I see. So, what happens to me if I am found here at night without you?"

"You can figure it out for yourself," Ang'ote said. He made some clucking sounds at the big mother who appeared like she carried a sizeable litter in her ripe belly and she scampered away into the thatch.

"They can give you a choice, you know. If they like you, that is. It is either they gnaw a bit at your toes, or nibble off part of your ears. If you kick at them, they get irritated—rather easily, I must say—and might carry it a bit further. But then, they really are not that nasty as you think. We've got a sort of code made up between us. I supply them with leftovers from my meals, and they look after the place while I'm away. Sounds reasonable, don't you think?"

"Don't you have a lamp in here?" Ombima asked, amazed that someone should talk so intimately of rats, of all creatures.

"You need one?" There was a baffled look on Ang'ote's face.

"It's gotten dark in here—and rather creepy too. Why don't you light one?"

"Why don't I light one?" Ang'ote repeated the words, in the way a seasoned drinker will let a new grain brew linger on his tongue a bit. "Why don't we just say I don't need it? Nevertheless," he held up a finger as if he wanted to make an important insertion, "If you really need one, you are at liberty. There is one on that hook over there on the wall." He indicated a cobwebbed spot above Ombima's head and, as he rose to bring it down he hastened to add, "I hope you brought along your own kerosene."

"You mean…" and then Ombima caught the interference of Ang'ote's words. By then Ang'ote was rolling over with laughter.

"I say, what kind of life do you live here?" Ombima shouted, astounded. "You mean you can't even spare a few coins for kerosene?"

"You know, I try to keep it as simple as I can. With the prices of commodities that keep going up, who knows, a bit of prudence could save the day when they eventually shoot through the roof—way beyond the reach of ordinary folk like us."

"But you got your pay only this evening! I mean…"

"You are right," said the other man calmly. "But then, let's just say I've got other uses for it."

They were silent awhile, Ombima twirling the tea grounds at the base of his cup idly, and Ang'ote scratching half consciously at an itchy toe on his right foot, which he had drawn up onto his seat atop the plastic water drum. A cool breeze blew in through the open door and stirred the smoldering embers in the hearth. A wisp of smoke curled lazily up from a dry stalk on the floor just out of the red core of the fire. The curl of smoke crackled into a thin long flame, which danced delicately in the breeze in a languid fluid motion, like a nubile Akamba dancer. Together, with the soft whistle of the wind coming in through the open door, Ombima and Ang'ote were like two strangers sitting around a witch fire in some underground place in a story. The darkness seemed to contain a lot of what needed to be said, and in the wind the cypresses outside seemed to be whistling the secret.

"Ombima?" It was Ang'ote who eventually broke the silence.

"Huhh?"

"I've been thinking."

"What about?"

"About Rebecca. I want to propose to her."

A smug expression that, thankfully, Ang'ote could not see in the dark appeared on Ombima's face. "I see," he said simply.

"I'm serious, Ombima. She has been on my mind almost all the time lately. I think I'm blind in love with her."

"Well, why don't you tell her then?"

"I tried to. Yesterday. But, for some reason, I found that at the crucial moment the words deserted me."

"Why?" Ombima tried to exude mild surprise, although it was all that he could do to keep the shock of the pronouncement from coming out in his voice.

"Why? I suppose it's because I'm afraid she's going to laugh at the whole idea."

"I see."

There was another uncomfortable silence. Ang'ote cleared his throat. "Do you think we really can marry, me and her?" There was a strange note in his friend's voice, which made Ombima realize he was listening to his most tender feelings.

"I can't tell you for certain," he said. He really didn't want to commit himself, mostly because he considered himself an amateur in such matters. "You know, Ang'ote, I'd suggest you talk over the matter with her, preferably as candidly as possible. Don't hide anything from her, and also let her not hide anything from you."

"Yes, you are right." Ang'ote scratched his right cheek vigorously, and it sounded like the skin of some lizard in the silence of the dark hut. He poked about in the fire, trying to revive the dying embers. Then he raised his face and stared at a point in the obscure corner where broken pots and other bric-a-brac were heaped. "I want your honest opinion, Ombima, man-to-man. What do you really think?"

Ombima sat up. In the dim light, a strange look clouded the other man's eyes. They were almost sad and pitiable, but Ombima was going to be straight with him. Clearing his throat to rid it of uncomfortable phlegm that had formed there he said, "Ang'ote, honestly, I think she is too old for you."

"Is it?" There was surprise in the other man's voice.

"You asked for my honest opinion, remember?" said Ombima, now seeing how it was starting to be, suddenly uncomfortable with the topic.

"I'm not exactly *young* myself."

"Frankly speaking, Ang'ote, I don't know exactly how old you are," Ombima answered lightly. He resisted the urge to laugh.

"You mean?" Ang'ote started. It was at this point that he always laughed. But his face was set, deeper, more disturbed. "I'll tell you—and this is coming off a troubled man's lips. That woman, for all her grandmotherly appearance, is only twelve years older than I am, Ombima—she told me herself."

"*Twelve?*" This time Ombima did not know whether to laugh or be shocked.

"Are you surprised?" said Ang'ote, trying to find his friend's eyes in the dark.

"But that's too..."

"That's too what? Go on."

"Ang'ote, don't you think you need to be older than her? I mean, don't you think men need to be older than their women?"

"Who says?"

Ombima paused, weighing his words. He slapped at his upper arm where a mosquito was just biting. "I think it's only natural. I mean..."

"Oh, so *you* say! But, while you are at it, do you stop to consider what if the two of us love each other, eh? What if we are just comfortable in each other's company? What has age got to do with that?" Ang'ote was suddenly angry. "You want my opinion, Ombima? I think age has nothing to do with matters of the heart. Not at all!"

Ombima whistled softly, the way a gambler might at his last losing hand, his eyes seeking Ang'ote's. He took a long hard look at his friend. "I can see that," he said, rather resignedly. "But why then are you getting so heated up about it, Ang'ote?"

Ang'ote sat up straight on the plastic drum, now aware that the argument could be slipping away from him. "Look, Ombima," he said rather irritably, "I don't think I need your opinion anymore."

"Only because I am stepping on your tail, isn't it? Well..." he shrugged with indifference, stretching his foot to ease a cramp in his muscle, "you are not paying me for my opinion, anyway. So why should I bother?"

The two friends regarded each other for a while. They were two people with a delicate problem hanging between them that neither could solve. Shaking his head, Ang'ote said, "You know what I think, Ombima? I think you are envious."

"Am I?!" Ombima said, his eyes widening. "And just why should I be?" He was quite surprised at this new turn.

"I don't know. I just have the feeling," said Ang'ote with an averted gaze. "Are you not?"

"Ang'ote, I think you are actually in love with this woman," said Ombima, nodding slowly with understanding. "Yes, it must be that. You see, you've become suspicious all of a sudden. You now weigh your words carefully when you speak. You were never like this."

"You think she has cast a spell on me, perhaps?" asked Ang'ote. He sounded like a child who had found a strange, beautiful bug he wanted to keep but had been told it would cast a bad spell.

"Perhaps she has," said Ombima, seeing that his words obviously were not going to make the other man alter the course he had opted to travel.

Ang'ote bit his thumb thoughtfully, the glow of the fire reflecting off his sloping forehead. Then a look of comprehension slowly crept into his tiny eyes, which were focused at a point on the floor. "In that case, I don't mind her adding another spell," he said and he sounded decisive, as if he had seen what he was going to gain and what he would lose. "To be honest with you, I've never felt like this before, never."

"Are the two of you happy together?" Ombima asked, more from curiosity. Ang'ote arched an eyebrow, his lips working as he mulled over the question. His eyes appeared to sparkle as a slow smile lifted the corners of his mouth. Then his face broke and he smiled broadly.

"Come to think of it, we are never quite… er… *happy* the few times we are together. The truth is we argue over every other little thing. You know, I never really thought about it until you brought it up."

Ombima laughed, trying to picture Ang'ote and Rebecca fanning it up over whether to eat their *chapatis* as they rolled off the pan, still hot, or wait for them to cool down and pile up so that they should sit at the table in a more decent way. The more the picture formed in his mind the louder he laughed.

"Well... has this now become a laughing matter?" asked Ang'ote, the suspicious look returning to his face. "I thought we were trying to find a solution here..."

"I am sorry, Ang'ote. I got carried away."

"Well, what do you think?" he asked rather anxiously. "Can this thing really work between Rebecca and me?"

"I think that if the two of you argue a lot then it is an indication of love."

"Is it?" There was a puzzled look on the other man's face, not certain if his friend was just flattering him.

"I think so. If you argue most of the time like you say, then it is an indication that you are comfortable with each other. If you ask me, it is deceptive if any two people truly serious with each other have everything going smooth for them. It might just be that the two of them are afraid to let their true feelings show, and that what they actually are doing is working hard to keep their ugly side hidden from each other."

"So, in other words, you are actually telling me that I am on the right path?"

"I'm not pretending to be some expert in such matters, am I?" Ombima said.

"You know what, Ombima?" Ang'ote wore a thoughtful expression, as if what he was about to say was a conclusion that had been forming in his head over a long while. "I think I am going to propose to her tomorrow."

"Huh?" Ombima exclaimed, mildly surprised. Then he thought of something. "What about all those grandchildren..."

"What about them?" said Ang'ote, his eyes boring into his friend.

"Er... I don't know, it just occurred to me that they will also need caring for, I mean..."

"Oh, I know that!" Ang'ote said, his voice straining in a slight snap. "I know full well what I'm taking on, my friend,

Ombima. Do you think I don't?" Ombima knew Ang'ote too well to know when he was lying to himself and the other man was himself aware of when he told himself lies. "You know what, Ombima?" Ang'ote said, starting to laugh. "I am going to buy you a drink at Eregwa's tomorrow—that is a promise."

By the time Ombima took his leave, the full moon had ascended the sky. A rectangular pattern of its silvery light shone on the floor through the open door. Upon this lit spot bigheaded ants were searching for a morsel to eat among the unyielding debris littering the floor, quite oblivious of the tentative issue bothering the hut's occupants. Ang'ote walked his visitor up to the path as was customary, even though Ombima's own compound was just a stone's throw away.

Outside, the once familiar country was now awash in the dazzling moonlight, the scenic landscape softened into barely perceptible folds and curves. Some of the silhouetted shapes on the hazy periphery were etched sharply against the dull grey backdrop, quite in contrast with the smooth curves of the rest of the sketch. They were like thin flying buttresses holding up the expansive night sky. Yet other shapes were more rounded and softer, like balled-up porcupines crouching amidst the towering silhouettes, ready to discharge their darts at the slightest provocation.

It was hard to imagine that there had been a downpour just the other day. The sky was now clear, and there was hardly any wind blowing at all. The air was turgid and warm, the deep grey November sky spangled with a million stars amidst which majestically hung the immense silvery ball of moon. Floating in this stillness were the murmured voices of the village children who came out to squat in the dappled shadows thrown by the moon, conversing in whispered tones, too awed to go to sleep. It was a warm dreamy night that made one feel young again.

"I can't go any further than this," said Ang'ote when they reached the entrance to his compound.

"Is it? But you have barely stepped on the dew, my friend. You could at least get me round that bend." Ombima offered his hand, which the other declined to shake.

"Hey, people don't shake hands at night. I don't know if in your clan you turn into witches when darkness falls, you know. You go in peace, my friend. And also," he paused as he was turning back into his compound, "do remember that what we just talked about is strictly between you and me. I trust you not to forget that. I don't want you talking about me, you see."

"Oh, I can understand your nervousness, Ang'ote," said Ombima, turning to go. "I was that way too when I was courting Aradi's mother."

The two friends parted with a good laugh that ricocheted far in the still night. Ombima walked on down the path, a low whistle coming to his lips as he reflected over the evening's events. As he drew closer to his compound, he noticed someone on the path ahead, coming in his direction. It seemed like whoever it was had just emerged from his compound, although he wasn't certain of it because he had been walking with his head down, lost in thought. Whoever it was came closer and he saw that it was a woman. She wore a white woolen shawl about her shoulders, and her stocky build was familiar.

"Ombima, is that you?"

That voice was unmistakable. Madam Tabitha wore a light perfume sometimes after she had taken her evening bath, the scent quite unmistakable in the wind along where she had passed, mostly because no other woman wore the same. In fact, no other woman in the village wore perfume, anyway.

"The day is old, Madam," Ombima said in salutation, a little surprised to meet her that late.

"Yes, indeed it is, Ombima."

Standing this close to her in the soft moonlight, Ombima could clearly make out the outline of her soft rounded plumpness. More so, in the deserted stillness of the moonlit night there was radiance about her that only the very wealthy carry about with them. It was this that overwhelmed Ombima a little.

"I was just leaving. Indeed it's good that we met." She had come to a stop just about a meter in front of Ombima and her voice, for some reason, was soft and relaxed, quite different from the domineering one of her tycoon husband. The contrast made Ombima feel slightly ill at ease.

"I came by to ask a favor of you, Ombima."

Ombima waited, unable to imagine what someone like her might come all the way from her warm house to ask of him at this time of the night. But then, what Madam Tabitha said next almost knocked the breath out of him.

"I've been going round my garden this evening, Ombima," she said, raising a polished fingernail to scratch at a speck on her cheek, "and I must say I am rather disturbed. Someone, it seems, is stealing from the garden. There is obvious evidence of this, although it's not too plain because whoever it is seems to be doing it carefully. However one can tell if one looks closely." She paused, frowning. "There are places in the vine where a pumpkin or two are clearly missing, while I don't remember harvesting any lately. Or some tomatoes plucked, a banana tree felled. Now, Ombima, I don't have the vaguest idea who this might be, although I must say I'm quite disturbed that anything like this should be happening at all." She was talking with calm, the way an employer might address the most trusted employee. "I've been thinking it could be one of the women who started working for me last week, especially that lot from Kivagala—they've got this look about them. One wonders why they should come all that way to look for work this way. However, it could be anyone else. I would like you to keep your eyes open as you work alongside them—especially that Kezia of Mwelesa's—and listen for any clues that might lead us to the thief, you know, like a careless slip of the tongue in conversation, or such. Could you please do that for me?"

Ombima gasped, afraid for a moment that his drawn breath would tell. And then he stammered, "Most obligingly, Madam." He was standing partially in the shade of an old *mtiva* tree that grew outside his compound. He hoped she couldn't see the expression on his face. "I wonder who that could be, doing such a thing, *tch!tch!*" he broke off in a mutter.

"Please do that for me. I'll be most grateful. The whole thing is really a bother because it has never before happened in the garden. Er... could you report to me anything you come up with, say on Monday after work?"

"Even earlier if I should find out, Madam," said Ombima eagerly. "You know that this news is a shock to me as well. I would like to find this ungrateful person for you, Madam."

"I'm sorry I'm putting you to the trouble, but I feel that I can trust you to do it for me, Ombima. Please do be careful, though, as you go about it. You know that any thief will naturally turn dangerous should they find out they are about to be uncovered," she said with a soft laugh that revealed a glimpse of her shiny white teeth, her dark eyes sparkling briefly with mirth.

Ombima mumbled a not-to-worry as she turned and prepared to depart, hugging her shawl closer about her shoulders. He watched her walk away, casting a figure of easy elegance in her unhurried stride. And as he watched, it didn't escape him the way the shawl wrapped about her, causing her dress to dip at the base of her spine. He let out his breath slowly and turned into his compound, his thoughts suddenly scattered all over inside his head.

Chapter Five

A HEAVY CLOUD of anxiety, which doubled as loneliness, hung over Ombima the whole of the following day. It seemed to him as if, somehow, the other workers understood that he was there to watch them, and that every one of them was suspected of the theft in the garden. He saw and interpreted their demeanor toward him as reserved and cold, not an outright rejection, but quite close to it. He thought they simply exchanged niceties whenever he was within earshot and worse when he was not hearing. He felt like a stranger in his hometown.

The hours dragged on. They were working in a section of the garden under pineapple bushes. It was tough going amidst the jagged, saw-tooth leaves. The leaves cut their limbs, however cautiously one moved between the lines, and into the cuts seeped some their sweat, stinging.

There was also very little fruit, harvesting having been done just the other day, and so there was little to steal. They could only gaze at the few unripe pineapples left and imagine how the soft flesh inside would have melted on their tongues, were they ripe.

Of course not a single one of them could cross his or her heart and claim never, at one time, to have stolen something from the garden. It could have been a maize cob, a guava, or a fallen mango. At least every one of them had secretly pilfered one of these as they left at the end of the day when no one was looking. This brought a mix of complex guilt, which was not really guilt, but a shamefacedness, a knowing silent conspiracy which prevented anyone from casting a first stone. Hence, a rule, itself silent, was observed that no one reported another for palming the odd fruit. This, along with their meager wages and the distance between them and their employer, bound them together as workers.

Ombima felt he had broken this rule and felt that the sense of brotherhood that had prevailed was now replaced with caution and suspicion. Everyone was watching their back, expecting heads to start rolling soon. And they all knew how hard regular work was to come by in these times. One might find work for a day or two, and then for the next two or so days the family would have to make do on those little earnings. Maybe one might find a farmer who paid well and also took as good care of the workers. But then, as far as investment went, Andimi was in a class of his own. No one had so much land under crop.

Ombima was pretty confused. He had been given the responsibility of catching the thief, meaning he had been set upon himself, and was expected to submit a report at the end of the day. So, just how did one catch oneself? He really wondered.

And then there was the other possibility: could it be a ploy? Did Madam Tabitha know who the thief was, and in reality was she just extending him the opportunity to reform?

But as much as it was confusing, there was this other angle to it. He was in the clear at least in the partial sense, to continue with his activities. He could, of course always heap the blame on someone of his choice. There was Musimbi, that loathsome, dull woman who was always getting warts all over on her hands and feet and whom no one wanted to work beside. Ombima thought she made an inviting option. He decided he would give it some thought, probably present her name as one of the suspects. For Musimbi, he had no misgivings, given that he hadn't much to lose by her dismissal anyway.

Besides Musimbi, there was a host of others to choose from. There was Kidavasi, the old man who trapped termites and whose son had just the other day nearly been stung to death trying to steal from Iduru's hives down in the valley. Everyone knew that the people from Kidavasi's family line had light fingers, and it was not something that had started yesterday. For him, Madam Tabitha would have little doubt.

Then there was Debra, the one with a few bolts loose in her head who had chased away her husband with a club the previous year for drinking the money he had traded their goat in Mudete for. She was also known to pick up people's things and stash them down her *rinda*. Ask any village woman and they would tell you that they wouldn't spread their washing next to Debra's when they went laundering at the river. The woman was known to pack up someone else's shirt or two among her own things. And perhaps the most curious thing was that that particular shirt would never again see the light of day. Her son didn't wear it to the evening football matches, or her father when he came visiting. And neither did she sell it to anyone. So one was left wondering exactly where the stolen garments disappeared to.

The list went on. Ombima could think up as many suspects as he wanted while the afternoon stretched on.

When finally they took their hoes back to the store preparing to depart for their homes, Ombima hung around to inspect the farm, rather secure in himself now that he had the confidence of the lady of the house. He looked at the beans hanging on their stems, fat huge pods a healthy green gradually turning yellow as they neared ripening. He inspected the little earth mounds covered with sweet potato vines, the leaves yellowish as they slowly wilted in the sun, the dry earth around the roots caked and cracked, a sure sign that the potatoes in the ground were engorged and mature. He inspected the pawpaws, one of which had startled him as it fell out of the tree on the first stormy evening he had snuck back here to steal. Birds darted in and out of the torn leaves, pecking leisurely at the mellow fruit. He thought of his own garden back home.

He found Madam Tabitha in the chicken yard at the back of the house inspecting the feeding of the broiler chicks her husband had recently bought. She had just changed from her school clothes into a plain print dress cut like a gown, giving an easy, comfortable fit. She had on sandals and her hair was slightly disarrayed now that she had taken out the pins that had held it. Her bright schoolmistress eyes were still the same: clear and alert. Ombima wondered why he always caught himself taking in such details about her.

"Good day to you, Ombima," she called out. "How was work today?"

There was a brightness about her that made Ombima quite at ease. "Fine, Madam," he said equally cheerfully. The sheen to her rounded cheeks, this close, was almost girlish. Standing there in front of her in his sweat stained work clothes, Ombima felt suddenly self-conscious. He waited for her to ask about the assignment she had given him, but it seemed she too was waiting for him to speak. And so he said, "I've been observing everyone, Madam, and I must say that I am quite baffled." He saw her eyebrow rise, as if to say "How so?" And so he cleared his throat and carried on, "Indeed I must say that if there is a thief among us, then whoever it is must be very clever. That is because everyone is acting normal to me... no one is giving anything suspicious away."

"I see," said Madam Tabitha, nodding with comprehension, her eyes darkening a shade. "Or maybe since you've been working among them all day, their mannerisms appear natural to you?" She stood with her hands on her hips, her legs slightly apart, a very mistressly pose that somehow humbled Ombima. Her teeth, a near perfect cornrow but for one of the two big ones at the front that was slightly crooked, flashed white as she spoke.

"Hmmm... perhaps yes, Madam," Ombima answered a trifle nervously, afraid that the responsibility she had entrusted in him might be slipping away too soon. He licked his lips, which had suddenly gone dry and hastened to add, "but I must say there's this woman who acts rather suspiciously to me though."

He had without thinking it decided there was probably little harm in prematurely playing his trump card.

"*Ehe?*" Tabitha's eyebrows rose again with interest, and she moved closer. "Who is it?" There was a look of genuine concern on her face now, as if she couldn't wait to find out who this was that had been causing all the havoc.

Ombima pursed his dry lips yet again. For some reason, he had found that this time around he was unable to meet her penetrating gaze. It was as if she was seeing right through him, reading his innermost thoughts. "Musimbi," he said calmly.

There was a moment of silence in which she seemingly absorbed the information. And then she took a step back as a look of genuine surprise slowly spread over her soft face. "Musimbi... the quiet one, is it?" Her brow knit into a couple of shallow lines. "Hmmm... well, one would never guess with some people. I suppose she has always baffled me too." Her eyes shifted from Ombima to a spot on the ground between them. "She never speaks much, that woman, and is always withdrawn from everyone else. She's the kind of person one does not easily notice if they are absent. *Hmmm... might be...*"

"It is still pretty much suspicion, Madam," Ombima hastened. "I beg that you let me investigate further, before we can start pointing fingers at anyone."

"You are right." Her eyes lifted from where they had been riveted on the ground and traveled upward to the blue sky behind him, as if some fresh thought had occurred to her. "Why don't you hang around the grazing field on the other side of the garden for a while later in the evening?" she suggested. "I'm certain the thief, whoever it is, normally comes at that hour. It can't possibly be in the night because then the dogs would surely alert us."

"That sounds like a good idea." Ombima knew that the dogs were usually released from their kennels situated at the back of the kitchen building at around nine at night, after feeding time. Nodding apprehensively, he said, "I'll sure come around this evening."

"I hope we catch that thief," said Madam Tabitha pensively. "Whoever it is, they are really doing damage to the garden. Well," she shrugged, coming out of her distant thoughts, "you go on home, and try your luck then. You know, I really appreciate the effort, Ombima."

"Thank you, Madam," said Ombima shyly. "It's no big deal, really. As a matter of fact, I'm equally perturbed myself," he added.

* * *

As Ombima left the compound, he bumped into Mudeya-Ngoko just outside the gate. The man was in a hurry as usual, returning from the weighing center to submit the records for the day. He carried the carbon-lined receipt slips extended in front of him as if they were valuable prizes, his eyes in a squint, obviously busy computing figures in his head. They said the fellow could barely read and write, that he actually just followed the weighing clerk's black pen as it scribbled in the receipt book. Then, really what happened was that he wrote along with the clerk, being able to perceive the numerals one to nine out of his rudimentary experience with arithmetic earlier on in life. Be it true or not, one could hardly ever slip something to do with figures past Mudeya-Ngoko's nose.

"Ageng'o, how was the day?" Ombima called vaguely, startling the other back into the present world.

"Oh, busy as usual, Ombima. How are you?"

Mudeya-Ngoko always made a pretense of being in a great hurry to get wherever it was he was headed, even late in the evening, always carrying around that thoughtful expression of his. For those who knew him well, this expression sometimes provoked laughter after they found out he was probably rushing home for the warm meal that the portly maid, Midecha, kept heated up for him by the fire back in Madam's kitchen.

"Well, the day was no easier for me either," said Ombima, avoiding Mudeya-Ngoko's shifty eyes.

"I see." Mudeya-Ngoko indulged in a characteristic habit of his. Raising his right hand, he quickly dipped an index finger into and out of his ear and made a *tut tut* noise at the back of his throat that only he knew how to make. "So, how was work in the garden today?" he said in the same officious tone, as if he was just mildly interested, having so much waiting for his attention. Yet in reality, he was anxious to hear Ombima's response.

Ombima knew the man resented his appointment by the lady of the house to work in the garden. He obviously perceived it a slight to his authority. In his thinking he had to be consulted on such appointments.

"Not so bad," Ombima said after a pause, amused at the effect it had on Mudeya-Ngoko's face. He hesitated as though waiting to hear more. But Ombima had said what he intended to say. With pretended indifference he shrugged and passed on into the compound, his lips pursing in an off-key whistle. Ombima couldn't help glowing with a bit of pride at his new-found position on the farm. Perhaps he could just dislodge Mudeya-Ngoko... Say, what if he planted the whole thing on him? Not such a bad idea. It would certainly be worth watching the man try to prove his innocence. Come to think of it, Mudeya-Ngoko was about the only person permitted anywhere on the farm at any given time without his necessarily having to explain his presence. This thought brought a dry laugh to Ombima, which almost shocked him. The more he reflected on the idea, the more absurd it appeared. And yet it also started to feel plausible.

It was still early when he got home. Sayo and the children were out on the farm tilling the ground in preparation for the coming season's planting. He found a machete and went out to join them, seeing there was nothing for him to do around the house.

Saliku broke from what she had been doing when she saw her father and ran to meet him, her almond-shaped face beaming, saying loudly that she had come second overall in her class that term. School had closed earlier that day.

Ombima reached down and swept her up into his arms, whooping with delight. She was so excited at her school performance and he was so proud of her he immediately decided on the reward he was going to give her. This was regardless of what Sayo was going to say about it.

Aradi, on the other hand, wasn't quite as excited. It turned out that he had managed position thirteen, two rungs down from the previous term. He had talked so much about making it to the top five. The results were hard on him. Seeing the boy's disappointment, Ombima patted him on the shoulder. Position thirteen was good enough, he told him. "Think of the poor child who brought up the rear, just what is he feeling right now?"

But, despite everything anyone said, it was clearly Saliku's day.

The farm wasn't a big affair, really. It was a ribbon-thin stretch of fairly good farmland that ran down to the twisting stream in the overgrown valley on which they grew bananas, cassava, maize, and vegetables. There was a patch of it at the fringe of the valley under tea, just about two hundred bushes. Ombima had started the crop experimentally. Already he could see it eating its way up the slope, encroaching on the patch set aside for maize. All the way up the slope was mostly good red soil where, in a good rainfall year, the family always made fairly good returns, where their neighbor to the left, Ambuvi, who worked for the Town Council in Mbale, had to put up a struggle to get anything out of his rocky parcel. The rest of the land on the upper part next to the path was taken up by the homestead.

From up where they were working, their two cows could be seen grazing on the tough valley grass that they had been feeding on all their lives, tethered to *makuyu* bushes that flourished in the swampy valley. Sometimes when the rains were particularly good, Ombima dug trenches all the way across the farm to check the downwash, this in order to keep the loose topsoil from being washed downslope into the valley. Then, with the tiny farm divided into these symmetrical patterns, it looked like a pretty patch that had been slapped onto the overgrown hillside. On the tiny ridges of shoveled earth formed along the trenches he planted napier grass which, nourished by the drain-off that collected in the trenches, shot out of the red earth with a vigor that defied the harvester's sickle, so that just weeks after the onset of the rains it was so high it could conceal a standing man. This Ombima used to supplement feed for the two cows.

Sayo had once grown sweet potatoes along these ridges, but had soon given up when a horde of squirrels from the tea bushes invaded the potatoes. She had silently harvested the vines for the cows to eat.

Sayo was working with the big hoe that Ombima usually used. Clearly too heavy for her slender back, she had to curve her torso at an angle every time she lifted it as she hacked the hard ground, already cracked from the hot sun.

"*Aaai!* This ground is so hard!" she lamented as she brought down the hoe with everything in her slight, hardy frame. "And yet it rained only the other day."

With the sighting of the new moon the previous week had also come a full twelve hours of sunshine, a blessing in some ways and a curse in others. For one, the sun was in time for ripening the beans that had been planted that season. Likewise, those who farmed tomatoes, like Arubati, the village carpenter's son, recently graduated from secondary school with bookish expertise, were smiling from ear to ear. Their fruit was juicy and red, and this fetched a good price at the market in Mbale every Saturday.

But for the owners of grade cattle, the dry spell was bad news. Foliage was scarce and those who grew napier on their farms wouldn't sell. Or if they did, it was at such a price that nearly all the milk the cow gave went into paying for its feed. As a result there was hardly enough milk. The young man from Munoywa who normally passed by evenings with his bicycle buying at six shillings a bottle, and who it was said later took it to the dairy in Mbale where it fetched a good ten shillings, no longer came.

One thing the sun prevented were animal diseases that came with the rains. Only the brown and blue grey ticks clinging to the dewlaps and undersides of the animals seemed unaffected, well-fed and engorged rain or shine.

The children were really just making a pretense at digging. Their little worn hoes bounced off the hard ground in violent recoil every time they struck at it, raising puffs of red dust that billowed around their feet, coloring their shins the fine red tint of the earth they upturned.

"You should try to make time for digging in the morning," advised Ombima. "Then, the ground is still soft and accommodating after the night's dew." Whenever he was not reporting at Andimi's, Ombima usually worked his farm in the early mornings. He found it much easier than when the sun was high in the sky. Sometimes, when they had planted and there was little left to do on the farm as they waited for the weeds to break through, Sayo accompanied him to seek work at Andimi's.

Ombima was clearing the ground with the machete. As he slashed at the tall weeds, grasshoppers and crickets jumped off in all directions, startled out of their hiding places where they had been driven by the relentless rays of the midday sun. Little pink and white butterflies with black patterns flitted among the brightly colored wild petals, dipping their long thin sucking tubes into the heart of the flower. After they exhausted one flower they took to wing again in search of another bright blossom. Then, when they had had enough of the plant's honey, they hopped away and soared on the breezy wind into the golden sunshine.

In the soft breeze, the torn banana leaves and the willowy branches of the eucalyptus trees in the valley beneath swayed gaily, whispering softly.

"Father, is Christmas this week?" Saliku asked, mesmerized at the picture of a rain of leaves shaken out of a tall eucalyptus tree pouring down across the valley.

"No dear." Ombima was following his daughter's gaze, and he felt the excitement too. "We still have a whole three weeks to go."

"But Mideva and her mother are already planning to decorate their house in patterns. Just the other day she told me they would be going down to the valley to search for the white clay." Mideva was Saliku's school friend, her closest friend. Her home was on the upper part of the road, close to the church.

"It doesn't matter if they do it now. They'll still have to wait a whole three weeks all the same."

"So, can we smear ours?"

"I guess so. You can ask your mama here."

"Shall we have new clothes for Christmas, Father?" Aradi wanted to know.

"Oh you can be sure of that, boy," Ombima said with a reassuring smile at the boy. He hoped that he would have raised enough money in two weeks because right then, there wasn't much in the savings tin to make plans on.

"And shoes too," added Saliku on hearing they were going to get new clothes. "You know my old rubber shoes are starting to pinch at the toes. I'm afraid I might not be able to wear them to the choir performance, Father. Or, if I do, then everyone will think I have chiggers in my toes from the way I'll be walking" Aradi snickered, mumbling something about a comment Saliku's gait had drawn from one of the village children who had seen them on a recent trip to Mbale.

Saliku had this pair of green canvas shoes that she usually wore to church on Sundays, handed down to her from Sayo's sister as a visiting present after her own little girl had outgrown them. Aradi's own, which had come down from a cousin in much more the same way, were now practically beyond use after one of them was carelessly left out of the metal clothes trunk one night and a hungry rat, who had chanced upon it in her nighttime scurrying in the hut, had wasted no time chewing out most of the front part of the tough leather upper. The hole that the rodent left was just too big to be fixed by the village shoemaker.

Deep in his heart, Ombima hated his children inheriting things other people's children had outgrown. He wished for them to have, at least for once, what they desired right from the shop counter, in order that they could also delight in the joy that came out of unwrapping the cellophane around the box just like other people's children. But then, where was he to get the money?

He was looking forward to the new year, when he hoped to get better returns from his tiny tea crop. From the lump sum end-of-year bonus pay, maybe all these things could be possible.

Ombima paused for a while in his work and looked across the valley toward Chugi. There were the new zinc houses people had put up late in the year, reflecting brightly wherever he looked. On the light breeze, he could discern the sound of a *fundi's* hammer summarily driving nails through stiff new sheets somewhere: *tong! tong! tong!* The new zinc roofs shone through the trees like silver medals marking a hard-worn achievement, and in their own way mocking those like him who still lived their rainy nights under rotting thatch.

"What are you looking at, Baba Aradi?" Sayo said, following the direction of his gaze. Ombima averted his eyes, pretending instead to survey the purple-streaked evening sky. But not before she saw what it was that had held his attention. When, however, she turned to look at him, he was surprised at the fierce resolve he saw in her eyes. It was as if she was saying: *we shall make it too some day.*

A thin weary smile spread over her tired features, and he felt comforted inside because he knew he had someone who shared in his dream. One day they would build a decent home. And then their children would enjoy the things that other people's children had. They would have enough schoolbooks and school uniforms and shoes. They would have enough to eat on their table too. And they wouldn't have to labor for other people to meet their daily needs... some day.

A cold chill slowly crept into the evening air as the sun started to drop in the west. Hundreds of birds came out of the trees and trafficked about in the clear December sky, their excited chattering ushering in the evening. A drum sounded in the distance. Soon others took up the beat all over, and on the wind the voices of children practicing in the church choir could be heard from the distant ridge. On a faraway hilltop, a firewood seeker burned wet branches hacked off a fallen tree, the smoke rising upward in a straight column as if God was receiving his burnt offering. And on the village path, the young women idled about on their way to the river, hardly in a hurry to get there, their water pots balanced delicately on their stylishly plaited heads. They chatted incessantly about a hundred and one things, mostly about other people. It seemed like the coming festivity pervaded the air, infecting everyone who breathed it, young and old.

Ombima, still lost in thought, descended into the valley to help his son untether the cattle. As they had grazed, the animals had gotten their long ropes badly entangled in the *makuyu* shrubs. Ombima and Aradi led the two animals, bellies swollen more to one side than the other, slowly uphill on their way home. Sayo and Saliku walked on ahead, their hoes slung over their shoulders. The overfed cows took their own sweet time laboring up the narrow path, gasping from the effort. A warm grassy odor drew the fat blue dung flies to their backsides, darting effortlessly from the cows' flickering tails. The cows leaned against the hedge lining the narrow path, brushing their shiny coats on the rough cypress, enjoying the caress of the untrimmed branches. And all the time their huge jaws chewed and chewed, slimy white froth dripping out onto the stubble of spiky hairs around their sweaty muzzles.

On the farm behind where the departing family had just been working, the squirrels and field mice crawled out of their burrows and stood on their hind feet surveying left and right before they advanced on the spot that had been dug to see what had been uncovered, hopeful they would find a starchy morsel to eat.

Chapter Six

THE NIGHT WAS humid and warm, buzzing with the call of cicadas upstaging the continuous droning of a million other night insects. The deep purple sky glittered with countless stars and a thin sliver of moon revealed the late evening shoppers hurrying from the village *duka* carrying their purchases wrapped up in discreet little old newspaper parcels. The pearly light also concealed the night witches, waiting motionless in the shaded hedgerows, tense with malicious intent. The village path was mottled in shadow, the leaves in the tree canopies whispering in the slight night breeze.

Ombima walked at a brisk pace, hurrying to police Andimi's garden as he had agreed to. Under the thin nylon shirt he wore, his skin had erupted in goose bumps, his breath rasping through teeth chattering partly from the chilly bath he had just taken. He was secretly excited about something. He did not know what. His heart fluttered as if it had grown wings. He wondered what he was going to steal today, now that he was "officially" licensed to conduct his nighttime business.

The rich man's garden was bathed in shadow, the tall gaunt banana trees like silent sentinels slouching against their support-ive, forked wooden poles. The fence creaked only slightly as he crawled his way underneath, his breath heavy with the excite-ment that mounted within him at the sight of so much wealth in farm produce arrayed in front of him. He felt, as usual, that he was entering some secret garden forbidden to people like him—a place trodden only by those few of noble birth. Inside, he stalked through the lines of tall banana trees, his stride soft as a cat's, his ears cocked, listening. Up above in the hanging, dried leaves, bats flapped about, disturbed by the stalker underneath who had disrupted their serenity.

Occasionally, the bats startled him as they darted out from the underside of a leaf where they hung upside down all day. As they sped away into the night, their shrill calls echoed in the tall trees, their tiny rat-like eyes shining red in the dark with a meat hunter's glee.

Ombima took his time to inspect the ripe fruits on the tall trees. It was while he was doing these rounds that he suddenly stopped short in his tracks, his ears cocked. For some reason, that peculiar sixth sense that he had acquired in the past few days had communicated a warning message. A cold fear came over him as he realized that he was not alone. There was another presence somewhere in the garden, someone who was right then watching his every move. He had often felt that way as a child. Sometimes he was mistaken, but then this time it was too strong. Suddenly the moonlit air hung thick with lurking menace and all the shadows that had just a moment back been mere harmless dark patches assumed life. The slightest shift in light became cause for alarm.

Ombima stood very still, swallowed in the embrace of a banana tree's crown. He felt a warm breath of air blow down his spine and he wanted to run. He cocked his ear for sound. A twig snapped. It was close. Then there was a rustling sound. He stood transfixed, sweating. Those sounds were certainly not the whistling of the wind in the dry banana fronds. He wanted to call out. At the same time he wanted to bolt out of there.

So there really was a thief after all!

He turned on his heel very slowly, poised to scream his loudest for help should the shadows shift, now quite certain he was not mistaken. The drooping wilted fronds of a banana tree just a couple of yards from where he was standing parted with a rustle and a figure slowly emerged.

Ombima's throat had gone dry. His tongue stuck against the roof of his mouth as he watched, everything he had planned to do suddenly evaporating from his head.

That was before a soft feminine voice that was quite unmistakable sounded, and it was calling to him by name. "Ombima, do not be afraid. It is only me."

Madam Tabitha stood there in the space between the tall trees with the moonlight pouring over her shoulders. In the pale light she might have been naked, save for a translucent gown made from some flimsy silken material that draped her rounded plumpness like a sculptor's cloak might drape a marble piece. She looked like someone who had walked out of a dream.

Ombima took a moment to regain his senses. She was walking calmly toward him, her feet confident in her stride, like someone who was accustomed to walking in the dark. Her gaze, however, was directed at an object beyond him in the garden.

"Good evening. You took your time coming." Her voice was husky and Ombima could not tell if it was from displeasure at the fact that he had come late or something else.

"I'm sorry, Madam," he mumbled, still unable to believe that it was really her there in the garden. "Have you been here long?" he stammered, for lack of something to say. What he had really meant to say was that he had not been aware there would be the two of them guarding the garden that night.

"I've been here quite a while," she said, reaching to scratch at her bare upper arm where some insect must have bitten her. "Unfortunately for me, nothing has happened so far." She paused to flash him a speculative look, and then walked on past, as if absorbed in inspecting her fruit. As she passed him the pearly moonlight fell directly on her and he thought he saw nearly every curve of her body through the nightgown's flimsy material. This close, her eyes looked puffy and her skin clear and flawless, almost pale in the light. She could not have been long out of bed.

She walked on past, her stride sure and purposeful, and he followed, feeling slightly awkward. He was like a schoolboy caught by the science mistress with his head in his lap on a very important stargazing assignment.

"I was really hoping to catch the thief tonight," Madam Tabitha was saying. "*Mzee* was very cross about the theft that took place last Friday. He was mad at every one of you as a matter of fact, and said you just couldn't be trusted."

For a while Ombima did not know what to say of it. He cleared his throat and ventured, "I'm confident we'll catch the thief, Madam... whoever it is." He was not quite sure what she implied with her statement. Did it mean they could no longer be trusted to work in the garden? This was duly confirmed by what she said next.

"And you had better hope that the thief is found," she said in that tight inscrutable voice. "We are thinking of taking on a new group of workers from Kigama to work for us on a permanent basis. We really don't know about you people of Ivona." Suddenly her tone became condemning. "We give you everything you could possibly need and yet you turn back and bite the same hand that feeds you!"

She had turned around and was facing him. In the wane moonlight he saw her rounded nostrils flare as if she was smitten, her ample bosom pushing against the robe's thin fabric in her passion.

"Tell me, Ombima, just why do you people steal from us when we do everything we possibly can for you, eh? I mean... I just can't understand..."

Her agitated stare went through him and he was forced to look away, stabbed by the guilt of their betrayal.

"I'm sorry, Madam. It really is selfish of us not to appreciate what we are given." He swallowed, searching for something to add. "I... I promise, I'll do everything I can to catch the thief," he mumbled, feeling quite uneasy because of her riveting stare.

"I'll take your promise, Ombima," she said at long last when she saw that he was not going to raise his eyes to meet hers. "In the meantime, I'll try to contain my husband's fury. I must ask you not to tell everyone else about the plans he has concerning the new people from Kigama. Naturally, I'll expect you to treat it in confidence."

She stood a while, contemplating a spot at her feet. A chilly draft swept through the garden and she clasped herself, her dark eyes still focused on the ground, her thoughts unobstructed. He watched her troubled face from the discretion of his lowered eyelids, mesmerized, at the same time frightened at the way her full lips moved in her thoughts. A huge night bird suddenly broke out of the crown of a banana tree close by and noisily flew away into the silvery night, furious wings beating against the torn leaves, disturbing the calm night.

She led him round the garden through the banana and pawpaw trees, pausing to inspect where a pumpkin had been plucked from its mangled vine and cassava stems gouged out of the ground. Then, still seething, she bade him to keep up the watch and left in the direction of the house.

He watched her depart through the banana trees, her gown drawn close because of the chill, her arms crossed over her chest, her light slippers slapping softly against the white soles of her feet. She exuded an aura of wealth and comfort far beyond the realms of a common villager. Ombima burned inside with shame, her words still ringing in his ears.

He watched her until she disappeared behind the trellis fence coiled with passion fruit, and then he turned and went back to his duties.

* * *

Shortly after, Madam Tabitha was undressed and snug in the rosy sheets on her side of the huge carved-wood bed, staring up at the ceiling. The wide room was in partial darkness, save for a long triangle of light that fell across the thick brown rug by the bedside from the door, now slightly ajar. In the next room she could hear the soft cursing of her husband, accompanied shortly by a dull drumming on the solid wooden desktop.

Andimi was sitting at the desk in his private study adjoining the master bedroom, hunched over his record books. He was having some trouble debiting some figures against his expenditure for the day. As usual, there were anomalies when it came to balancing his accounts, which he was strict about keeping in order. This was the one part of the business that he never left to chance, however tiring the day may have been. There were many small articles from his numerous businesses that needed to be entered and double-checked. Occasionally, he broke off to count away on his thick stubby fingers. Or he just sat a while, biting the ballpoint cap, already disfigured into a flat caterpillar from habit, between his sharp little teeth. This happened whenever something did not appear to go the way he wanted it to.

A mug of coffee that the maid Midecha had made for him had gone lukewarm. He wore his pajama bottom and an undershirt, and bedroom slippers that were made of fur. The soft skin of his plump biceps and brow was covered in a thin film of moisture. The forearms, resting on the sheets of paper that were strewn all over the table, left damp patches whenever he picked up the pen to write.

In the other room, Madam Tabitha lay on her back listening to the sounds of the night creatures outside, merged with the untiring *tick-tock* of the tiny winding action clock on the bedside table. Sleep would not come easily. She had a hundred thoughts milling about inside her head.

* * *

Ombima was equally thoughtful as he entered his compound a while later. He was walking with his head lowered, oblivious of everything else around him, lost in conversation with himself.

He almost bumped into Sayo, coming from the direction of the little thatched latrine. She was carrying a twisted old scuttle, her hands covered in ashes. She had been sprinkling ashes from the hearth around the latrine hole to keep out the smell and the flies, usually her last chore of the day.

"Hey, don't you announce yourself in the dark, woman? I almost bumped into you there."

He drew up alongside her and made as if to walk on to the house but she held him by the arm and said, "Wait, Ombima. I'd like to know where you have been. It is now almost midnight."

Ombima felt the tension in her even in the dark, her breath whistling out between clenched teeth in anxious little gasps. She must have been waiting out there for him a long while.

The door of the house was open and he could hear the children talking inside, arguing over something they were roasting in the fire. A flash of white beyond the cabbage patch revealed their neighbor's dog scurrying away into the banana trees, frightened by their presence. It had been scavenging around for edibles in the dirt Sayo had thrown on the pumpkin heap.

Ombima looked at his wife, standing close to him in the semi-darkness, her eyes boring into his, trying to find a sign there to prove her suspicion. She was not very tall, coming up to just about the level of his shoulder, and was slight of build. Her dark, oval-shaped face was serious in the faint light, her features slight and shapely, almost plain. She was standing very close to him and he could feel the warmth of her flesh through the old cotton dress. He suddenly had this urge to put his arms around her.

"Where have you been, Ombima? You've been gone almost three hours. And you were certainly not at Ang'ote's because I've just come from there."

"I've been at Andimi's, Sayo. Working," he said calmly.

"Working?" There was surprise in her voice, and her eyebrows drew inward. Then she seemed to recall something. "Oh,

I remember now. Madam came by the other day. Was it some work she wanted you to do for her?"

"Yes, it was."

This time she gave him a most odd look, as if to say, *I wonder*, and then she turned and walked on toward the open door. Ombima hurried and caught up with her, remembering what he had meant to tell her. "Wait, Sayo. There is something I've meant to ask you for sometime."

"*Eh-heh?*" she stopped and turned around. There was that firmness in the set of her mouth that told him she was aware it was not a suggestion he wanted to put to her seeking her approval, but something he had already made up his mind about. So well did they know each other.

"Sayo, I'd like us to visit this year's show in Kakamega. I hear it's on in a few days' time. I think it would be a fitting present for Saliku for her good performance in school, don't you think?"

"When did you think this up?" Sayo was holding her head tilted to one side, her eyes narrowed to slits. As much as she was surprised at the idea, which sounded quite remote and out of the ordinary to her, she was still levelheaded enough to see through to its implications.

"Oh, it came up just this evening," Ombima lied, stroking his beard, conscious of her gaze on his face. "Now look, Sayo." He rested his hand on her shoulder in a gesture of affection that he knew defeated her, "It's not as if I have suggested we make a trip to Nairobi."

"I know you only too well when you've made up your mind, Ombima," she said at length, sighing defeat. At the same time she allowed herself to come into his open embrace, seeing there was nothing else for her to do. She rested her face on his chest, listening to the strong steady heartbeat hammering away inside her ear. Then the tenseness slowly went out of her and she relaxed against him, sighing yet again, savoring in the folly of his rashness that had many a times cost them greatly. "Oh," she whispered into his nylon shirt. "Just how thrilled the children will be when they hear the news!"

"Just you leave that to me, dear," he caressed her lean back, once again realizing just what the world she meant to him.

As for her, she purred contently, leaning against him in the smoky shadow cast by the moon. She wanted to ask him where the money to finance the trip would come from, but she was too humbled and at peace in his embrace to think of starting an argument. In any case, she knew only too well that it would have to come from their savings tin, meaning the plans for the new house would have to be shelved yet again. Then again, this was the month of Christmas and people were supposed to enjoy themselves.

They walked side by side into the house to announce the news to the children, their hands linked, just the way they used to do many years ago when they were courting.

Later that night, Sayo put to Ombima the same question she had a few days back. Was there another woman in his life? And yet again he vehemently denied the accusation, in witness of the bright silvery moon and countless twinkling stars.

Chapter Seven

THE TRIP TO Kakamega town was going to be exciting for the whole family. Ombima was secretly thrilled, partly by the inane mindlessness of the whole thing. Here they were, about to squander a chunk of their hard-earned savings on pleasurable things. He had not told Sayo exactly how much he projected, knowing full well how she would react. This indulgence would set back their dream of putting up a decent house. Well, that was quite a setback, he was honest enough with himself to admit, but then, he also just did not care. Sometimes in life one needed to let go and just *live*, he comforted himself, at that moment feeling like a boulder that was rolling downhill, heavy with that benign, frequently delusive, self-bolstering that overcomes even the hapless pauper.

It was still early and the market town of Chavakali had not yet roused. They stood by themselves waiting at the deserted bus stop. The only other people were the sleepy touts perched atop an upturned handcart. They shared a cigarette in the miseries of mornings like these that only small town *matatu* touts understood. There was also the madman Ababu—a permanent fixture to the market place night and day—curled up in a bunch of greasy old rags on a shop verandah, fast asleep among many of the town's stray mongrels, which usually guarded him. A fat nanny goat, belly hanging with perpetual pregnancy that she never seemed to relieve herself of, scavenged for edibles in a heap of garbage the townspeople had put out in the night. The old garbage man, leaning on his long broom made from *viraji* shrubs, labored his way slowly up the street. Other than these town folk and creatures, everything else was still asleep.

Ombima stood beside his family, head held high with pride. Everyone had come out in their best dress. Aradi's plastic shoes, bought in Mbale just the other day to make up for his old pair, were as bright as a bundle of roadside leaves would get them with a quick polish. His wife's were slightly worn at the unaccustomed raised heel, pointed at the front with the old leather stiff and cracked. She had spent much of the previous afternoon polishing the chrome buckles on them, and now they shone as if the shoes were denying their twelve years. Saliku on her part was like a bright flower that stood out from the rest of them in her bright print dress with puffed sleeves. She now looked at her domineering elder brother with barely disguised pride following her good performance in school.

The family had to contend with the morning chill for a while before a *matatu* came along. It was an old contraption that belched black diesel fumes, like an old man on his last stretch of a long and tortuous life. It rattled noisily into the bus depot, horn wheezing like someone with tuberculosis. It was as if the driver was at liberty to make such loud noise this early in the day, before the arrival of the flashier *manyanga* minibuses, when his old heap would have to get off the road.

With its arrival, the horde of touts who had been sharing a cigarette sprang to life. There were two passengers already in the *matatu*: an old man who seemed asleep on his walking stick, which was planted firmly between his knees, and a pretty girl sitting opposite, who might have been the old man's granddaughter but for her sophisticated dress and coiffure, which surely could not have spent the previous night underneath the same roof as the old man.

Ombima and his family settled themselves on the narrow benches that served as seats and waited for the *matatu* to fill up. They hardly talked, all of them pensive and apprehensive now that the trip had actually begun. Ombima sat Saliku on his lap, knowing the touts would eventually ask him to do so in order to make room for another passenger on the narrow bench. The little girl rested stiffly against him, looking out of the grease-splotched glass window at the familiar market town, her anxiety betrayed by her strained breath. And there was reason too for her anxiety, for this was her first ride in an automobile.

Presently, a handful of other passengers trickled to the bus stop. The touts shepherded them into the *matatu*, reminding them they might be in for a long wait if it was the bus they wanted. The driver, tiring of firing the engine and honking, got out and banged the door shut. He told one to the touts to push a rock underneath the front wheel to keep the car from rolling away, since he had left the engine running. Perhaps he was upset because the vehicle was not filling up fast enough. He ambled away to relieve himself on the garbage heap on which the she-goat had been foraging, a disconsolate whistled tune playing on his lips. Afterward, he lit a cigarette and stood surveying his vehicle, maybe puzzled at how it managed to hang onto the front suspension. They had to wait for him to finish his smoke. And then he hurled the glowing butt onto the garbage heap, spat on the ground and jumped into vehicle. He gunned the croaking engine repeatedly before he leaned out the window and threw a couple of shillings on the tarmac for the touts to fight over. The *matatu* crawled out of the stage with an engaging jolt, dousing the touts in black fumes as they ran after it, shouting insults at the driver for cheating them first thing in the morning.

It was fascinating country that rolled alongside the road—deep endless valleys painted in a fine carpet of green that merged with the straggling little hills sprawled languidly on the periphery, their invisible tops shrouded in curls of grey mist. There were trees, tall as pillars that rose out of the gently folding earth. Scrawny black birds perched on these trees and watched the speeding vehicle with sleepy insouciant eyes, knowing full well the heap of rattling metal could not harm them. And from the little huts dotting the hillsides, one by one emerged the people who dwelled in this country. They were squat, dark, and without haste letting out their cows or chickens for yet another day.

They saw a group of young men on a roadside farm urging on a team of oxen yoked to a plough, their rawhide whips snaking through the air and coming down on the shiny coats of the oxen with an explosive *twap*! At every strike of the whip the sturdy beasts dug into the task, heads lowered on their powerful shoulders, muscles rippling. Inch by inch they churned the earth a steaming rich red in readiness for the seed of the coming season.

There was more traffic on the road as they slowly approached the town. Battered farm trucks transporting loads of produce to the local municipal market competed side-by-side with the sleek sedans that took the office people to work. In between these wove the loathsome handcarts, cutting at tight angles into the road as if they had right of way, and yet they could not pick up enough speed to keep up with the flow.

The townspeople walked along the paved streets, looking like people from another world in their immaculate dress and delicately poised movement. Mingling with these were the conspicuous inassimilable country folk who had trekked from afar to come and do whatever business it was brought them to the town, their bare cracked heels covered in the country's fine red dust.

Elegant flat-roofed buildings dominated, their wide glass windows reflecting like huge mirrors set in the plastered walls. They stood among the trees, competing for height like a new civilization, a far cry from the rusted zinc-roofed shops of Chavakali. There were no crows perched on sagging power lines and no buzzards circling lazily above the town slaughterhouse. Neither were there flat headed lizards crawling up cracked sun dappled walls, nor goats fattened on banana peels lying with their kids in the shade of huge gum trees in the marketplace. Here, all was clean and orderly, even a little cold.

Ombima herded his family along a wide paved road that led to the showground, feeling a measure of pride as he walked amid the townspeople crowding the sidewalk. He told them to link hands as they made their way in the swirl. There were many people and it was noisy, with everyone shouting for right-of-way. The wide road along which they walked was packed, the honking of impatient motorists mingling with the piercing ringing of the fidgety *bodaboda* bicycle riders who ferried people to and from the market square for a fee. One would assume the milling crowds were all destined for the fairground. It was almost impossible to detach themselves from the solid column in the event they were being led the wrong way.

Ombima's big fear was that he would lose the children in the crowd, and he expressed this to Sayo. Then, he knew, they would not be found but for a stroke of luck. As for the children, they were speechless with awe at all that they were seeing, hardly conscious of the direction they were taking in the spinning traffic. Not even Aradi, for all his bravado, had anything to say out here, miles away from the familiar valleys and hills of home.

Ombima hoped they were going in the right direction. He had been to the town a long time ago to get a national ID card at the Government Registry Office. The other time he had been here was when he accompanied his father and another old man to see about papers concerning legal ownership of their parcel of land back in the village. On both occasions he had made as much time as he could to walk around. Even then, his exploring had been limited to whatever time he had before dusk when he had to find his way back to the bus park. From these two trips he had a general idea of the town's layout.

As for Sayo, Ombima did not know exactly how much she knew, even though she claimed she had often passed by here as a child on her way to the settlement scheme in Lugari, where she had relations. All the same, whatever she still recalled did not seem much, judging from the rather baffled expression on her face every time they rounded a bend. She was like someone seeing the place for the first time.

Luckily, the place didn't need to advertise itself. Indeed, like the announcement over the radio had said, there were many people on this second day following the official opening. Most of the people in the streaming crowds were headed there too.

In front of them, rising twelve feet above ground, was a perimeter wall that shielded the grounds so no one could see what went on inside. From the other side of the wall emerged the electrifying sound of a brass band accompanied by a rolling *parum-pam-pam* of a hundred drumsticks on tightly stretched skins that made one want to scale the walls and join in the fun.

The entry was through narrow passages in the walls, past a turnstile that let in only one person at a time, and which was manned by a posse of guards. There was just no way to get in, unless one queued for a ticket at a tiny grilled window beside.

It was another world inside the perimeter walls—a world miles apart from the noisy hustle and bustle of the town. There were people everywhere one looked, all neatly dressed and jolly of face. Only they were not elbowing and shoving like those on the streets outside. There were many colorfully decorated stands that the exhibitors had put up on straight avenues lined with flowers, to which people streamed to see what was displayed. Some exhibited tractors as well as other complicated farm machinery, and others the processed products that came from the farm. There was a stand where cabbages grew as big as pumpkins, the leaves a healthy green, and another where grade cows as big as two of those in the village put together were on display. Aradi and Saliku wanted to see them all. They were so excited they could hardly keep still.

"Let's go and see what that man over there is doing, Father, *please*," pleaded Saliku. The object of all the attraction close to where they were standing was a snake charmer who was busy with his act. Just when they got there, he was in the process of inserting the head of a shiny black serpent coiled like a rope about his shoulders into his wide-open mouth. Sayo recoiled from the scene, horrified. No wonder a hush had fallen over the crowd of spectators.

There was a stand close by in which a leopard and a lion were kept in cages, besides other scary wild animals. The two cats gazed through the mesh wire at the hollow eyed showgoers with eyes laced with ire, pacing their tiny cages with barely contained restlessness, as if they were not amused at their confinement.

"Can't they tear through the wire?" Aradi wanted to know, getting as close as he dared, greatly captivated by their close realness, so different from the pictures in books.

"They can if you get close enough and they feel you can make a juicy meal," warned Ombima.

Just at that moment some daring boy ventured close to the cage and touched the grills, whereupon the glaring lion uttered an angry roar. The bellow was so deep and spine-chilling it sent everyone scampering in all directions. The cage keeper ran after the boy who had irritated the lion, threatening to whip him.

By midday, it was quite hot and dusty. Ombima took his family to the arena where a series of shows were in progress. They sat in the shaded stands and bought cold sodas from a passing vendor at double what they usually sold for back in Chavakali. A tiny cream coated cake for each one of them was even dearer. It did not matter though. What their eyes were feasting on more than compensated for their extravagance.

It was cool in the shade of the covered terraces. Sayo rested her head on Ombima's shoulder, closing her eyes when a slight, dry wind blew across them. The children were playing a little distance away with three other children they had made friends with only the way kids at a big gathering do.

"We are spending all our money, Ombima," she said rather dreamily. She kicked off her shoes, which were a trifle tight, judging from the corns of pale skin that had formed on her little toes. She was idly wriggling the toes, more the way she used to during those evenings long ago when they met on a flat well-side rock in her maiden village on their first date. Her eyes, closed like that, reminded him of the timid young girl who was afraid of snakes and centipedes, and who dreamt of a romantic distant place where the sun never quite set, and where the nights were starry and warm whenever she ate lots of *vusangula* berries just before she went to bed—a shy young girl who had never been alone with a boy before.

"What does it matter, Sayo?" he said, pulling at his soda straw. "We didn't steal it in any case, did we?"

She looked at him, then directed her gaze far across the stadium and shrugged. "True, we didn't."

They were sitting in the topmost terrace and so he could safely slip his arm around her waist. There were many other town women seated on the terraces with their families making Ombima realize that Sayo's dress was certainly not the most fashionable. Earlier in the day as they had left home, he had thought she would pass for the most immaculately dressed lady of the occasion.

He looked at her face, burned by the sun of the open fields over the years, but still remarkably smooth and blemish free, save for a few wrinkly lines that were just starting to show around the eyes from the endless worrying. Her beet-root lips, which had just a moment back been scaly and cracked from the anxiety that country people experience when they came to a big town, were now softened by the soda. Her sensitive nostrils dilated slightly as she breathed in the cool wind blowing over the terraces from the direction of the trees beyond the stands.

An impulsive urge suddenly came over him, watching her sleepy face resting on his shoulder, and he called out her name. She muttered a reply on her half-open lips without stirring, eyelids drawn half over her eyes in her light snooze.

"You know I love you?" he said thickly, an affectionate tightness at the back of his throat.

She raised her eyelids an inch and looked sideways at him, assessing the look on his face as if for honesty. Then a weak smile played on her lips and she whispered, "In front of all these people, you mean?"

"No, not in *that* way, silly!" he slapped her cheek playfully.

She laughed softly, her teeth glittering in the afternoon sunshine. "I'm not quite sure," she mumbled in the same sleepy tone, still not opening her eyes fully.

"Well, you had better believe it," he said, reaching out to caress her chin. "Because it is true." He looked at the faint scar beneath the hairline that she had once told him came from a childhood accident out cultivating the fields alongside her elder sister. It was significant because he had a scar on his face too, a tiny shallow pock above his left cheekbone just underneath the eye, which he had sustained similarly in his childhood. Perhaps their two scars bore some deeper meaning, he thought.

"I truly love you, Sayo."

She did not say anything for a while. And then she sighed and turning to face him, buried her face in the hollow on his shoulder and roped her arms in her lap over the black leather purse she carried, and which he could not remember when it was it had come into her possession. She liked to pose that way whenever she suspected he was pulling her leg.

"It is true, Sayo," he whispered into her hair, tightening his hold about her slender waist. "Please say you believe me." He did not know why he had gotten sentimental all of a sudden. He was looking at her intensely, waiting for her answer.

A couple of youth who were eating ice cream close by were looking at them with interest, probably wondering whether the way they were holding each other wasn't rather old fashioned. Realizing they had a keen audience, Ombima quickly withdrew his arm from her waist and looked toward where the children were playing.

There was a parachute display by the Kenya Army about to commence in the arena and crowds of spectators surged forward to watch. On the public address system the announcer sounded hysterical with excitement. Ombima took Sayo's hand and led her down to the lower terraces, hurrying after the children who had rushed to the edge of the arena with the mounting excitement.

There were belly-filling roars as the large, camouflaged military helicopters passed over the arena and, one by one, the battle-drilled paratroopers dropped out. Poised up there against the clear blue sky they looked momentarily like tiny black ants the huge winged insects had defecated, just before their motley parachutes unfurled, drifting slowly down to earth with their long limbs sticking out like those of a weightless flying bug.

The crowd cheered and clapped every time the showmen hit the ground and rolled, sprinting to the sidelines as they pulled in their chutes.

After the show, some officials took the dais to offer a lengthy speech in praise of the fine showmanship displayed by the daring soldiers. The children promptly lost interest as, one by one, they sauntered off toward the green and white striped marquees where a band's sassy music enticed.

There was just enough money left to buy the children the ice cream they were clamoring for and pay for a carousel ride inside one of the tents. Thereafter Ombima realized that he was left with barely what would pay for their fares back home.

The early evening sun had softened and the shadows lengthened on the ground when the sweep of the swirling crowds changed course and, in little groups, the show goers started leaving for home.

"Let's go now, before we miss our *matatu* home," Sayo said, drawing her shawl closer about her bare arms because a chill had suddenly crept into the air, blowing from the direction of the forest. The day's many events had left a calm, over indulged expression upon her face which, though inscrutable, certainly was not unimpressed. She had clearly enjoyed herself, regardless of the misgivings she had earlier on.

For the children, their windblown faces were expressive of their weariness, sleepy eyes glazed with the effect of too much excitement crammed within a short spell of time. They looked like they would drop off right there on their weary feet.

Ombima hoisted the girl onto his shoulders and they slowly made their way toward the town bus park, sandwiched between crowds that reeked of sweat and exhaustion, everyone anxious to get home. They were just in time for the last *matatu* for Chavakali and they squeezed in, trying to fit into the cramped space left inside the cab as best they could. Right then, it did not matter if they were trussed up like chickens. All they wanted was to get home to bed. The lights slowly blinked on all around as a shroud of darkness slowly descended on the endless populous town.

Chapter Eight

MADAM TABITHA WAS furious when Ombima reported late for work the following morning. She was waiting for him by the toolshed, and the look she gave him when he emerged with his hoe intending to rush and join everyone else in the garden was not pleasant at all.

"Ombima, just a moment," she said, coming toward him, an angry look that Ombima had never seen before in her eyes. She stopped just about a yard away with her hands linked behind her back, her head held at angle, mouth firm and no nonsense at the corners.

"Where were you yesterday?" her piercing eyes flashed slightly as she spoke. "It was a workday and you went off without informing anyone, why?" she continued even before Ombima could open his mouth.

Mudeya-Ngoko was hovering about behind her, idly holding a sheaf of ink-stained papers that he intended to take somewhere. There was an expression of unconcealed amusement on his face, his protruding mouth twitching in even more rodent-like convulsions. He obviously enjoyed the dressing down Ombima was receiving from Madam.

But he was not to savor Ombima's ill fortune for long because Madam Tabitha soon became aware of his presence. "Go on, you!" she turned on to him, her eyes blazing. "What are you standing there doing while you know well you should be out there with the other workers?"

Mudeya-Ngoko hastily pocketed the papers and vanished in the direction of the chicken houses, his fragile pride smitten by the outburst.

"Stupid!" she added after him, for good measure.

Ombima stood there shaking, the worn hoe held by his side.

"I thought I was speaking to you, Ombima. Where were you yesterday?" She had really worked herself up. He could feel the tension between them—she the furious employer, and he the truant farmhand.

"I went to Kakamega, Madam." He decided to come out straight with it, telling himself he certainly had not broken any binding rules.

"*You* went to Kakamega?" There was a hint of shocked surprise on her face. For a while her mouth hung half-open while she took a good look at him, as if digesting what she had just heard. Then some shadow crossed her padded brow and she asked, "You went to Kakamega, to do what?"

Ombima swallowed, not certain how exactly she would receive the news, but deciding there was no harm in saying the whole truth now that he was out with it. "I went to the show," he said calmly, averting his gaze because he thought he could not stand her piercing stare.

This time her eyebrows shot up as an expression of bafflement spread over her face. He even thought a look of slight disbelief crept into her eyes. He caught himself wondering at her manner of questioning.

"You went to the show?"

"Ye… yes, Madam," he stammered, now quite certain that he was going to be fired. And, strangely, there was a curious exalted feel about that awareness, as if the truth would set him free. He waited.

But then, quite unexpectedly, he saw her face change. The furious expression that she had worn crumbled as she planted her hands on her hips, just before she gave forth a lengthy laugh.

Her ample bosom heaved as her rounded body was racked with spasms of bemusement.

He felt himself grow hot around the ears, not quite sure he wanted to be the object of her callous laughter. He was about to tell her so when she stopped suddenly and, rubbing her teary eyes, said amid gasps, "I'm sorry, Ombima. I really didn't imagine..."

She did not complete the sentence and gave him a most odd look before bidding him join the rest of the workers. As Ombima turned to go, quite puzzled by her whole behavior, she reminded him he still had not caught the thief like he had promised.

"I will stay out up to midnight today, Madam," he promised, thinking it was only in order that he should make amends for his absence the previous day.

"And you had better, too." There was a different note in her voice as she said this, which caused Ombima to pause in his step. "Yesterday while you were away, I lost all my ripe pumpkins as well as some cabbages, together with a number of pawpaws. Just when I had set my eyes on them for the coming market day in Mbale."

All of a sudden, Ombima understood the odd look she had had in her eyes just a moment back: he goes absent without explanation and everything disappears in one night.

As he walked off toward the garden, his hoe slung on his shoulder, his head was whirling with thoughts. What Madam Tabitha had said greatly troubled him. Was she directly blaming him for the theft of her produce, and if so, could he exonerate himself from her accusations? All at once, he found himself in the sticky muckheap he had been planning for Mudeya-Ngoko just the other day. But, even as he pondered his situation, he also realized that there could be another angle to it. *Could she actually be suspecting him of the theft?*

Only then did he realize just what a fix he had gotten himself into. Here he was, claiming to have taken his family to

Kakamega to attend the show, and yet at the same time he could not offer substantial proof to support it. Who had seen him go? Not even his closest friend Ang'ote was aware of it. How come? And then the garden had been raided. It was difficult to convince anyone that he had not stolen the pumpkins. Now, if at all he was certain it had not been him, then who had? This was the one question that he could not begin to answer.

The day passed slowly, and the hangover of the day before that weighed over him did not serve to lessen the confusion of his situation. All of a sudden it seemed a crime for one to take his family to attend an agricultural show in a town far from the common market town that they were used to. In fact, to Ombima, it seemed the other workers were looking at him with a cold reserve beneath the thin coat of cordiality they pretended to extend. It was as if they were envious of him for having dared, and in effect, achieved something far beyond the realm of their rustic imagination.

By midday, he was already contemplating quitting work on Andimi's property. He could seek work elsewhere, perhaps in a neighboring village, where not everyone would have to know what he had for supper last night, and what his family did when they were not laboring on other people's farms for a pittance. It was a welcome relief when evening came at last and he was able to go home.

He left the wealthy man's estate and went down the dusty path toward his own compound. He was weighed down with thoughts, knowing full well he would have to report back later in the evening to catch the thief. He had just had a tour of the garden and seen for himself what damage had been done—it was a pretty messy job. Hitherto luxuriant with well-mannered crop, the garden was now an ugly mess with ripped vines and fallen support poles strewn all over. It was as if a troupe of baboons had descended on it for the better part of the night, intent on not only stealing as much as they could carry away, but leaving behind a streak of destruction as well.

Ang'ote confided in Ombima that evening that Andimi had been furious when he learned of the destruction. It was now openly feared that he was thinking of dismissing all the garden workers. Apparently, he had already issued a warning to those who tended the chickens and the cattle. Everyone was worried that they would not be able to find other employment if matters should come to that.

Of course there were numerous other tea farmers in the area who could employ a farmhand, but then those mostly took on workers when there was a peak, such as when tipping tea was coming up after pruning during the rains. Otherwise they normally tended their crop with their individual families.

Ombima left Ang'ote's house a genuinely worried man. But there was no peace for him at his home either. One of the cows had broken its tether earlier in the day and wandered into a neighbor's young crop of cassava. Now the fellow, an ill-tempered old man with nasty mood swings, was engaged in a heated war of words over the fence with Sayo.

Ombima tried to put up with the exchange for a while. But it became too much and he snuck out the back door into the banana trees carrying a bar of tallow soap, which was also used for laundry and dishwashing, toward the valley for his evening bath.

The stream was pure and crystalline inside the patch of bush where the village menfolk normally bathed, the sparkly water cascading over the sun-warmed rocks in singsong splatter. Sometimes snakes and lizards crawled out of the bushes to warm themselves on the rocks, but then it was said snakes normally did not bite in water. A small crab, its carapace stained a muddy color by the silt at the bottom of the stream where it normally resided, walked sideways across the flat rock, hastening its funny shuffling when it sensed a presence.

Ombima sat on the rock and started to undress, the distant look in his eyes indicative of his wandering thoughts. The rock was warm on his bare bottom, still retaining the warmth of the day even as the sun sunk in the west.

He squatted on the rock and washed his nylon shirt in the tumbling stream, beating it against the rock to squeeze out the field dirt and odor of sweat, knowing well that it would dry by the time he finished bathing. Rinsing it in the bubbly water, he spread it out on a branch where the evening breeze touched it, and then set on the task of scrubbing his dirty heels with a small flat rock with a coarse surface that was rounded with use. He rubbed the rock against the soles of his feet until the skin was white and smooth, taking his time because he was not in any hurry. He scrubbed and bathed the rest of his body, massaging his long sinewy limbs, trying to get the lather to flush out from the skin all the dirt from the long sweaty day. He lingered in the cool clean water that sprang out of the rocky hills of Kisangula, enjoying himself.

Bathed and scrubbed, he then lay back on the warm rock and allowed the shimmering droplets of water to dry off his cooled skin. The gentle breeze, filtering through the branches, felt pleasant against his closed eyelids. He just lay there, still, trying not to think about anything, the sound of the rushing stream all over inside his head until the breeze turned to a chilly wind. Then he got dressed and rose to walk back home.

* * *

Later on in the evening, as he crouched in the banana trees in Andimi's garden waiting for the thief to show up, a sweet scent similar to the one he had smelled from some wild flowers in the valley just that afternoon wafted up his nostrils.

The moon was shining brightly and from a distance the night air pulsed with the repetitive drumming of one of the many youth bands roaming the village in song and dance through the night, in early excitement of the approaching Christmas. A faint breeze was blowing and the sound of the young men's singing rose and fell with it, this minute the lyrics of the song clear and crisp on the wind, and the next subtle and faint, overpowered by the pulsing throb of the long drums. The music kept the night alive. Ombima thought that the aroma he had caught on the wind came from one of the flowers growing in the rich man's front garden. It didn't.

Madam Tabitha was coming down the path that wound through the bananas from the direction of the house. In the bright moonlight, her night robe swished about her feet like that of a queen.

Ombima's breath caught in his chest at the sight of her, freezing still where he was squatting as he waited. As she came closer, he saw that she carried something rolled up underneath her arm. She did not seem to know quite where he could be from the way she kept glancing in the shadows, although it was apparent from the look on her face that she expected him to be there.

She stopped just short of where he was and scanned the shadows briefly, before calling out his name in a soft whisper that sounded oddly conspiratorial. Ombima was stunned beyond words, mesmerized by the sight of her clad in that feathery dress, standing in the moonlight. For a while not a sound escaped his lips. He had never quite seen Madam Tabitha this way. There was a scared look on his face as he crept out of the shadow of a hanging banana leaf onto the lit path. His throat had gone dry and his heart palpitated wildly inside his chest. He felt like a thief.

"Ah, there you are." There was only the slightest lifting of a dark eyebrow and a sparkle from the depths of her dark deep eyes as she came toward him. There was this odd dreamy sheen to her face this particular night, one he had never seen on her before. And as she came closer, he saw that it was a small blanket that she carried rolled up under her arm.

"Good evening, Madam," he managed, shuffling rather uneasily on his feet. She smiled rather sweetly in reply. She stopped a couple yards from him and stood surveying him awhile, her shiny dark eyes roving from his toes slowly upward to his hair. The smile deepened.

"You had a bath in the river, didn't you?" she said, more the way a child might make an observation. "You smell of the *muti* soap."

A wave of embarrassment assaulted Ombima and he almost retracted back into the shadows. But then he saw that she was smiling and had said it in good cheer. He stood nervously through her appraisal, wondering what she could possibly be thinking. Then, after a length of time, she said, "Come," in a firm soft voice that he was compelled to obey.

She walked toward the patch of ground underneath an old pawpaw tree that the women had been weeding that afternoon. As Ombima followed, electrified by the mystic aura that she exuded, a thought rang inside his head. Perhaps he just might not have come to catch thieves.

This realization dawned on him with a sense of dread, the invigorating flowery perfume that wafted about her encroaching on his fair judgment, dulling his senses. He could only watch dumbfounded the way the curves of her full body strained against the flowing silk, the thin fabric of the gown wrapping about her in many cascading folds as she moved. He felt like a farmyard boy in a dream about a distant place where people didn't have to shovel dung.

She stopped when she reached the old pawpaw tree and let the blanket drop to the ground. Then she turned to face him. In the silvery light her eyes shone and her nostrils moved to her shallow breathing. She looked wild and untamed in that agitated state, as if she had intoxicated herself on some substance in the thin night air. Her gown was slightly disarrayed and her dark complexion washed in the light of the moon. Ombima wanted to bolt out of there.

He looked at her hair, coiled in a thick round bun on top of her head, and then he looked beyond her at the disheveled garden.

"It was you who did all this, wasn't it?" he said in a thick raspy voice that wasn't his own.

For answer, she smiled wickedly at him and folded her arms across her chest, causing the many plastic bangles she wore to rattle against each other like a *mganga's* sorcery beads.

"You did it deliberately?" he added utterly confused.

Still there was no answer.

He looked into her eyes, dark wells of feminine mysticism that, in that pale witches' light, had a powerful, almost hypnotizing effect on him. She remained still and calm.

And then, all of a sudden, she closed the gap between them and flung herself at him, her supple arms encircling him. There was an animal strength in her, her breath warm and moist on his face as she reached up to touch his cracked dry lips with her soft fingers. She opened her mouth an inch and closed her eyes, her hold tightening about him. And then she was kissing him passionately, almost violently. "You fool! You stupid, insensitive fool," she mumbled as their lips crushed against each other. "Can't you tell when a woman is sending a message to you?"

For a while, Ombima remained transfixed, his body stiff, immobilized by fright. And then the intensity of her passionate attack on him swept upward from his stiffened toes, planted resolutely in the cool earth and he felt himself melt away, like lard in a pan heating over the fire. He uttered a low groan deep in his throat as a spasm ran up the constricted muscles at the back of his thighs. Unable to sustain his reticence, his arms went around her soft full waist and his languid body slowly surrendered to her embrace. Soon afterward, he lost all control of himself.

* * *

Later as they lay side by side on the rumpled blanket, her hand snaking idly inside his nylon shirt, lingering over his breeze-blown tiny nipples and goose flesh skin, the fear crept back on him. His chest rose and fell slowly and his breath whistled against the insides of his slightly parted teeth. And then suddenly he was stung by the enormity of what he had just done. Frightened, he raised his hands and buried his face in his coarsened palms.

"What is it?" she asked, rising on one elbow, surprised at his unexpected gesture.

"Uh... nothing, Madam." He avoided her slanted gaze, which was roving slowly all over his bony chest with its few tufts of crinkly hair.

"You are not afraid by any chance, are you?" There was a faint edge to her slurred voice, which might have been sarcasm, as well as a serene, satiated look on her rounded face, like someone who had just scaled a big mountain.

"Uh... not at all, Madam."

She eased onto her back and sighed. Her hand was still under his shirt, and she twirled her fingers idly in the coarse little hairs on his sternum, just at that tickly point where Sayo liked to fondle. "Let's do it again, then, if you are not scared," she said in the manner of a challenge.

He lay still, listening, appropriate words to turn down her challenge deserting his dried lips. He gathered enough courage to turn over on his elbow and look at her, lying prone on the coarse blanket, the way he had seen white people do in pictures when they sunned themselves in Mombasa. The moon poured through the wide gap in the leaves above them, illuminating all the curves of her naked body. A warm inviting smile slowly suffused her pretty features at his keen appraisal.

"Come on, Ombima," she cooed, her eyes shining with impish mischief. "You don't have to worry about a thing." She reached up to touch the tip of his nose with her fingertip. "You know that you can come here today and tomorrow, and every other day, and we can be happy together, you and I. What do you say?"

Her voice was like honey, her gaze like *vulimbu*, the sap that is boiled over a low wood fire and used on traps to snare field birds. He looked long at her, feeling every inch like an unfortunate animal caught in a trap. Then his gaze shifted to the shadows beyond her and, pursing his dry lips, he uttered a barely audible, "No."

She rose up on one elbow, a look of mild surprise on her smooth rounded face. At the same time her hand rose to trace a thin feathery line down his jaw with a long fingernail. "Why?" Her voice was teasing. "Am I not beautiful enough?" A soft low laugh exploded somewhere at the back of her throat. "*Eeh?* Am I not?"

Ombima was stunned, his gaze fixed on hers, which seemed to dare him look elsewhere, his lower lip trembling with uncertainty.

"It's not that…"

"Then what?" She didn't let him complete his sentence. She looked every inch set to dominate his every being, pinning him down with her piercing stare. "Why don't you want to?"

"You know why, Madam." He tried to make his stare as level as he could, but he was not very successful.

"No, I don't," she countered, her hand traveling deftly down his cheek and under his chin. There was a challenging look still in her eyes. Ombima fought with his thoughts, wishing he could close his eyes so he would not look at her, unable to. At last, he saw the futility of his struggle in this staring game. A mist had settled over his mind, making it difficult for him to think straight.

"You are someone's wife, Madam, that's why!" he blurted.

She looked at him wide-eyed for a moment before she threw her head back on her shoulders and gave a soft laugh. "How you make me laugh, Ombima," she said, her white teeth shining in the moonlight. "You are so full of amusing answers this evening."

He watched the muscles in her throat jerk with laughter and, despite his situation, found himself thinking how so silken the soft skin under her chin looked. He made a soft grunt in his throat.

"Well, well," she said after her laughter had subsided, "I am someone's wife, so you say. And you are someone's husband, and so?"

She flicked a finger in his face, as if it was a simple piece of arithmetic that he should work out with ease. Bright tears sparkled in her eyes as she fought to contain her amusement.

He looked at her beaming face long and hard, not quite believing what he saw.

"You are a wicked woman, Madam Tabitha," he whispered at last, getting to his feet decisively. He started buttoning his shirt, moving away.

But he was not to go a step further before she was onto him, halting his process with a firm hand on his shoulder. "Wait." There suddenly was a very cold look in her eyes when he turned to look back at her, and it hit him with a little jolt.

"What is it?" he asked nervously.

She was tying up her robe. "I want you here tomorrow, same time." Her voice was firm.

Ombima knew a threat when he heard one, and there was no mistaking this one. Then she added as if by the way of explanation, "We can be happy with each other, you know? And all the while, no one needs to know. Good evening, Ombima."

He turned and started walking away, her parting words still ringing in his head. He walked through the moonlit banana trees like a man waking from the dead. His legs were suddenly stiff and leaden, the import of her words sinking in. He did not even pause to look back, imagining her slipping away into the shadows in the direction of the house, going back to bed. All of a sudden, the world seemed like a very small place, the hitherto distant horizon at the fringe of the hills an encircling wall of solid stone hemming in a poor hapless soul from all sides. All he could think of right then was how he would slip past Sayo into the bath shelter behind the house to wash the woman's strong perfume off before she caught a whiff of it. Then, he knew, there would be no denying, because no one else in the village wore that scent. Indeed, no other woman in the village wore perfume.

As for where he had been all this while, that would be fairly easy. What he did not know right then, even as he plotted how best to keep the evidence from his wife, was that he was not going to spend that night in his bed at all.

Chapter Nine

IT HAPPENED AS Ombima lay on his back gazing into the liquid darkness swirling and twisting with all manner of shapes above him, hands linked beneath his head, unable to go to sleep. Beside him Sayo was fast asleep as her shallow regular breathing indicated, her arm resting unconsciously across his flat belly underneath the threadbare blanket. The children were also asleep in the adjoining room. All was quiet, save for the usual chewing sounds coming from the cattle pen in the kitchen as the cows worked on the cud they had accumulated in the day, something that could go on the whole night. The night outside was still, the cypress trees rustling softly like they usually did, even when there was the faintest of breezes. In the distance, the dull thud of a weary drum sounded as another restless soul beat out his sleeplessness. Out of these regular night sounds suddenly came a sharp gasping sound, as if someone was gagging. It was followed by a coarse wheezing sound like breath grating against an unnaturally elongated uvula blocking the back of the throat, the sound someone who was being strangled might make.

Ombima sprang out of bed and raced to the adjoining room where the children slept, a cold finger of alarm clawing at his throat. The horrible sound had stopped and now there were thumping noises as if a scuffle was taking place. He searched about with his hands for a lamp and a box of matches, hardly able to see a thing in the dark. He heard Sayo come into the room, woken by his sudden springing out of bed.

"Here," she whispered at his elbow, fear evident in her voice. She pushed a box of matches into his hand.

He struck a match and threw the room into yellow light, touching the flame to a tin lamp close by.

Saliku was lying on the floor in a tangle of bedding, having rolled off the mattress of old sacking she shared with her brother Aradi.

In the lamplight her half naked slender body was contorted into an unnatural shape, one arm twisted at an odd angle backward over her head and the other trapped beneath her. Her eyes were squeezed shut and her face pale and horrid, the color of cold ashes. Her mouth was twisted at an angle, a line of spittle dripping down the side of her face toward the light. As they watched, the tiny body that was their child gave a jerk, and then she was convulsing in a series of spasms that saw the narrow hips and torso lifted upward and then slammed back on the hard floor with a hollow thud, the neck sticking out on stiffly bent shoulders as the powerful throes died out.

"Quick! Saliku is dying!" Sayo suddenly sprang forward, throwing herself upon her daughter's sprawled form.

It was Ombima who recovered first, everything quickly coming into focus. He pushed his wife aside and picked up the almost lifeless child from the floor, cradling her in his arms as best he could, despite the fact that her head and limbs stuck out stiffly, unbending, as if the very life was shooting out of her.

He bade his wife find some warm clothing as he carried the sick child outside. "And stop that screaming, for the love of God! Just you keep calm, will you?"

But then he was not the closest to calm himself either. Aradi walked beside him on the dusty path, his dark face shiny with sweat in the bright light of the moon, having been startled out of sleep to the shocking sight of his sister writhing on the floor in what appeared like the throes of death. The boy was considerably calm for his age, although there was a wild unfocused look in his eyes, the twisted iron bar he carried on his shoulder—which his father usually took with him for protection whenever he attended a funeral on the other side of the village at night — serving to exemplify his state of near panic. The boy's mother, bringing up the rear, was even the worse for dread.

Sayo was struggling to keep the tin lamp from blowing out, cupping the palm of her hand over the flame. In the dancing light her face was a mask of despair, her thin figure hugged by a smoky old shawl she had hastily thrown over her shoulders. In the crook of her arm she carried her husband's old woolen coat, which she had been unable to hand to him because of the great strides he was taking at the head of the trail, bearing the almost lifeless form that was their daughter, wrapped up in an old blanket. Sayo was shaking uncontrollably.

The family made their way along the winding village path in silence, making for the direction of the church where the compound of Senelwa, who worked in the government health center in Mbale, was situated. As they passed the compounds along the path, dogs rushed up to the entrances from their masters' shaded thresholds where they had been sleeping to bark at them. The night, which had been warm just a moment back, had suddenly turned chilly.

Normally, it was not a very long way to walk from Ombima's compound to the village church. Tonight it seemed like a mile. They hurried up the moonlit path, going as fast as the weight of the sick child would allow them. But still the church's high, whitewashed wall would not show through the cypress trees round the bend. In the dark, Ombima's face slowly became shiny with sweat, and his breath rasped through his clenched teeth.

He was relieved of Saliku by his wife for a while so he could rest his cramped muscles. A thin whining sound was issuing from Sayo's lips, which served to aggravate matters that were already grave enough. He wanted to ask her to stop it because it was making him scared, but thought better of it. As for the boy, he was all right, although he appeared greatly shaken. A heavy silence had descended upon them. All their attention focused on the motionless Saliku, uncertain what her fate would be.

At last the moonlight's reflection off the church walls showed through the trees ahead. Senelwa's compound was in partial darkness, screened off by the towering eucalyptus trees that formed a canopy around his little brick-and-wattle house. There was a movable gate of trussed poles at the entrance, which they had to push aside because it was already drawn closed for the night. The moment they touched the makeshift gate, two huge hounds came bounding at them from the direction of the house, their sharp yellow teeth flashing in the moonlight, growling savagely.

"*Bayaa!* The owner of the home! It's only us," Sayo called out, her voice trembling with fear.

Senelwa's wife appeared holding a powerful flashlight, which she shone around their chests, ascertaining who the "us" were, not quite raising the flashlight to their eyes because it was considered taboo to do so. Certain that they weren't thieves she barked an order to silence the dogs. Then she eased aside the gate to let them in, all the while as calm as only a medical practitioner's wife can be in an emergency.

"When did it all begin?" she asked as she relieved Ombima of the load. Sayo explained to her as best as she could in a shaken voice.

Senelwa was at his desk looking over some papers, a huge tome on human anatomy lying open at an illustration of the heart and its various tubes. He set aside his pen when they entered and calmly asked that the patient be laid on the leather examination couch built against the wall, next to his desk. He put on his long white coat, which hung on a nail above his desk, and eased the long tube he usually examined his patients with around his neck. Then he came over, carrying the kerosene lantern he had been using to read. The heavy tortoise shell glasses he wore when studying made him look older and more authoritative, quite different from the cheerful young man Ombima usually met at beer drinking parties in the village.

He invited them to sit and went to examine the sick child, who lay inert on the leather couch, her limbs still sticking stiffly out, her eyes partially open as if to welcome death.

"When did this start?" He put the same question to them that his wife had just a moment back.

"Just about half an hour ago." Ombima was sitting at the edge of the old sofa, same as his wife and son, the way ordinary folk of the village do when they come to a modern house.

The *daktari* touched Saliku's face and chest, and massaged the side of her neck, aiming to elicit some reaction from the immobile child. Failing, he went to an inner room and came back shortly with a tiny penlight, the "listening" tube dangling from his neck. This piece of equipment so scared the village children almost everyone of them would promptly take to their heels whenever they sighted Senelwa dressed thus, well aware that the next minute one of them was going to get a jab on the buttocks. A shadow crossed his face as he listened for a heartbeat with his instrument.

Ombima and his family sat nervously on the sofa, waiting for the *daktari* to finish his examination. All the while, Saliku remained motionless, her face pale in the light of the kerosene lamp. She looked almost dead.

The *daktari* put his finger to her eyes and rolled back an eyelid. The eyeball was white and pale, slightly protruding, dry of any fluid. He shone the thin penlight into the eye, searching for something. He then pried open her mouth and aimed the light at the back where the tongue disappeared into the throat. He appeared a bit disturbed by what he saw. Yet again he put the same question he had asked them, and Ombima replied in the same way. He then put the penlight back into his pocket and asked his wife to prepare an injection.

"*Tch! Tch!*" he kept saying as he drew up a straight-backed chair on which he sat, facing them. Rubbing his soft office worker's hands on his pressed grey flannel trousers, he finally etched onto his brow those two lines doctors usually have whenever they are disturbed by the condition of their patient.

"You say it started thirty minutes ago. Was she perfectly alright when she went to bed?"

He combed them with his scholarly gaze, unsettling them further. Across the room, his wife yawned into her palm, perhaps feeling sleepy, as she delicately lifted shiny old steel equipment out of a drawer. Sayo and Ombima looked at each other, they both nodded yes.

"She played about in the evening like usual?"

"Yes," said Sayo, taking charge because she saw that Ombima did not know. "She played with her friends outside, in the field outside our compound and, I must say, she acted quite normal to me. I don't know where these demons came from, I tell you. My girl was quite fine."

"I see."

There was a moment of silence in which the *daktari* brought out more medical things from a small white bureau by the couch that had its glossy white top stained with blotches of pink methylated spirit. There were a couple of vials, a roll of gauze, a swab of cotton wool, and a plastic syringe, together with two clear jars full of tiny pink and white tablets. He placed the objects on the table, arranging them neatly side-by-side, more the way a surgeon in an operating theatre might do.

Ombima felt his son seated next to him stiffen at the sight of the equipment. The boy had a phobia for doctors and hospitals.

"She wasn't taken ill recently, do you remember?" asked the *daktari*, taking his time with his preparations, as if someone wasn't staring death in the face right there in front of him. His casualness was starting to unnerve Ombima, who was everything but calm and patient.

Sayo now fumbled inside the folds of her dress for the child's clinical records card, which she remembered to bring along as they had left. Senelwa pushed his chair closer to the light. He looked over the card's contents written in a chicken scrawl that only the tutored medical eye could read. The card marked the child's progress in life from a hapless infant just out of her mother's womb right up to where she was then. He flipped through the stapled leaves in the book, running his finger slowly down the entries. Then he put the card aside and took off his spectacles, rolling up the sleeves of his coat.

There was a tiny thermometer that he had placed underneath the child's arm a moment back, which he now withdrew and studied against the lamp's flame. He artfully maintained the blank expression on his face that gave nothing away, prudently taciturn about his findings to Ombima's family. He wore that inscrutable face doctors learn to slip on and off in the course of their practice that makes them indubitable custodians of a terminal secret.

Senelwa returned the thermometer and rummaged about inside the drawer, humming softly to himself, until he found a queer looking piece of equipment that had a little round rubber ball dangling from it. Aradi watched keenly as the *daktari* strapped the padded flap on Saliku's lifeless arm and started pumping the ball slowly in his palm the way someone would knead a ball of *ugali*. He wondered if the equipment was pumping something into his sister's arm, air perhaps?

Senelwa's wife had boiled some water in a stainless steel pan, which she now brought to him and he set about preparing the injection. He used a pair of tweezers to pick up a sterilized needle from the steaming pan and stuck it onto the plastic syringe, plunging in the stopper with a little pop sound. He drew some of the steaming water into the chamber and pumped two or three times until only air squeezed out of the syringe.

"I'll give her this injection to revitalize her," he said as he pierced the rubber cap of the vial with a clear liquid inside. "And then I'll give her another to control the fever, which I must say is running pretty high. However," he shook his head for the very first time, allowing a troubled look to creep through his practiced mask, "I must caution you that this is not a cure for her illness." He paused to make his point clear. "Let me be candid with you. This illness appears quite serious to me. Indeed there's not much I can do to help her tonight other than the two injections, not until I get to examine her ailment in the lab that is. To do that, we must get her to the hospital in Mbale first thing tomorrow morning, and then we'll see how it goes."

He wetted a swab of cotton in clinical spirit and applied it to the mound of flesh his wife had exposed out of Saliku's disarrayed clothing.

The boy was watching keenly, totally motionless, as the *daktari* softened the spot on his sister's skin where he would push his needle.

It was as if Aradi saw himself there on the couch. He momentarily experienced the terror of lying there motionless, listening for the prick of the needle and, even worse, the searing sharp "hotness" soon after the doctor squeezed the plunger, forcing the contents of the syringe to spread into the taut flesh. He wanted to shut his eyes.

Saliku did not flinch throughout the two jabs that were administered. She remained as motionless as a log, not even uttering a whimper. It was as if she wasn't conscious of what was happening to her. It made Aradi very scared to think of this, for he had been waiting for her scream. What could have happened to his sister?

Later, they left the doctor's compound in silence, Ombima carrying Saliku on his shoulder. Senelwa had flatly refused to be paid the fifteen shillings Sayo had carried in the knotted corner of her *lesso*, saying he would not take any payment from them as yet—at least not until the child was feeling better.

This struck Aradi as a bit strange. The *daktari* was well known in the village as a man who didn't quite ask for payment for his services—at least not in words—but who, nonetheless, never overlooked it either. He entered the names of his debtors in a big black book he kept stacked away in his desk drawer, which he brought out only when they were conducting the "shaving" ceremony for a departed soul, when the deceased's debts were read to his beneficiaries that they may inherit them together with the estate. Other than that, only on one occasion had Aradi heard he declined payment for his services when he had a case on his hands that appeared well progressed beyond salvaging. Then, he politely refused to be paid, however hard the patient's people might persuade him to accept. In other words, this was his way of telling them that he saw no hope in the case and, therefore, wouldn't take any money. Aradi could not imagine that he had refused payment for the later reason.

Aradi walked behind his parents, engulfed in the same cloud of silence that hung over them. He could not see Saliku's face because an old baby shawl covered her head. But even beneath the fabric he could see that her neck hung onto her shoulder, too limp to hold up her head. Her arms were limp too, just like her feet dangling down her father's sides like a second set of limbs.

Aradi wanted to offer to carry her part of the way, but he knew that he would not bear her weight for long if he were allowed, judging by his father's labored breathing. All the same, he wished they would get home soon because he was weak in the knees with fear. He wanted just to crawl underneath the blanket and shut his eyes and ears to everything.

Later, when they were in bed and the lamp had been blown out, Aradi willed enough courage to reach out and touch his sister's hand. She was very cold to touch and completely unresponsive, her breathing so shallow he could barely hear her. She lay stretched out, stiff as a banana stem. Instinctively, he withdrew his hand.

He shut his eyes tightly in the dark and mouthed a silent prayer to God, beseeching Him to kindly turn his sister back from the journey she had embarked on and make her strong and lively again. This was because if He was going to let her die, then Aradi would have no one left to be with. He drifted off to an exhausted sleep soon after he had completed his prayer.

Chapter Ten

GOD MUST SURE have heard Aradi's prayer, because his sister did not die overnight. That hour when the birds were starting to wake up in the trees, the gaunt-necked *engonye* bird perching in the bare branches of the tall eucalyptus tree in the valley, with its hooded eyes dolefully watching the eventless marsh and sodden plumage too heavy to carry it to another branch, found the family on their way. The first rays of the morning sun struck as they crossed the rotted wooden bridge that led to Chugi, their load having changed hands once already.

Saliku was barely conscious all the way to Mbale. Occasionally she groaned, as if in discomfort, but other than that she slouched limply onto the back of whoever was carrying her, her head resting on their shoulder because she could not hold it up straight, even for a short time. Sayo dabbed at her damp face with a cloth. At home, before they set off, Saliku was offered food but would not eat or drink even the warm milk given her. The injection and the sleep had revitalized her a little. At least now she didn't appear as helpless and weak as she had in the night when the illness had struck. Her eyelids were half drawn over her pale eyes, as if they couldn't go all the way up and she gazed from underneath them at whoever was talking to her like she couldn't remember ever having seen them before. Her mouth hung slightly open, lips flaked and cracked, like they sometimes turned when they had to work long hours in the hot sun out in their garden. Only her nose twitched weakly now and then. Otherwise everything else about her looked pallid.

Aradi brought up the rear of the foursome, trotting along to keep pace with his parents, who were walking fairly fast. He had put on the faded brown jersey he usually wore to school, worn at the elbows and on the underside of the sleeves where his hands rested on the school desk as he wrote in the exercise book. Despite the relatively warm clothing, he still felt the morning chill. He carried a small parcel made out of one of his mother's headscarves that contained some sweet potatoes leftover from the previous day's meal and a thermos full of tea. Sayo had hastily packed this food just in case Saliku were to be admitted in the ward. There was fear in her that her daughter's illness might just prove even worse than it had appeared the night before.

Ombima huffed on at the head of the trail with the child on his back, his nylon shirt dampened by his sweat and some of his daughter's. His face was grim, quite different from the heedless abandon of just the other day when they had been so happy at the festival in Kakamega. The show now appeared like something from the distant past. Suddenly, his face was deeply etched, lips set firmly together, eyes focused ahead unseeing.

It was a long while before they saw the buildings of Mbale through the trees ahead. And just then, they started to meet the first people coming down the road, mostly early rising business people returning from running their first errand of the day. There was this elderly villager who walked hunched over, thin hands clasping his frail body, numb fingers just barely holding onto a clean plastic jerrycan, on his way from delivering milk to the dairy. Why he couldn't send his son, Aradi could not imagine. And then there was this band of young men struggling to get a squeaky old wooden wheelbarrow to town, laboring with it every inch along the rutty path, careful that it shouldn't tip over and spill what it carried. The oddly angled, huge spoked steel wheel, barely oiled in the young men's haste, screeched its protests all the way. Covered over with fresh banana leaves on the wheelbarrow was the carcass of a freshly slaughtered cow being delivered to the butchery from the slaughterhouse down by the river.

This early in the morning people glanced at others they met only briefly, hardly bothering to exchange greetings, in a hurry to get where they were going. It was almost as if what they were doing was slightly criminal.

When they finally got to the health center, the admission wing was not open yet. They had to wait for the official time when government health workers report to work. The family was restless with anxiety.

They found a seat on the benches outside made of long planks of wood bolted onto sturdy metal frames that defeated the town's vandals, the polished wood stained in places with what one preferred to imagine was truly just wood polish. They shared the bench with a couple of goats, which lay on their bellies at the other end as if they were patients too, waiting for the doctor, chewing idly on their overnight cud as they gazed out beyond the shaggy cypress hedge that ran around the hospital and toward Manyatta across the valley yonder. Looking in that direction, Aradi could see the government's earth moving machinery at work, leveling the ground at the site where it had been proposed sheds be built for the district's idle youth to engage them in meaningful *jua kali* industry. Other than the goats, nothing else stirred at the hospital this early in the day.

After some time anxiously waiting, a light went on in one of the windows and the screech of a rusty hinge opening was heard. Ombima sprang to his feet to investigate. But it turned out to be only a sweeper who had come early to clean the place before the arrival of the orderlies and doctors. Disappointed, Ombima peeked through the one-way glass in the dusty window, hoping to arrest the attention of the subordinate staffer to the plight of his child, but soon gave it up. He came back to sit with his family and wait, hoping Senelwa would show up as he had promised.

Saliku was stretched out on the bench with a blanket wrapped around her. She shivered continuously with the fever. Her mother kept dabbing at her face with the damp cloth. She had given up trying to make her drink some of the hot tea in the flask. Beside them Aradi wrung his arms in his lap in silent nervousness, trying not to look at his ailing sister. Ombima found it hard to sit still and instead paced the paved waiting yard restlessly, hoping someone would show up.

The sweeper came around with a broom and bucket and started cleaning the long corridor that bisected the hospital block, gathering the numerous round black goat droppings that covered the floor into the bucket. He was a stoop shouldered old man who cursed all the time, his displeasure directed at the goats perched atop the wooden benches the cause of all his miseries. Pausing now to put a trash basket hanging askew on its mounting back in place, or to fix a trailing plant that had detached from its trellis, he gave the impression he had been there a long time.

At long last the nurses started arriving in little groups of two's and three's. They paused on the paved walk to chat over the day's news as they straightened their freshly starched white and blue uniforms with little white caps pinned into their hair. They stopped in the waiting yard and looked at Saliku with assessing eyes, more the way a farmer might look at a bullock up for sale at the local market that seems unlikely to last a couple of hours at the yoke.

They offered some instructions to loosen the blanket around the face so that the wind might circulate freely on the patient's face and to give her a little water to keep down the temperature. They then went on down the corridor, their regulation black shoes beating an echoing *tap! tap!* down the narrow hall.

Senelwa took his time. It was when the short hand of the clock mounted above the Records Officer's window approached eight that he breezed in through the open gate. He offered a lengthy explanation about the rough path that came from the village, which in the circumstances was quite needless.

Saliku was taken to a brightly lit room furnished with a table, chairs, and an imposing steel filing cabinet in which were stored files dating back probably to the first days of the establishment. In the corner a tiny bed on castors was hidden from view by a bright orange screen that rolled on huge oiled rings suspended from the ceiling.

Sitting at the table was a thin bespectacled man whose wiry hair was greying at the sideburns, and who had just been browsing through the morning newspaper. Neatly arranged on the table were four trays of equipment, including the tiny steel pans similar to the one Senelwa's wife had sterilized things in last night. Perhaps the hospital had provided them with some to practice from their home villages, Aradi thought.

There were blades and needles and scissors and tongs of all sizes and shapes, all shiny and clean as if they were waiting to pierce the first patient. Laid in neat array like that, they filled one with dread.

Senelwa, who briefly had gone into another room, came back wearing a white coat similar to the one he had worn last night, his intimidating stethoscope hanging from his neck. The man with the newspaper said something to him in rapid London English, after which he asked Aradi to wait outside. Somehow, inside the hospital, Senelwa did not look so dominating as he had done in his house last night. Aradi thought he even looked a little subdued.

Aradi sat on a hard white bench in the corridor outside with his ears open, dreading what they intended to do his sister that required him to leave the room. There was the powerful odor of the hospital that the few flower bushes lining the cement walk could not dissipate. Aradi hated hospitals.

An old man came slowly down the corridor led by a small boy who held onto his unsteady wrist, and who looked to be his grandson. The old man leaned heavily on his walking stick, the nails in his worn *akala* shoes scraping the smooth cement floor irritatingly in the cool hospital surrounding, his feet shuffling along as if he didn't have much strength left in him. He looked very ill, his dirty woolen coat hanging heavily on his thin shoulders. Perhaps he couldn't even see where he was going, so weakened by his illness, because as he walked he kept tapping the floor ahead of him with his walking stick the way blind people do. When they reached where Aradi sat, they aimed for the bench, almost as if aiming to sit on Aradi. The boy jumped up from his seat.

"Who moves there, Onzere?" the old man asked in a weak raspy voice, his grey head cocked slightly to one side as if he was listening. His thin lips, deeply etched with a network of lines and slathered with slobber, now trembled with suspicion, bushy grey eyebrows knitting. Indeed he was blind, because he felt about with his hands. His opaque eyes, which were watery and a bit frightening when he looked one directly in the face, focused right ahead, wide open yet unseeing.

The boy, seeing that the old man would not sit down, held onto his hand reassuringly, a gesture that not only appeared shy on the part of the boy, but which also appeared familiar to the old man because it eased some of his tenseness. "It's only a boy, *Guga*," said Onzere, eyeing Aradi shyly. He whispered right into the old man's ear when he spoke. Thus reassured, the old man allowed the boy to help him sit on the bench.

After he sat the old man turned in Aradi's direction and paused, his watery grey eyes moving slowly left and right. Then he pursed his lips and said, haltingly, "Good day to you, my boy." He held out his right hand, thick skinned and much wrinkled with age, in the direction of Aradi.

"Hold my hand here, will you?"

There was a look of deep concentration on his face, his gaze fixed at a point above Aradi's head.

"You know, I can't see you," he said with what Aradi thought was a tinge of regret.

Aradi raised his hand and placed it into the man's, quite unnerved at the way the grey unseeing eyes were focused on him, assessing every part of him as though they could see. It felt a bit eerie to be examined like that by those unseeing eyes. "Very good, my boy," said the old man after he had found Aradi's hand. His quivery lips curled slightly upward at the corners, as if he was really pleased as he gently squeezed Aradi's hand. It was a long handshake, the old man seemingly not wanting to let go of Aradi's hand. It felt odd, as if by holding his hand the old man had made an achievement of sorts. "Good, now come on, sit down here beside me." He patted a place on the bench with his palm that had just a moment ago been cold and a bit clammy in Aradi's hand. His voice cracked at the end of every word, his speech marked by his wheezing breath, which sounded as if his weak lungs were making a great effort just so he could speak. "I am sick and old, but I certainly don't bite small boys, do I?" He directed the question at the boy who accompanied him, his sightless eyes still roving left and right in his pleasure.

"No, *Guga*, you don't," answered Onzere.

The boy had a heart shaped girlish face and an easy, shy smile that Aradi liked. But he looked the sort of boy Aradi would easily beat in a fight in school. He wore an old cardigan with the picture of a smiling cat knitted in front and a pair of old plastic sandals that were sewn with wire where tears had formed, but which the boy nevertheless looked immensely proud in, as if they were the most expensive shoes. Aradi decided that there was probably no harm in sitting with them.

"Good. That's my boy," said the old man brightly when he felt Aradi settle on the bench beside him. He offered him a wide toothless smile and reached out to touch his head with his cold hand. "What's your name, son?"

Aradi told him in a slightly shaking voice, a bit uneasy at the way the old man's hand was roving all over him.

"Aradi? That name comes from Imavi, doesn't it?"

"I come from Ivona," said Aradi coyly.

"*Ooooo*… I see," the old man said, nodding his grey head slowly. "My daughter was married to a man from your village, and so you can see I am really no stranger there." Once again he rested his gaze on Aradi. "Do you know Savatia? He who knows how to trap moles?"

Aradi did not know many grown-ups from his village by name but he lied to the old man all the same, figuring he implied the man the village kids called Segese, who came from close to the village *duka*. He trapped moles too, although those women who hired him to work on their potato fields said he trapped the potatoes along with the moles.

"Yes, that one," said the old man, licking his lips, which Aradi now saw trembled whenever he spoke. "Yes, that weasel!" he burst out after a short length of silence. "You should really be ashamed to admit he comes from the same village as you, my humble son." He paused as if to muster a callous rage deep inside him. "That snake locked the door on us once when we came by your village to visit. Yes, indeed he shut it on us!" There was an agitated expression on the old man's face now where it had been senile and sickly before. He brought up a crooked finger and wiped at his nose. "Savatia, that son of somebody, slammed the door on us, right in our faces. *Us!* His kinsmen. I was really shocked!"

The old man shook his head as if he was reliving the details of that incident from days gone by. "He must have thought we had come by to solicit for the bride price for our daughter. You know, the wizard never paid even a single cow's tail in bride price… never!" He appeared quite bitter as he narrated this. "Not a single tail. You can ask this boy's grandmother. But then, we really hadn't come to ask for the bride price like he thought. Whoever heard of people going to do that, my children? No, a woman is not like a kilo of meat you might go buy from the butcher. Anyway, we only meant to pass by and greet our daughter and maybe ask for a drink of water, given we were on our way from the cattle market in Mudete and we were tired. We only came with greetings, for the *amahoru* we felt for our daughter. And that snake… I swore there and then to this boy's grandmother that even if I were to be carried on a bier, I wouldn't ever set my foot in Ivona again, never! Not while I was still alive in this world!"

The old man's outburst had been so intense that when he finally came to the end, he was almost breathless, his gaunt figure bent over the crook of his walking stick like a sickle, heaving alarmingly. For a while he was racked by a sudden bout of asthmatic coughing that rattled his thin shoulders. Then it passed and he brushed at the brownish spittle that slaked his lips.

Aradi glanced across at the other boy, surprised to see him calm and unmoved, while for a moment he had feared that something dreadful was going to happen to the grandfather. The boy on his part smiled back in a reassuring way, as if to say there was no cause for alarm that the old man often reacted that way whenever he was excited.

They were silent for a while afterward, the old man lolling on his walking stick with his eyes shut, as if he was feeling sleepy. Aradi sympathized with the boy. He wondered what it was like to have to lead the blind old man by the hand all his life. It must be a great burden thrust on his shoulders. But then if it was, the boy was not showing it. He must be quite proud of his grandfather, concluded Aradi.

There were noises coming from the room in which Saliku and his parents were. Aradi sat up and listened hard, wondering what might be happening. He hoped it was not anything serious. Probably the doctor was only taking his time to attend to Saliku as best as he could. Saliku would come out shortly feeling better. All the same, in the deepest vestiges of his mind, a thread of fear lurked. He didn't know why.

The old man suddenly stirred in his doze and said rather groggily, "Those people in there, aren't they coming out?"

There was a thin film of moisture on his face and a worried look in his eyes.

"Not yet, *Guga*," said the boy dutifully.

"I wonder what they are up to, *tch! tch!*" he muttered, his head shaking left to right on his weakened shoulders.

"Are you feeling unwell?" asked Aradi, by then feeling fairly comfortable in their company.

"*Unwell*, you say?" Once again the old man turned his blind gaze in Aradi's direction, and once more, the boy cringed inwardly from the naked coldness in those depthless eyes. They looked like those eyes on a wooden carving, still utterly lifeless, however deft the sculptor might be with his tool.

"I have been unwell almost all my life," said the old man, unleashing without warning a long stream of brown spittle that landed with a splatter on the newly swept cement floor. It was an angry gesture. "I have been unwell every other day! Today my back, tomorrow the joints of my legs... Just the other day the doctors said they might soon have to tie the urine *bombo* in my loin to keep some of the pain away. Anyway, they need not to do that after all. I told them there's no need. I'll probably die soon, anyway."

"Please don't say that, *Guga*." It was the first time that Onzere had interrupted his grandfather. "Please don't say you will die." There was a pained look in his clear eyes.

"Why?" the old man turned to face his grandson, as if he had just uttered something strange. "*Eh*? Why, Onzere? Why shouldn't I say that I am going to die?" There was a faint hint of irritation in the old man's voice. "Haven't I said to you before that some people must die so that others can live?"

"Well, I meant—" the boy started to speak, but the old man cut him short.

"Whatever you meant...!" he started and then stopped. "Hey, someone, look at me arguing with my grandchild—the 'iris of my eye'—over nonsense. What a mean old man I am, so ungrateful to my loving boy here!"

Despite the circumstances, Aradi found that he was amused at the great understanding that passed between them, the generation separating them not withstanding.

"Anyway," said the old man at length, "to answer your question, my other grandson from Ivona, I am really unwell, yes. Indeed I didn't sleep at all last night, nor the whole of the past week, like my grandson here can tell you. I have come back for some more of my medicine, even though the day the doctor appointed me is still a week away. That is because I've already finished everything he gave me—and the pain still won't go away!

"You know, son, I've become so dependent on the medicine the few days I still have to see the sun rise and set in this world. I actually revolve around it. It's like a string that's holding me to this world. Otherwise I might go on to meet my forbears in the next one. All the same, sometimes I think it is this medicine that's going to be my undoing. Yes, it is this medicine really that is going to kill me!"

By then, a good number of people had arrived at the waiting area, all suffering from diverse ailments, brought by their family members to seek the attention of the doctor. The patients carried little exercise books like those used by pupils in lower primary, the first page of which bore the government stamp from the hospital. Most of them did not understand why they had to bring this little dog-eared book along every time they came. After all, they usually paid for the consultation and had to go to the *kemisti* across the street for the drugs the doctor prescribed. These days they had to dip into their pockets for everything, right from the needle and syringe the doctor would use on them, up to the water that would mix the *abrokeini*.

It made the blind man look back with longing and nostalgia at the good days when one didn't have to sell their only fowl to pay for an injection, or for the gloves the midwives would wear while attending to his wife, or anything for that matter. The days long gone when everything under God's sky was free.

Eventually, the door to the examination room opened and Aradi's parents came out. They looked tired and rather pale, as if whatever they had been doing in there had not quite gone the way they had expected. Mother was carrying Saliku on her hip, and she looked even more wan than when she had gone in.

The people who had gradually gathered on the white bench in the corridor surged forward when the door opened, suddenly alert, each hoping yet apprehensive that they would be next inside. They were aware that if teatime found them still in the queue, then they had better just be setting off on their way home, the doctor would leave for his tea and would probably not be back for a long time.

Aradi sprang to his feet and went to his father's side. He looked at Saliku, his fear returning. Then Senelwa came out of the room, perspiration on his face this early in the day. He patted Aradi's father on the shoulder, showing him the direction to the lab where they were taking the child for tests. He then went back into the room and closed the door.

Aradi followed his parents down the long corridor, fear clawing at his heart now because of the deep silence into which they had both fallen. His father did not even seem to recognize that he was walking there by his side. He wondered what the doctor had told them inside there that had made them so quiet.

Saliku was now so weak that her legs and arms dangled on her mother's side as if she had become a child again. Her eyes were drawn almost shut, leaving only pale yellowish slats that were sickening to look at because they gave her face an even graver, ashen appearance. Aradi instinctively knew that he could only look forward to worse to come.

The lab technician who took and prepared the samples for observation in the machine that had many sighting glasses on it was a friendly type who chatted them up and went out of his way to reassure them that everything would be fine.

As they waited on the bench outside for the results, Ombima spoke for the first time.

"Did you bring any money with you, Mama Aradi?" His voice was thick with anxiety.

"Yes I've got some. Although I'm not sure if it will pay for all this." She tapped the knotted corner of her *lesso* where she carried the few silver coins that she had found in her savings tin. Her voice betrayed her own anxiety.

"Let's hope it will," said Ombima, stifling a yawn in his roughened palms. His long narrow face was deeply inscribed with worry.

"I hope they won't charge too much," Sayo said.

"I hope not. If they do, then we can go to Senelwa for help."

Sayo nodded and then sat still, her gaze focused on a big toe that showed through the hole in her old canvas shoe, waiting. They fell back into the earlier silence. Saliku lay curled up in her mother's lap, underneath the cloth that covered her. Her chest rose and fell weakly with her shallow breathing. In front of them, nurses and medics, resplendent in their pressed uniforms, passed to and fro, their richly polished shoes clicking confidently on the hard cement as they went about their endless business. Some paused to inquire about the child while others passed on as if she were any other patient. Some walked with their hands linked, their laughter ringing gaily down the corridor. They made one wonder if they ever suffered the same illness that their patients did, or indeed if they had any troubles at all.

Everywhere in the health center it seemed as if only *Kisuaheli* was spoken, making it hard for one to depict the exact mood for the speaker, like one would easily do in the case of a *Lulogooli* speaker. Perhaps it was the language behind which they hid their true selves, a sort of cosmetic salve that concealed the spots of their soul. The doctors had their sorrows and joys, which should never show while they were on duty.

They waited for what seemed a long time for the results of the lab test. Meanwhile, Saliku's condition deteriorated. She became even paler and was unable to open her eyes. By then

Aradi could no longer bring himself to look at her. She looked like someone he had never seen before. Because of that he hoped that his parents would send him away, back home. His sister's plight was just too much for him to bear.

Then the lab technician came and gave them a slip of paper. They returned to the consultation room and had to wait their turn yet again because a sizeable queue had formed outside the doctor's door. They pleaded with the people there to let them see the doctor but no one moved.

"I'm even worse off than you are, lady," said a man in the queue who had a fat wart growing on his nose that was discharging a yellowish ooze. "I am supposed to be in Kakamega in thirty minutes to attend to some serious business. And yet here I am, patient like everyone else."

Luckily for them, Senelwa chanced to glance out of his window and on seeing them, signaled that they come over. Not pleased at this the other patients in line complained loudly of some people "who thought themselves superior to everyone else just because they knew someone."

After his parents went inside, Aradi wandered off to sit on the wooden benches in the waiting yard. He still had the bundle containing the potatoes and flask of tea and he wondered if it was alright for him to eat some of the food. His stomach was grumbling.

As he was debating whether to open the bundle, his father appeared down the corridor. He looked left and right and on spotting him, came in his direction. His strides were long as was usual with him. However, he wore a worried look on his face.

"What is it, Baba?" Aradi walked up to meet him, suddenly worried too. He could tell from his expression that something was wrong.

But his father would not speak. He walked him back to the waiting yard with a heavy hand on his shoulder and asked him to sit down. He then sat himself down at the edge of the bench and gazed out across the mown lawn, toward the line of hills that showed in the distance far beyond the borders of the little town. He remained that way awhile, gazing fixedly into nothingness.

Then he stirred and opened his mouth, the gum at the corners holding together his dry lips. He now spoke in a very low tone that Aradi had to edge close to hear.

"Saliku's illness, it appears, is more than we thought, son." He took a dry swallow of something that had constricted at the back of his throat. "It looks like we might be in for a long wait. Perhaps she'll even have to be admitted in the ward."

Aradi took in the news with a sense of trepidation. He was afraid for her. He had never known her to get this ill before. It had always been the flu or, at worst, a bad fever that the strong smelling fever leaves boiled in her bath water always effectively controlled. When the illness persisted, they never went beyond Senelwa and the village healer, Oresha.

She had had a stomach ailment once when she was younger, and which the village women said were "snakes" in her bowels that needed to be flushed out. Despite the many herbal concoctions given to her, the problem had persisted. She had suffered pains that worsened in the night, causing her to moan and toss restlessly as they lay side by side on the mat. In those days, they had shared the inner room with their parents. Eventually, after many days, Oresha had conquered the stubborn "snakes" with bitter concoctions forced down Saliku's throat at mealtimes. There had always been a solution, so it seemed. It was only a matter of finding out where it lay hidden.

But now this. Aradi wanted to ask his father just how serious it had gotten, but was scared of that distant look in his eyes. He had heard horrible tales about the wards at the health center. That patients admitted there were treated badly, fed on under- or over-cooked food and weak soups.

Even worse, it had been said, when night fell and the wards grew dark because there was only one functioning light in the corridor, ghosts of the long dead came to torment the sick. There was also a chilling thought that one might wake up in the morning to discover that the person sharing their bed, and with whom they had been talking just the evening before, was cold and stiff. Most of the stories people told were of course outrageous, and Aradi knew that he really shouldn't believe them. But even then, he still didn't want his sister admitted there.

It was a big relief for him when his father suggested that Aradi should leave for home while he and his Mother waited. "Someone needs to guard the compound," he said. He asked him to take the cows down to the valley to graze and to make some porridge if he felt hungry. "I hope one of us will be coming over soon, and that we'll let you know what has transpired."

Aradi handed over the bundle of food he carried and left, trying to stay brave while his father's gaze was on him. As he walked down the town's lone street, he was weighed down with a feeling of something indefinable that was going to happen, a feeling that refused to go away, looming over his every thought.

Chapter Eleven

MUDEYA-NGOKO REPORTED unusually early that day and the maid, Midecha, knew that there could only be one reason for it. He needed to have a talk with *Mzee* alone, probably about some favor he needed from him. They all knew that the best time to talk to *Mzee*, that is, Andimi, was early in the morning before he left. Experience had taught them he was at his most generous then.

Midecha watched him through the kitchen window as she prepared the morning meal, lounging aimlessly about in the yard, peeking into the dog kennels and upsetting pots and pans as if he meant to put them in order. The big dog, Simba, had never quite liked him, and it made its discomfort all too clear with its low growling when Mudeya-Ngoko approached the cage. He moved back. Very few, it appeared, were comfortable with this man around the compound. It was good that he did not live here, thought Midecha as she flipped over a rasher of bacon on the charcoal brazier, casting an eye on the recipe she was working from in Madam's big black book. Probably none of the kitchen staff would still be working here if Mudeya-Ngoko worked there, what with the man's disgusting habit of sneaking up on people just as they were leaving the workplace and demanding to search what they carried, just when they least expected. And, anyway, what could he be doing here today, anyway? One would think he would be at home preparing to go to the funeral. After all there would be no working today.

It was as Mudeya-Ngoko was pacing up and down thus that an idea suddenly occurred to him and he turned and came purposefully toward the kitchen.

"Good day to you, *Mkeere!*" he called in salutation. "That sweet smell sure reminds me I'm hungry!" There was that smug cheer on his narrow pointed face, as if it crossed his faintest imagination that he would one day sit at table with *Mzee* and have *her* serve *him* breakfast. She smiled as candidly as the vile thought would allow and went to scuttle some more coal into the big stove in the corner where the food that would be taken to the funeral was boiling. Even then, she kept an eye on Mudeya-Ngoko, just in case he had ideas inside her kitchen.

There was a pile of rags on the shelf by the door. Mudeya-Ngoko selected a clean one and tossed it into a pail together with some soap powder and went back out in the yard.

"Going to wash the car?" Midecha asked, leaning out of the window.

"Yes, *Mkeere*. I thought it looked a bit dusty." He opened the garden tap and the strong jet striking the brim of the pail splashed all over the front of his shirt before he could position the pail well underneath the tap.

"But I thought Matayo cleaned it just yesterday," said Midecha, stifling a laugh. She had been just about to ask him to cease using that name on her. She was not an old woman. Mudeya-Ngoko looked funny with water all over his shrew-like face.

"I'll just do it yet again," said Mudeya-Ngoko, wiping the water off his face. "You know Mzee shouldn't drive a dirty car around when he has all of us working for him."

As he lumbered round the bend with the frothing pail, Midecha caught herself wondering what could be on the man's mind. He certainly didn't want to see Matayo fired, did he? In any case, she had not been told *Mzee* was going anywhere. She thought that they were all going to the funeral. Not giving further thought to it, she went back to her duties where the faint smell of burning bacon.

Andimi was in the main hall when Midecha brought in the breakfast on a tray. He was standing in front of the wall-length mirror adjusting a new wine red tie a friend of his had recently sent him from London. He was dressed in a cream suit that he rarely wore, and there was a self-satisfied look on his face.

"Good day to you, Midecha," he beamed, turning around so she could inspect his work. "How do you find my new tie? I think it matches well with this suit, don't you?"

"Oh, they are just perfect, *Mzee*. It is really beautiful!"

One thing Andimi did not lack for was style. He chose his clothes well in the morning, something that had never ceased to amaze Midecha. An old rag might appear like the finest linen on him, she thought.

"Thank you, my dear. Just what I need right now. You know I am going to meet someone important today."

"*Ooooo*, I see," said Midecha, turning to go on into the dining room. "I hope everything goes well for you."

"It certainly will with you wishing me luck first thing in the morning. I know you can bring me luck."

"Thank you, *Mzee*," beamed Midecha, a bright smile on her face as she walked on into the dining room. Madam was inside arranging napkins on the solid wood dining table.

"Good day, Madam. I didn't know you were up already," said Midecha, hurrying round with the tray. "I hope I haven't kept you waiting for the food."

"Oh, not at all, and good day to you too, Midecha. Just place the tray over there. I'll set the table."

"Thank you, Madam." She set down her load and uncovered the silverware and, checking that the cutlery was in place, left the room. Andimi was still standing in front of the mirror in the hall and this time when she passed by, he was busy with the tie and did not turn around. He still wore that self-satisfied expression as he went about grooming himself, a plastic jelly comb stuck in his curly black hair, which he had freshly brilliantined. On the floor by the outer door was his old alligator skin briefcase that he claimed also brought him luck, the gold hasps and trim shined with Brasso, waiting.

When he finally went into the dining room, Madam was seated at the table, her plate in front of her. She had not yet served herself. She seemed to have been waiting for him. The whistle that had been playing on his lips slowly died.

"Well, you are up early today. I thought you were still in bed," he said, the slightest bit of surprise showing on his face. He hooked the toe on his calfskin shoe under his chair and pulled it out, the heavy mahogany dragging on the rug. "Well, well, what have we here! *Ummmm...* My favorite. Fried eggs and bacon!"

He dragged the bowl with the bacon to his side and smelled the spicy flavor trapped underneath the aluminum foil. "*Mmmm!* I love this!"

Madam got up without comment and went to ladle the food onto his plate. "Hey, wait a moment there. What is the matter, my dear? You certainly don't look very pleased." He had been too busy admiring the food to notice her mood. Now as she stood beside him, he felt the tension in her. "What is the matter, Tabitha?" he asked holding onto her hand.

"Nothing," she said shrugging off his hand.

"Oh, come on," he stood up and went to her, resting his hand on her shoulder. She was still in her nightclothes and through the lacy fabric he could feel her tremble slightly. "Come on, tell me, my love," he implored.

"Okay, sit down."

She took her seat across from him and waited a moment, composing herself. Andimi watched her nervously, his finger tapping idly on the table.

"Andimi, you are not going out, are you?"

The question took him quite by surprise as he had been expecting something else.

"But of course I am. What do you mean?"

"I mean, you didn't tell me you were going out."

He gaped at her a while, and then, comprehending, he nodded slowly, "I see. I am sorry, Tabitha."

"And you had better be, because you are not going on your journey." Her eyes lowered to her plate where she was idly fiddling with her fork.

"What!" Andimi almost jumped out of his seat. He dropped his spoon and leaned forward, his sweaty hands resting palm down on the richly polished table.

"Just that. You are not going."

He stared at her a while, reading the changing expressions on her face. His chest was heaving slowly. And then his eyes narrowed and darkened.

"I see," he said softly

"You are not going anywhere, Andimi. You are going to the funeral with me, I say."

"Look, Tabitha, you had better hear who it is I have to meet first," he said at last, his tone persuasive, seeing he would get nowhere getting angry with her. "There is this man from Mombasa I've been wanting to meet for a long time concerning the hotel partnership. I remember once telling you I was planning on expanding the hotel business in the new year. Now, I've just got wind that this man is coming to Kakamega on some business and naturally, I've arranged to meet him there. I was even hoping I might persuade him to spend a day here in the village with us. He is the key to penetrating the tight tourist circuit that you know as well as I do is pure profit. Now, Tabitha, I'd think you'd see more sense in the importance of a meeting like that."

"Andimi, will you *please* listen to me?" Her eyes rose slowly until they locked with his, arresting him. "You are going back inside to take off that suit, then you are coming with me to the funeral, hear? We have a reputation to uphold, and you are not convincing me you are going off on business as usual when one of our workers is bereaved – no, you are not!"

"But this is important, woman!" Andimi was losing his calm. "I mean, you can well represent us at the funeral. I have to make money, can't you see? We need to make money, or are you too daft to see that?"

"*You* need to," said Madam, rising to her feet and placing her hands on her waist. "*You* need the money, Andimi," she gestured with her finger in his face, her chest heaving in agitation. "Look at me, *eh*? You think I need money?"

"I suppose not," said Andimi, rather calmly, lifting his heavy mass out of the chair with a little difficulty. "You are too busy spending it to realize you also need to make it, anyway."

"*Ohoooo*, so that's what it's all about, *eh*?" Madam rushed across just as he prepared to leave and planted herself solidly in his way. "That's what this is all about. You think I am only good for spending your money, *eh*? Well, I'll just remind you in a moment that we are indeed married, and that I deserve some respect as the woman in this house! Yes, you lend me your eyes here, Mr. Big Man. I think I've tolerated your attitude long enough!"

And then, before Andimi could comprehend what she was saying, Madam Tabitha dashed across with the speed of lightning and grabbed hold of the coffee pot on the table. The coffee inside was rich and dark, still steaming straight from the imported coffee machine. She lifted the pot and threw away the lid, and the next minute Andimi was drenched all over in steaming hot, black coffee.

"My, you are *mad*! Mad, woman, *mad*!" he could hardly believe it, his eyes widening with shock. "My suit! My good luck suit! Woman!" He stared down at the damage, then a wild rage filled his eyes and he lunged at her, his hands slapping and tearing.

The maid, Midecha, heard the commotion, and Mudeya-Ngoko too, who had been drawn by the raised voices. They stood at the door looking at each other, uncertain what to do. And then it registered on them that Madam and *Mzee* were actually fighting and they rushed in to help.

The room was in total disarray with expensive crockery reduced to shards and food spilled all over. Madam was resting against the wall with her chest heaving and her hair in disarray, her gown torn. There was a wild look in her eyes. Andimi was standing above her, looking like someone they fished out of the marshes down in the valley, his expensive suit stained dark.

He turned around slowly when he realized Midecha and Mudeya-Ngoko were in the room. "Get out, the two of you!" he snarled, his tiny eyes like pits of fire. They had never heard him so angry. "Go on! Get out of here! *Shenzi!*"

After they were gone, Andimi stayed a while surveying the damage with his bloodshot eyes, weighing costs. Then he turned on his heels and stormed down the hall toward the bedroom, a curse escaping his snarling lips.

* * *

So many people had never before come to their compound. The villagers flocked in and out, discussing the matter in little groups according to peer, all looking downcast because of the misfortune that had visited their village. The women sang sad songs that served to deepen the somber mood even further, their unceasing wailing even worse than the deed. They crowded around the thatch house in the middle of the compound and, one after the other, squeezed in like beads into a tiny gourd.

Smoke billowed around the hut all day. The customary *mahengere* meal of maize and beans, a convenient necessity for a mourning ceremony, was being prepared in large pots borrowed from the neighbors. At these times, the bereaved family need not bother because the village women took control of the kitchen, feeding the fire with dried tree stumps and adding water to the cooking pots until the grain was cooked, swollen, and burst.

When the vehicle that brought the coffin from Mbale had arrived the previous day, the village children, who were playing on the road and in their front courtyards, had been drawn out by its continuous hooting. They ran alongside the procession with their paper planes whirring between their clenched teeth, the game of *idwaro* they had been playing in the sand forgotten. Some of them thought it was Kiradi, the truck driver, delivering sand to someone who was going to put up a stone house in the village. But then they saw the strange little pickup truck and wondered who it could be. They looked among themselves and waited to see into whose compound it would turn. Some of them tried to climb onto the tailgate but a mean faced turnboy shooed them away, but not before they saw the little wooden box in the truck, which they knew people were put into when the village pastor wanted to lower them into the ground. And then word went around that it was indeed one of them. They became confused and didn't know what to do.

The children had previously thought that it was only the old people who died, together with cattle that drank water from the stagnant pools in the marshes far down in the valley.

Saliku had died in the night shortly before the dawn of the second day at the hospital. Sayo had been by her side, lain in a narrow iron cot in the ward, but had not witnessed her passing because she had momentarily dozed off. Sayo had finally succumbed to the weariness that dogged her for hours after keeping vigil by her daughter's bedside, talking softly to her and sometimes singing a soothing song she recalled from her childhood. She had flatly refused to leave for the village, despite the pleas of the ward matron that visiting time was up, insisting that she would stay with her daughter or, if they tried to force her, strip off her clothes and throw such a tantrum they would have to call the police. Even then, it was already dark by the time Saliku was admitted to the ward after an attempt to transfer her to the better equipped hospital in Mukumu failed, due to lack of transport.

Ombima had gone home earlier in the evening, tired of the long hours at the health center, just sitting doing nothing. He intended to borrow some money that they would certainly need, together with fetching some food for his wife who had had nothing to eat since the day before. Perhaps the village shopkeeper would be kind enough to lend him some money, which he could repay later after he resumed work at Andimi's. He hoped to be back before nightfall to see how they were getting on, or if night caught up with him, then early the following morning.

For two days the village trampled the compound until the grass was squashed flat underfoot. In the night, the young mourners came with a band of drummers and had an argument with the old men who had lit a fire in front of the house because they wanted to warm the lax skin of their drums at the fire and the old men wouldn't let them. They then danced round and round the compound, singing at the top of their voices. This went on such that the churchwomen, who had gathered around the shed containing the object of all the honor, gave up their own singing and waited sulkily in the ring of light thrown by the bright pressure lamp Andimi had provided, which hung from a long pole shining like a sun that lit up the night.

When the young mourners eventually left, the now sleepy church women tried singing for a while, but they were too tired and one by one, slipped into the warmth of the hut, where they curled up on the floor, long old woolen coats covering their feet and heads. Only the old men remained chatting around the dying fire outside. Even Sayo, who must keep vigil beside her departed child in the banana leaf shed singing from a hymnal to keep up her spirits, soon tired with no one to help her. She drew her old coat closer about her and leaned back in her smoke stained folding chair and fell asleep.

At the burial many people who had known Saliku during her short life spoke. With their fluid eloquence, they decorated a warm child who hardly ever wished ill on another and who was a cradle of humility, respect, and goodness. No one told of the Saliku who punished her brother with the corny nail of her big toe whenever they could not agree on how to share the common blanket on a cold night. For one, they who really knew the departed hardly ever got the chance to speak and also, it was taboo to say such things about the dead. They might not be pleased wherever they went.

The little compound was crowded and the relentless overhead sun bore down mercilessly, as if it was angry. Conspicuous among the important mourners in the banana leaf shed the boys from the village had made against the fence was Andimi and his wife Tabitha. They sat patiently on the best folding chairs the neighborhood could offer, the wealthy man with his face partly hidden by the wide brim of the expensive leather hat he wore. Even then, his face was moist in the heat and his colorful *kitenge* shirt damp under the arms. Beside him, Madam was resplendent in a red cotton dress and bright silk headdress, her face somber. Mudeya-Ngoko squeezed between the wealthy couple and the village pastor, looking rather ludicrous in a bright nylon cravat tied askew over his creased *mtumba* shirt. Senelwa too was there, together with several schoolteachers and a handful of other dignitaries. It was a touching gathering that had found time from their regular engagements to come and grace the humble home.

Ang'ote was at hand to attend to them all, seeing to it that any new arrival promptly found a place to sit. A red roadside carnation in the lapel of his old tweed coat that normally hung on the sooty wall clearly singled him out as the master of ceremony. The rest of the villagers settled themselves all over the compound where they could find shade, some on the long blue benches that had come from the church, and others on the bare ground on which they spread their *lessos* and sweaters to keep their white church clothes from staining.

Like all burials, it was to be an unnecessarily long, droning affair in which people said almost the same thing as the speaker before them. That was until the wealthy couple started getting visibly impatient and the village children, bored, started wandering away in search of better occupations. Ang'ote had no choice but to cut off clan members who had yet to address the mourners and hand over the program to the village pastor.

Aradi stood at the fringe of the neat square hole underneath the scarred old guava tree they used to play on and listened to the pastor ramble on in his shaky voice. The boy was in a daze and could hardly hear a word they were saying. Next to him stood his parents: Father in his woolen suit that his brother had sent from Nairobi and which usually lay at the bottom of the clothes trunk, and Mother in her white church dress, which had been ironed for the occasion. Father looked dour, the lines on his brow deeply etched, the look in his eyes unreadable. But for Mother, the entire world had come to an end. She was really just being brave. Underneath the surface she did not even have the strength to last the solemn ceremony. It was a good thing indeed that a relation was at hand beside her, a gruff dark woman whom Aradi had never seen before, just in case she couldn't take it anymore. Her face was puffed and tear stained, her eyes red from the crying. She looked at you and you knew she was not looking at you at all because her eyes were focused on something that you could not see. She had become so thin and haggard all in the space of three days. It broke Aradi's heart to see her looking that way. Unable to bear it, he turned his eyes away just as they started to fill with tears.

In front of them the little coffin balanced delicately on two sisal ropes placed across the grave, parallel to each other like a thin road that would take the body to God up above. Four old men from the clan held onto these ropes waiting for the pastor to finish. They might have been holding onto a little carton box stuffed with papers because the coffin seemed so light. Aradi couldn't see inside, the lid having been nailed shut. All the same, he could not help wonder what it felt like in there, all alone in a clean white dress in a bed of pure white lace, gone to sleep with the entire village watching over you.

The pastor bent stiffly and dirtied his clean hands with a fistful of the red earth that ringed the little grave. He held it high above him and read some more from the big book of God that balanced in his left hand, the leather cover old and starting to fray at the spine. His spectacles, which rested at the end of his nose, were misted over and had a thin film of dust. Watching him, Aradi was certain that he was not reading from the book at all because, despite the fact that his unsteady lips were moving, his eyes were actually squeezed shut, the rambling words coming from deep inside his throat as if from memory.

The pastor opened his fist and the clod of earth landed on the box's varnished lid with a haunting hollow thud. Soon after, he closed the Bible and the old men relaxed their hold on the ropes, lowering the coffin down into that place where it would never be seen again. The young men started shoveling earth into the hole. Aradi closed his eyes and turned his head.

Overcome by emotion at the sight of the little coffin in the grave, one of the mourners, a woman from Kisangula who had once trained the children's choir, started wailing loudly, beating her breast. Two others joined in and there was a commotion as the stronger women rushed to hold them and keep them from jumping into the grave. The soloist launched into a dirge, and it was only after the song floated above the somber gathering that emotions were calmed enough for the young men to continue filling the grave. As the requiem died away two of the near-unconscious women were led away toward the back of the hut to rest in the shade of the banana grove.

The young men resumed their work, their muscles rippling under their moist shirts with every throw. Soon the coffin was out of sight in the bowels of the earth, the red wound in the moist earth sutured closed.

Thereafter, the women, their throats coarse like sandpaper from continuous singing, planted little yellow and orange flowers they had plucked from the hedgerows over the fresh mound. And then one by one they walked to the neighbors' homes where they would be served the *mahengere* that was by then cooked soft from the long hours on the fire. Some of the villagers who had not been in the column of white dresses and headscarves also joined the file, hungry from sitting in the sun for so long. Others went away to their own compounds to cook for themselves.

The village's old women lingered a while, uncertain which homestead to go to where there would be least company. The medicine woman who had saved Mudachi's grade cow with her concoctions just the other day had managed to drag her swollen foot to the funeral. One wondered at the irony of her being unable to cure her swollen foot, despite the fact she knew all the secrets of herbs. Perhaps it was a case of the skilled barber who could not turn the clippers on his own pate? She now stood by the fresh grave, watching the conversing clans people dotting the compound, her old eyes shifting and figuring. She leaned heavily onto her walking stick. Her small, multicolored, heavy woolen sweater framed her senile figure like a sodden old cloak. In one bulging pocket she carried a neatly folded black nylon bag that would carry some of the *mahengere* home to her grandchildren, who she knew would come running to meet her when she returned from the funeral. The bag was greasy from previous use.

She wondered what the young men in coats and ties could possibly be discussing that was taking so long. Perhaps they were not as hungry as she felt, she concluded, as she started dragging herself to the back of the hut, her thick walking stick, smooth and shiny with use, tapping the trampled ground.

Andimi was talking to Ombima a little distance from the house. From the way Ombima kept nodding his head, Andimi seemed to be promising him something. Madam stood a little distance from them, waiting for her husband so they could go in and have some of the food. She seemed preoccupied, as if her thoughts were in another place. Aradi watched them, sitting in the shade on one of the blue benches that the departing villagers had vacated. He could hear his friends play bus-and-conductor in the trimmed cypress hedge at the compound's entrance. They had tried to persuade him to join them, but he had declined. He just wasn't up to play today. He was wondering what the wealthy man could be telling his father.

Andimi and Madam went over to the smoke filled hut, and as Aradi watched them enter, he felt a tinge of shame. What would such people, accustomed to eggs and the cream of milk from their black and white grade cow, find worthy of their delicate palates in such a humble house? Perhaps it was only a sort of gesture because his father worked for them, and they were therefore under obligation to come to the burial.

He wondered what it would feel like when Mother had to present before them their chipped enamel plates and bowls. Aradi felt irritated. He stuck his little finger between his teeth and gnawed at it angrily, the way he usually did whenever he found that he could not keep his feelings under control. He spat on the trampled grass under his feet and rubbed in the spittle with his heel.

After the mourners had finally left, some of the village women came to help Sayo clear the compound of the church benches and clean up after the two-day ordeal. And then they too went away to their own compounds to cook for their children, and a deep silence descended as night slowly fell.

Chapter Twelve

ARADI COULD NOT go to sleep that night. He lay alone in the dark long after Mother had blown out the lamp, listening to the sounds of the night. There were other relations sleeping in the room with him, curled up at the far end on old mats that Mother kept for visitors. There was his aunt and another woman from her village who had accompanied her to the funeral, together with other relatives whom he did not know. They were fast asleep judging from their deep steady snoring.

Even then, the room still felt empty to Aradi. He touched the empty space beside him on the mat where his sister should have been sleeping, her warm body curled up like a porcupine, in the posture he remembered. She had always complained of a chill, even on the warmest of nights. Aradi wrapped the blanket about him and squeezed his eyes shut, trying to get to sleep. But it was not possible. The pictures swam around inside his head and refused to go away.

Finally he gave up and rolled over onto his back and stayed that way, staring up into the formless blackness. He could hear rats scuttling up in the thatch, coming down to see what the sleeping people had left for them in the old pans by the hearth. There was a whole army of them, scurrying down the sooty old poles with that unmistakable scratching of tiny sharp claws on dried wood. Outside, the tall cypresses whispered softly like they usually did. Otherwise, it was a calm night. Aradi tossed the blanket aside, rose, and reached for his shirt slung on a folded chair against the wall, disturbing a rooster that had been sleeping close by. He paused, listening to hear if anyone had been aroused by the noise. His aunt across the room turned over on her side and sighed, rustling the long coat in which she had wrapped herself to keep away the night chill. She was still for a while, and then she snorted and started to snore again.

Walking on cat's feet, Aradi stepped over the sleeping adults and groped for the bent nail that secured the door. He swung it back slowly and pulled the door open and slipped out into the cool night, pausing to ease the door back in place.

Only the faintest of breezes stirred the trees. The moon hid behind a dark cloud that dominated most of the western sky, though a scattering of stars twinkled weakly up there, too dim to light up the night. Aradi looked at the big cloud hanging in the sky, mesmerized at its dark immensity against the otherwise clear night sky. It had a bright silver lining all around that made it loom closer to the eye, as if one could actually touch it with an outstretched hand.

About him the compound was still, the shadows of the tall cypress lurking with hidden demons as usual. He looked at the great mango tree just beside the house, dark green leaves thickly knitted on its stubby branches, like the head of a woman who had combed her hair out straight. He wondered what lay hidden inside those barren branches that flowered profusely in the season but never came round to bearing even a single fruit. He had always had this odd feeling whenever he passed underneath the tree at night that the old witch, Ngayira, was crouching up there with her pet leopard, waiting for people to fall asleep.

A couple of doves nestled in the big branch toward the fence. Now, he thought, was probably the best time to catch them, a tempting thought that nagged at his mind. Just the other day he had stolen up to the nest and seen a pair of pretty, spotted grey eggs inside.

Dragging his eyes away, Aradi looked across at the twisted guava tree. There was that limb on the west-facing branch that was gnarled at an acute angle, as if it had been mangled at some stage in its growth, and which now resembled an old woman's emaciated, crooked elbow. It always brought to him the picture of his grandmother, bent over her long walking stick, a rotting old reed basket swinging by her side, full of worm-eaten mushrooms collected from the grazing fields down in the valley. He habitually paused at this point to catch his breath every time he climbed the smooth branch.

At the foot of the tree twisted old roots refused to remain underground. They were hard and knobby, like the corn on Father's little toe, dangerous to a careless toe swinging to kick a stray *makora* ball.

Beyond the guava was the little mound of fresh earth. Aradi looked at it and a chill passed over him. He clasped himself, his teeth chattering in a sudden spasm that wracked his body.

He stepped out of the shadow of the thinning thatch eave and walked toward the entrance, his feet wet from the cold dew starting to settle on the trodden grass. He walked with little measured steps, his head hung, as if he was lost in thought.

The village path was deserted at this hour, with most of the villagers locked inside their homes. Occasionally over the trimmed hedges, Aradi heard the voices of the occupants, some talking around the fire after the evening meal, and others making ready to go to bed. Passing by Nyaligu's compound, Aradi saw someone going to the latrine, which was tucked into the hedge, holding a tin lamp cupped against the night wind, the flame flickering back and forth as if in some macabre dance. It was Musimbi, Nyaligu's daughter. She was wearing a nightgown she probably wore in the city. Through her flimsy dress her breasts danced delicately to her step. She had come just the other day, visiting from her husband's place in Nairobi. The village children said she had brought her little siblings lots of gifts from the city. Aradi wondered just how it would feel to have an older sister who brought gifts from Nairobi.

Passing by Sambuli's little *siimba*, he heard laughter bursting from the hut. He paused to listen. There was the voice of Sambuli and then that of his friend, Adolwa. They had girls in there too, though Aradi could not tell who they were from their voices. In the background could be heard strains of crackly music. Perhaps Sambuli had purchased batteries for the radio he had bought from the village shopkeeper after selling his piglets. They were drinking *chang'aa* as they danced, going by the raucous laughter.

Aradi wished he were older so he could build a *siimba* of his own by the entrance of their compound and have a girl come visit him in the still of night, or his friends come over. Even then he wondered just what it was they did together when they were in these secret dances that so incensed the village chief and his headmen. Hardly a week passed before some of the older boys were flogged at the chief's *baraza* for some mischief or other. And more often than not, it involved girls. These adult things fascinated Aradi, more so because of the secrecy around them... that one could only be taught in the *tuumbi* after one was circumcised.

The great wood doors of Indimuli's shop were already closed and the shop sat still and mute in the night, quite unlike the hive of activity it was when the village children crowded at the counter for a kilo of sugar, or a measure of kerosene, or a cigarette for their father, or a fistful of *makaya* biscuits. It was all different now. A sliver of light showed underneath the door. A lamp was on inside. Aradi listened closely and caught the muffled voices of Indimuli and his wife Miroya, and even the chink of coins as they counted the day's take.

At the back of the imposing whitewashed building could be heard the voices of their children arguing over a late fire in the hut that was their kitchen, and in which they slept together with the cattle. They were never allowed into the shop unless they were bringing in a bag of sugar or tins of cooking fat they had brought from Mbale—and even then, strictly in the presence of one of their parents. They might dip their hand in the *makaya* jar on their way out, so said Miroya. And rightfully so, thought Aradi, because no one in their rightful senses wouldn't.

A short distance past the *duka*, Aradi took a detour to the well. There were two dogs on the narrow path, one white and the other a dark color, sniffing at each other as if they were onto some mischievous business. On seeing him, they scampered off, one into the tiny patch of pruned tea on one side and the other bounding into the trimmed euphorbia hedge around Indimuli's banana patch. Had it been day, and in another time, Aradi would have picked up a stone and sent it after the dogs.

He lost interest in the dogs and went on down the twisting path, going cautiously because the euphorbia and cypress hedges on either side were not trimmed and hung over the path, sometimes brushing into his face. It was easy to sprain one's foot in the small, hollowed footholds the village children had dug into the path to help them get their water loads uphill during the rains when it was slippery. These small steps, for all their helpfulness, turned treacherous at night, especially when one was going downhill on a drizzly evening.

Aradi's journey ended at the next compound down the path. Without intending to, he had walked all the way to the home of his sister's best friend.

Mideva often came to their compound. Indeed she had been at the funeral in the company of her mother, although Aradi didn't get the chance to talk to her. He had noted the distraught look on her face as her mother led her around. It was as if the woman wanted to shield her physically from the loss. Aradi recalled the hopelessness in her eyes as the older boys started to shovel the earth into the little grave. How he wanted to get out of his father's hold and cross over so he could sob with her, but it had been impossible. He recalled too the look of abject sorrow in her eyes as the procession sang, *In Jesus I stand, He is my Rock, my stay...* after all was done and everyone started to walk away.

Aradi now stood outside her compound, his heart palpitating with uncertainty. What could he possibly be doing out here at this hour? What would he say if anyone found him here? The thoughtlessness of the whole situation dawned on him.

Even then, Aradi dealt his heart a blow and proceeded on. He created a path in the euphorbia hedge and went in, checking that no one was coming his way. He was standing in a tiny patch of millet. In front of him was the grove of banana trees at the back of the house. And there stood Mideva's house, which was partly thatched with reed and partly roofed with rusty zinc sheets that her father had started to put on. He crouched in the shoulder-high millet, listening. There did not seem to be anyone about and so he crossed over into their bananas.

It was dark in the banana trees, and for a while he could not see anything. Gradually, his eyes adjusted and he inched toward the house, groping the smooth tree bark for direction. There was a moment when he slipped on a rotting stem and he almost lost his footing. But then he held onto some trailing dried leaves and steadied himself. It shook him a little though. He imagined crashing down onto his face and the noise it would make in the tranquil night. The next minute Mideva's mother or elder brother, Nasiali, would be shining a flashlight through the bananas, the bright beam falling squarely on his face.

Aradi inched on until his outstretched palm touched the rough wall of the little kitchen at the back of the main house. He stopped and looked around, trying to get his bearings, recollecting the layout from the memory of previous visits. By then, the moon was slipping out from behind the thick grey clouds. A silvery wash spread slowly over the banana trees, enhancing the shadows and illuminating the open spaces.

From the other side of the wall, Aradi heard the munching sounds of the black milk cow as it chewed its cud. Other than that, all was quiet. There was a lamp on, judging from the yellow dart of light slipping through a crack in the rough wall. He knew that Mideva slept in the kitchen, together with an older neighbor, Vutagwa, a girl who usually came over after the evening meal.

Aradi almost went round to the other side and tapped on the window, but just then he heard the bolt of the door to the main house pulled back in its rusty housing and a flood of lantern light spilled outside. Aradi withdrew quickly into the shadows behind the kitchen.

"Mideva—*eeh*?" It was the familiar sound of her mother, her slippers slapping against the old brick walk that led from the main house, the lantern she carried in her hand swinging to and fro.

"*Yooo*, Mama!" Mideva's voice from inside the kitchen was crisp in the night. For a while it had appeared as if there was no one in the kitchen, and indeed he had started to wonder if at all she was in, and what business they were doing with Vutagwa that made them so quiet.

"Have you remembered to add water to the pot like I said?" Her mother was coming to the kitchen.

"*Eee…* I was just about to, Mama," said Mideva, her voice straining, as if she was choking on the smoke inside the kitchen.

Aradi heard the kitchen door open, and then Mideva adding water to the boiling pot. Then her mother left saying, "And do sleep with one eye open tonight." Then she paused as if she had just remembered: "Tomorrow we are going to harvest that millet field in Inyali. Just remember we must get out ahead of the birds if we hope to finish by midday."

"*Yeee*, Mama," Mideva answered meekly.

And then the lantern light disappeared back into the main house and there was the sound of the door bolted shut.

Aradi waited a while, just to be sure. He heard Mideva cough, choked by the smoke from the fire. Then she started to sing a pointless tune that went round and round, and which Aradi remembered hearing Saliku sing too. He decided it was probably safe now. He went round to the little window and tapped softly, twice. She paused, listening. He tapped again.

"Who's there?" she called, surprised.

"It's me," whispered Aradi, glancing over his shoulder, half expecting to find her brother Nasiali standing there.

"Who's 'me'?" she asked suspiciously.

"It's me, Aradi. Please open the window." Goose bumps broke out all over Aradi's arms. He was scared, uncertain why he was there in the first place.

There was another pause, and then the tiny bolt securing the window was drawn back and the little window creaked, opening to the inside. In the poor light of the smoky tin lamp Mideva's clear eyes were rounded in surprise, still watery from the smoke, her oval face framed against the wall. She moved it closer to the window and studied him better in the light, her face pressed close to the wooden bars that ran vertically across the tiny window space. Aradi felt unnervingly exposed. Then she withdrew the light and said, "Aradi! What are you doing here?"

It was not as much a question as an expression of her shocked surprise.

"*Shhh*! Mideva. Can I come in?" He moved away from the ring of light and pressed against the wall closer to her ear. "I'll explain everything. Please."

She paused, considering, her dark face that was shiny from oiling after the evening bath knitting at the brow. Deciding there was probably lesser harm in him being inside than standing out there she said, "Wait," and went to open the door. Aradi rushed round and quickly slipped in through the opening, breathing hard. Mideva closed the door, and then came round to stand in front of him. She still wore that look of shocked surprise.

"Aradi, what is it?"

There was only her in the room, the other sleeping mat still rolled up with the blankets inside, pushed up next to the wall. Her bedding was spread out on the floor in the corner far from the fire, and on the rumpled blanket was a small book with a chewed front cover, as if termites had attacked it. It was the story about a girl called Owino, which Aradi remembered from two years back at school. In the kitchen's far corner, locked up in its pen of soot colored poles, was the black milk cow, lying on its belly, tied to one of the posts. The cow's jaws moved slowly left and right as it chewed, the little black hairs on either side spattered in white froth. Its wide unblinking eyes gazed steadily but languidly into the roaring fire, as if it was just harmless fire, seen everyday. Beside it slept a little calf, its wide ears moving only the slightest at the sound of strange voices, little muzzle resting on its outreached shanks.

The floor was swept clean, the little hearthside stools stacked against the wall close to the cattle pen. The few chickens they kept climbed over the stools, covering them with their black and white droppings.

Mideva was standing in the middle of the kitchen staring up at Aradi, a chewed pencil with which she had been copying from the book onto a yellowed slip of paper still held in her hand.

"Where is Vutagwa?" Aradi asked, feeling her eyes boring right into him.

"She's not here, why?" The baffled look she wore made her look older than her age. Aradi was watching the two perfect lines between her eyes, which made her look wiser too.

"Oh, I just wondered," he said lightly. "She sleeps here though, doesn't she?"

"Yes. But today she didn't come. Yesterday she was complaining about some stomach pains. I guess she's been taken ill." She moved to replace the lamp on its stand before she repeated, "So, why are you here? It's late."

Aradi tried to stare back at her, but her intensity defeated him. "Can I sit down?" he asked, looking toward the stools stacked against the wall.

"But we are ready to go to bed," she protested. "You should be home."

"Look, Mideva, there is only one thing I want to tell you, and I promise I'll leave after that," Aradi said. There must have been an appeal on his face, with eyes that didn't conceal the sorrow he felt inside. "Please, Mideva, give me a minute. I know it's not good manners coming here like this in the middle of the night, but then, I just had to."

Mideva looked at his shirt, at the big hole a flying spark had burned into the fabric around his belly button one evening as they fought over chicken entrails they were roasting in the fire with Saliku. She looked at his feet, toes white in the night-time dew he had collected from the grass, the skin thickened and wrinkled. There was a moment of hesitation in which she debated over what best to do. Then she pulled out one of the stools for him and went back to the lamp. "I'll have to put out the light, just in case my mother comes back."

All this while they had talked in whispers, afraid that someone passing outside would hear them. Aradi sat down facing the fire, watching the way the fierce flames greedily consumed the wood. The flames fanned out around the base of a huge pot like a fiery orange flower, hissing softly. The pot bubbled on, the enamel lid covering it vibrating up and down, held down by a round *ing'ingiru* stone. A steamy red froth ringed the wide mouth and spilled over into the fire, hissing angrily whenever it fell on the red embers.

"You are cooking *mahengere?*" asked Aradi feeling a little uncomfortable now that she had let him in.

"Yes. We'll have a lot of laborers on the farm tomorrow to help us with the harvesting."

There was a moment of unease in which Mideva went to push the smoking wet log deeper into the fire. On second thought, she withdrew it and left it on the floor to die out. Then she pulled up a stool and sat down. Aradi was watching her all the while from underneath his eyebrows, discreetly following her movements. She now sat wringing her hands in her lap, the glow of the fire playing on her face, waiting.

Aradi cleared his throat and said, "Mideva, I can't sleep. I don't know why, but my eyes are dry as day."

She raised her head only the slightest. And then she went back to wringing her hands, twirling her pencil stub between her fingers. It was as if she had not quite heard him.

Aradi waited. At length she raised her eyes to look at him. In the orange glow he was surprised to see a very different look from the one he had expected. In an instant her clear eyes became depthless. It was as if Aradi had scratched a thin surface to reveal the hurt underneath. Her voice had changed too when she spoke, going softer.

"I can't sleep either, Aradi." She didn't look at him as she said this. "I know it, even before I go to bed."

They were silent for a while. The flames lapped at the dry wood and crackled, fanning out over the sides of the pot. The cow shifted on her belly and belched, the smell of its breath strong like that of decomposing grass. The calf whined in response. Aradi felt a wave of something warm wash over him and he looked at Mideva, sitting just an arm's reach away from him. Her gaze was directed at her feet and in the dancing glow of the fire, he suddenly realized how much like Saliku she was, with her long dark eyelashes and dark curly hair and a slightly protruding chin that tapered almost to a point. Her mouth, though, was more curved—a sharp nick in the upper lip and thicker in the lower—a fullness that was enhanced by faint dimples in her rounded cheeks. She might have been smiling. And, yes, she was so much like his sister, looking down like that.

They had often played together, running after butterflies and *madagala* hoppers in the field outside Aradi's compound, or playing *chavana* in the clump of bushes behind Nasiali's little hut where her mother usually tethered their two goats. But there had always been three of them, Saliku included. Or when Aradi's friend, Kesenwa, came to join them, then they paired up and romped among the bushes in quest of fun. Now, sitting here in this smoky hut just the two of them, he saw her a bit differently. Again, he thought, she might have been his sister.

Aradi scratched at the floor with his big toe, at a loss for words. A thick hot ball had clogged his throat. He looked at Mideva's feet, her toe nails shining in the firelight, tiny and almost square, but for one on the little toe that curled upward and stuck out, refusing to be coaxed into uniformity by the trimming razor. A thin film of fine ash had settled on the petroleum jelly she had rubbed into her skin as she worked around the fire.

Aradi looked down at his own feet, one of the big toe nails cracked and not so well cared for. He wanted to hide them under his seat. He tried to swallow, but the taste in his mouth, like sawdust, wouldn't go down his throat. He looked sideways at her through his lowered eyebrows. She still had not looked up, and was very still. He wondered what she was thinking.

Aradi wanted to reach out to her. He lifted his hand as if to touch her knee but stopped himself. And then, before he realized it, he said to her, "I couldn't help thinking about her, inside that grave… all the soil pressing on her…"

"Saliku is not in that grave, Aradi," Mideva said without a trace of doubt in her voice. "Saliku is in heaven. And she is happy."

With that simple statement, there dawned upon Aradi an immense relief, as if the slightest opening had revealed itself in the haze that had been his mind. And with it came tears, first a drip, his sobs silent and then his whole body was tremulous.

Mideva extended her hand toward him and held his shaking shoulders. Then she moved her seat closer as he continued to cry the many tears that had filled up his breast and let him lean on her until he cried himself to exhaustion.

Mideva watched Aradi cry and she too was overwhelmed by a wave of emotion. She felt her throat clogging up, some hot ball squeezing up her throat into her mouth, choking back the words she wanted to say. Slowly, her hold on Aradi tightened. And for the first time in the long day, the heavy unwept tears flowed unashamedly from the depths of both their souls in the comfort of the concealing darkness.

Later, after their quivering bodies had stilled and they felt drained and pure, Mideva lifted her face off Aradi's shoulder and said, "Do you think she will be sad wherever she is in heaven?"

And Aradi sniffled and said, "I don't know that she will, but I know that the angels up there will keep her company. I know that wherever she is, she is happy. This is what I believe."

"True," Mideva whispered back, wiping her nose with the back of her hand. "God will make her one of the angels too."

* * *

Later, toward morning, as Aradi snuck back into the house with the slightest creak of the old hinges, his father in the next room was listening. Ombima had been awake all the while, unable to drift into sleep like his wife beside him had. His heart was in pain and he wished he could go to sleep, at least so it would take away some of the misery, even if only for a moment. He managed to doze off once, but then it had been only for a while, and then he was back awake, tossing from one side to the other in the narrow bed that, this night, felt even more confining. He had even contemplated getting up and going to seek solace in the cold night outside.

But even as he debated over it, Ombima still would not rise. For some reason his upper body felt too heavy to lift off the lumpy old mattress. Eventually, the approaching dawn's faint grey light seeping in through the narrow opening between the thatch and the wall found him yet to make up his mind.

His alert ears clearly heard the creak of the old door hinges and the hesitation, before the padded footfalls that followed and a soft whoosh of cold night air as the door was eased back into place. He heard soon after the soft rustling as his son crept into bed. He wondered where Aradi had been.

Chapter Thirteen

THE HEAVY FEELING dragged into the following week. The home was starting to feel like an enclosure in which one was bound to remain during the entire mourning period. Ombima longed to go back to work. He was sick of just sitting there doing nothing. Sayo did not talk much, and the boy kept to himself more and more. A man longed to slip off and go somewhere where they weren't known and have a big *gorogoro* of beer.

One such day, Ombima was sitting on a dead tree stump just outside his compound. It was a fine sunny afternoon, breezy with the light seasonal winds usually felt in the country toward the end of the year. The late afternoon sun shone golden through the tall trees and the calm was punctuated by the distant beat of drums as the village youth geared up for the choir competitions now that Christmas was drawing closer. Their voices sounded strained and passionate above the wind, as if winning the choir trophy was all that their dreams were made of at that moment. Sayo had gone off to the women's rehearsals, and Aradi too had disappeared off somewhere together with his friends. Ang'ote had probably gone off to the choir too, being such a lover of music. Ombima was alone and decided to go for a walk.

The village path was deserted. The fine sand was imprinted with a million footmarks the villagers had left behind. In the light breeze, yellowed leaves shook out of the swaying branches overheard and wafted down. They made Ombima think of his own childhood, of the long lazy days gone by when all his work for the day was to climb tall trees in search of bird nests and tramp the woods with his slingshot looking to shoot down anything that could fly. As these thoughts came back to him, he suddenly felt his age.

It was hard to believe that he had been a vibrant youth just the other day, with long dreams about what his future would be like. Then, the years had rolled on so slowly. Those evenings when he sat with other young men outside his father's compound evenings after he had milked the cows and completed his duties for the day. Everyone talked of saving up some money and going away to the big towns to seek work. They all wanted to live in the big towns with their families, and drive a car and put on shoes and a tie. If only they would get a bit of education at the local school to enable them to pass the school certificate, which would be their pass to the world they yearned for.

But of course not all of them had made it.

Some, like Onzere, son of the village pastor, had gone on to secondary school and then to college, and now they were nowhere to be seen. They had probably gotten so rich in their new jobs that they no longer lived in the same world as their old friends with whom they had dreamt. Some had proceeded to the village polytechnic and now were practicing artisans, like Elphas who had a metal workshop in Mbale. A good number of them had slowly trickled out of the village to seek greener pastures elsewhere.

Not so for Ombima. That bright future had been shattered when his father had broken his leg one day out felling trees in the valley. This fateful accident spelled the end of the old man's trade in charcoal, which he burned out of the trees he bought from other villagers and then carried to Chavakali to sell to the hoteliers. It was the little he earned that enabled him to pay Ombima's school fees. The old man knew his charcoal trade well, having been initiated as a young man. But then, like they say, a man's good fortune can only last so long.

It had been a cold rainy day, and those who had been with the old man said it had happened very suddenly. That as the tree they had been chopping finally crashed through the restraining branches, everyone had stood back with a sigh because it was going just the way they had wanted it to. Because of the rain, the ground was slippery, and as the huge tree struck down, the boom of the crash rang out through the thick woods, lifting the birds from the jungle's high branches in a twittering panic. But then that was not all.

Just as everyone was preparing to descend on it with their machetes to severe the many side branches, the huge tree, without warning, shifted in the thickets in which it had gotten entangled and the next minute it came sliding down the slope, its smooth bark unstoppable on the sodden surface. The old man had been standing directly in the way of the sliding juggernaut, bending down to collect his fallen axe. He hadn't had the chance to jump out of the way.

When the other loggers brought him out of the valley on a stretcher they had fashioned out of a khaki shirt and poles, Ombima looked at the old man's broken leg and felt all his dreams evaporate into thin air. Everyone went into a fright over his fate, the women wailing ceaselessly. But for Ombima, he knew it was all over.

There had been only one thing for him to do: get out and work for any villager who would pay doing any job they had to offer, to earn the little that they would need badly to put something to eat on the family table. It came as such a shock, but it was also frighteningly real. All of a sudden he, as the eldest son, had assumed the old man's role in the family.

He hoped all long that the old man's leg would set somehow, and that he would come out of the plaster cast and get back on his feet again. But it was not to be. The doctor, after months of prevaricating, finally got the cold reality across to the inquisitive young man: old bones are hard to set—and even when they do, they hardly ever go back to the way they were before. And truly they never did for Ombima's father. There was nothing else Ombima could do. It was such a cruel burden to be lowered onto the shoulders of a man still so young and ambitious.

Now Ombima passed the *duka*, he suddenly felt the urge to smoke. He did not know where it sprung from, given he had not smoked in a long time. All he knew was that, all of a sudden, he wanted a cigarette so badly he could not pass by. He dipped into his pocket and found a few shillings. He decided there was probably no harm in the old indulgence this once. He turned into the open gate and walked up to the counter. It was Miroya, Indimuli's wife, at the counter and when she saw him, her face suddenly assumed that downcast look he had come to loathe.

"I'm so terribly sorry, Ombima," she said after they had exchanged greetings. "She was such a pleasant child."

Miroya's rounded face looked comical, if sorrowful, and her dark penetrating little eyes might have been laughing. Looking into those shifty orbs, Ombima was not in the least fooled. The woman was anything but sorrowful. How could she, when she had been so hard on them, heaping abuse openly on his children whenever he sent them to ask for some groceries on credit, calling them such names the children were scared of going there a second time, even if with the money to pay for it. How could she possibly feel sorry?

"It's alright, Miroya," Ombima dropped his gaze, not wanting to look at her much longer. "We've already lived through the worst of it. Thank you for your concern."

The shopkeeper and his wife had not come to the funeral, both having been kept busy at the counter serving the people trooping to the funeral. They had not so much as donated a kilo of sugar for the mourners.

Even then, Ombima had lost count of the number of times he had received commiseration from people. They were difficult moments when other people had to express their concern because it only served to worsen the situation. He wished they would realize this and keep their words, however well intentioned, to themselves. He just wanted to forget everything that had happened, and having to be reminded by them all the time was certainly not helping.

The shopkeeper's wife was startled when he told her what it was he wanted, and, thinking she hadn't heard right, he repeated.

"Oh, alright," she said in the way people who are unsuccessfully trying to hide surprise do, going for a pack of what had been Ombima's favorite brand in his smoking days. He calmly unwrapped the cellophane, just like he used to, and tore open one top corner, tapping out a crisp new cigarette, which he wedged between his lips. He tucked the pack into in his shirt pocket, relishing in the momentary thrill of going back to an old habit.

As he walked away, Ombima felt Miroya's eyes on him. He was well aware that she could hardly wait to get the news onto the village grapevine. *Oh, let her!* he cackled deep inside his throat. For once he did not give a twit what anyone of them said.

He lit up and pulled a lungful of smoke, feeling heightened by the old leaf smell in the tobacco that had first lured him into the habit. His feet kicked the fine dust and the evening breeze got into his nylon shirt, causing it to billow behind him, its coolness slapping against his flat belly where a button had popped out. It brought on a heady sensation.

He passed the village church and the practicing choir's intonations sounded a thousand miles away, the beat of their drums like a vague rhythmic tapping somewhere deep in the mire of his scattered thoughts. Someone called out a greeting from the singing crowd. He did not respond.

Going past Senelwa's compound, the dogs came running to the gate and barked at him, recalling his scent from the night a few days back when he had brought Saliku. Senelwa's wife, who was herself a poor substitute for a tenor in the church choir, came out and shouted at the dogs. She saw him and called out a greeting. Ombima did not hear this.

There was an open field after the church on which the villagers were going to put up an office for the new chief who had been appointed in the area. A group of old men were examining the site where the foundation would be dug, debating over how much every villager would have to contribute toward the project. They looked up when he passed and Timateyo, the cross-eyed one, said, "That young man has really taken it badly." He was pointing at Ombima with a crooked finger, browned from stuffing tobacco snuff up his nostrils. The others nodded in agreement and watched Ombima in silence. Their eyes, like the shopkeeper's wife's, bored into his backside. He loathed them all. *Why couldn't they just mind their own business?*

The cigarette burned out and he lit another one close on its heels, wanting the refreshing taste of the tobacco to stay at the back of his throat. The smoke seemed like the only thing around him that would not open a mouth to utter words of condolence. The smoke and the wind. Perhaps those two were his only friends.

At the top of the hill he came to the road that led to Kivagala. In the soft afternoon sun heat waves trapped in the yellow gravel rose from the curving surface in thin feeble curls. Far beyond in the hills in Gamoi, a long snaky column of red dust billowed above the wind-whipped trees, heralding the approach of a vehicle.

Throngs of villagers walked in little groups alongside the road, coming from the market in Mudete, looking weary from a long day of activities. The old men walked with their skeletal arms slung over their walking sticks, which they had placed across their bony shoulders when they became too heavy to drag along. Ahead of them the boys who had accompanied them to the market pranced alongside the calves that they had bought, excited about getting them into the rest of the herd. On their heads the women carried baskets of groceries they had bought at the market, their babies slung on their backs in nestlings fashioned out of old *lessos* that they carried with them even to the farm. The women looked tired, but were bolstered on uphill by the anticipation of the excited looks on the faces of their children back home when the bulging baskets they carried were finally opened and the contents issued out. For once the women had run out of something to gossip about, their lips glued mutely together, swollen and cracked with thirst and the hot sun. Ombima knew some of them because they came from his village, and they stopped him occasionally to exchange greetings. Still, he was hardly conscious of the things they rambled on about and was only pleased when, realizing that there was nothing meaningful to be gotten out of him, they gave up and walked on.

The vehicle that had been sighted in Gamoi came closer and zoomed past in a thick cloud of red dust, which immediately engulfed the mass of weary market goers. It was the old Bedford truck that collected tea leaves from the buying centers, laden on both sides with stuffed sacks, looking like a rounded belly that was ringed with fat. It was soon lost round the bend in the direction of Kiritu, gone before the curses of the old men in the crowd it had blanketed in dust could get to it.

Ombima left the road at Kisangula and went up a rocky track that led into the hills. On the hillcrest he climbed was the school where Madam Tabitha taught. Here, too, would converge all the choirs from the surrounding villages on Christmas day for the singing competition. Then, young banana trees would be cut and planted along the road up to the school to mark the celebrations. And in the branches of these trees children would hang purple and pink bougainvillea petals they plucked out of people's hedges. It was a long while indeed since Ombima had last come here.

Up in the hills the air was cool and a little thin. The trees, not as tall or lithe as those in the valley, swayed gently in the breeze. Birds flipped upside down in the wind, the plumage on their underside flashing white and pure, before they were swept downhill on the air current. Their chattering filled the air, just like the collective buzz of the mountain insects. Above the twisted, stunted trees the clear, opal blue sky dropped gracefully behind the hills in the Tiriki country far yonder.

Ombima sat down on a flat rock, the surface of which was covered by veins weathered in the sun and rain. Inside the bigger crevices crisscrossing the sun-warmed surface lizards lay sandwiched, gazing out lazily at the world with their unblinking glazed eyes, entertained by the music the cracking rock made as it contracted with the changing temperature.

It was beautiful country that spread out on the other side of the hill. Mostly rocky, the hillside was painted with patches of farmland where the terrain allowed, on which the people of the hills scratched a subsistence living. Above these patches swayed two or three banana trees growing in a little groove that had somehow established firm rooting in the cracks in the rocks. These trees were short and stout, their trunks bent at an angle by the wind that constantly blew uphill. Those that had fruited carried four or five stubby fingers, fat and engorged on the mineral their wandering roots sucked out of their rocky foothold.

In the shade of these banana trees nestled a peasant's hut, the dome shaped overhanging thatch bleached white in the sun, positioned such that when he sat in the doorway enjoying his stuff in the evenings. The countryman could have a bird's-eye view of all of God's country. Where the peasant's hoe had not scratched the red earth, hardy scrub and bramble crept over the rocks, their slow growing branches covered with poisonous white thorns that protected the peasant's homestead from intruders as he slept in the night. Over this rocky country the late afternoon sun spread its golden rays so they painted the gnarled tree branches and jutting rock faces in soft color.

Ombima used the butt of the cigarette he had been smoking to light another one. He inhaled deeply and let out a long jet of smoke, which floated above the thorny treetops in long twisted curls, just before a gust of wind swept it away and it was lost in the golden haze. He drew in his bare feet and sat on the top of the rock with his arms wrapped around his bony knees. He remained thus for a long time, the breeze blowing over his hooded eyes, the cigarette burning out between his fingers. The cry of a lark close by mingled with the awesome buzz of the mountain insects soaring above the beat of the drums in the church choir many miles away. And then some instinct told him he was not alone.

He spun around, startled, at the same time as a shadow fell across the cracked rock face. Madam Tabitha was crouching on the rock behind him, pausing as if she had been creeping up on him, her rounded face bright with mischief.

"Madam!" Ombima was clearly startled, not having heard a sound all the while she had been climbing up the outcropping rock.

Seeing the wild look on his face, she broke out in a giggle. "I have a way of startling you all the time, haven't I?" she said, coming to sit beside him.

"What are you doing here, Madam?" Ombima asked, mouth agape in surprise. She was clearly the last person he had expected to find up here in the hills. She regarded him sideways, the amusement making her face glow like an excited child's.

"I came to see you," she said. "*Ehe*? You don't believe it, do you?" Her long eyelashes rose an inch and her eyes shone white like drops of milk. "Well, you had better, because it's true."

She wore a lacy white dress that was puffed at the shoulders, and which was gathered in numerous folds over her bosom with a silken cord. The skirt billowed around her folded feet like a child's on Christmas day. "*Ehe*?" she was looking directly into his eyes, reading his thoughts. There was a wild excitement about her this afternoon, like he had never seen in her before. "Tell me, Ombima, are you happy to see me?"

He looked at her teasing face, thinking he was probably dreaming. Her skin was soft and luminescent in the pale afternoon sun. He looked at her bare arms, full and supple, yet graceful and very feminine, folded meekly in her lap. He looked at her petite feet scrubbed pink inside her sandals, regularly oiled in jelly. "You are out of your senses, Madam," he whispered, letting out his breath slowly. He was totally confused.

"Am I?" she asked.

The cigarette he had been smoking was still burning between his fingers and, suddenly, she snatched it and took a long puff from it, letting out the smoke the way she had seen people do, her shapely lips pouting. Her exhalation was not strong enough though, and it billowed about her face. He watched her, bemused. She took another longer drag and choked on it, breaking out in a cough that made her eyes water.

"What are you doing, Madam?" He tried to take the cigarette from her but she struggled out of his grasp and took another puff, which she ejected full into his startled face.

"That," she said in a playful voice that was still raspy from the choking smoke, "is what I'm doing. I'm learning to smoke, that is." She then rolled back on her haunches and bubbled with laughter that made her ample bosom heave, causing tears to stream down her rounded cheeks. Her teeth shone white in the sun, and there was an overpowering presence about her.

Gradually, Ombima forgot all his fears and he found himself relaxing in her company. He was even moving up next to her, like a magnet to a tin of nails.

He paused to glance over his shoulder, not knowing what had come over him. The rocky country below was still bathed in the captivating golden sunlight. Surely anyone down there could clearly see the pair up on this high perch. Then he looked at himself: his clothes were frayed and going loose at the seams, his feet dusty, not as clean as her own. Tentatively, he reached out and touched her cheek. She remained very still, gazing fixedly at him. Her lips were full and soft, slightly parted, inviting. He gazed into the black depths of her eyes, trying to discern her thoughts. Then, before he knew it, his arms wrapped around her rounded shoulders, his hands wringing the bright bubble of joy, drawing it closer, squeezing. It was a very strange possessive feeling that had taken over him all of a sudden.

"Hey, you'll break my ribs, Ombima!" she cried, squirming out of his hug. But he drowned out her next words with his mouth pressed over her own, forcing open her full lips with his tongue so they opened like flower petals. He kissed her soft warm moistness, his whole body set afire in her invigorating heat.

"You will break my ribs, I say!" she moaned amid gasps, still trying to fight him. But he only carried on exploring her mouth with his tongue, seared by her secret warmth, tasting his cigarette on her soft pink tongue, looking to drink all of the warmness out of her.

It was the cigarette butt burning his side through a hole it had eaten in his shirt's nylon fabric that finally stopped him. He sprang back, wincing at the sudden pain that had bit right in the middle of a mounting wave of fierce passion.

"Serves you right," she said cheekily, enjoying a good laugh. "Is that the way you court a lady where you come from?" There was an open challenging look in her clear liquid eyes.

He jumped to his feet and grabbed at her, but she had seen it coming and was a trifle too quick for him. Flopping down on her belly, she quickly slid off the rock and fell into the grass and burr. She picked herself up and started running downhill, her laughter ringing out like a sparrow's twitter. He gave chase.

They roused a brooding quail out of the grasses and she flitted away in the direction of the maize farms with a raucous *purrrr*! He called out to Madam Tabitha to stop, but she ran on downhill, skipping over bushes and rocks, making for a long jagged crevice in the side of the hill in which a tiny brook trickled over the rocks down into the valley. He caught up with her just at the edge of the overgrown cliff. But when he tried to grab her wrist, she instead pulled suddenly at his extended hand and the next minute they both went tumbling through the tall grass into the little stream.

The crystalline water splashed in all directions as they sank to the bottom of the brook. And then the pearly flower closed back on top of them and they were completely submerged in the startling coolness.

Regaining his balance, Ombima tried to struggle out of the stream, his clothes soaked and plastered to his skin. But she grabbed for his ankle and pulled him back in, laughing all the while.

When the ruckus finally eased, he was resting on top of her and she was lying on her back in the streambed, the clear mountain water flowing over them. Her dress was like a big white flower floating on the surface of the water.

He rose to his knees and passed his hands underneath her and gently lifted her out of the water. Her eyes were closed and her oiled cheeks flushed with excitement. Her lips were slightly parted, showing the fine tips of the two huge, slightly crooked front teeth. She was covered all over in the fine moss that covered the stones on the stream floor, a few grains of sand stuck in her long hair, which was now damp and in disarray. Her nostrils were dilating slightly, the way they might do in a deep peaceful sleep.

"Look now what you've done!" said Ombima, his biceps taut with the effort of carrying her considerable weight. She pressed into him, hardly making an effort to help, her wet arms roped loosely about his neck. Looking at her face so calm and composed, he wondered for a minute if she could have gone to sleep in his arms.

When he finally made his way out of the stream, he stood on the wet grass, bearing his backbreaking load, contemplating what best to do with it. He gazed down at her. Her lacy dress, sodden like it was, molded the gentle curves of her full body like a second skin, drawing out every single contour. He felt a sudden burning deep inside him. But just when he was going to lay her down on the grass, one of her eyelids lifted lazily and in a faint slurred voice, she whispered, "Please carry me up to the rock, Ombima."

As he trudged on uphill his feet squashed the tall grass, causing scores of grasshoppers to flee in all directions. Pink and yellow butterflies wafted out of the valley and swept suddenly uphill, borne by a gust of wind. The skin on his arms erupted in goose bumps as the cold current engulfed them. She clung to him, trembling from the chill. Her flesh was warm against his, like a freshly caught deer might feel against the chest of the triumphant hunter.

He reached the top of the hill and rested her on the flat rock. She arched her back off the cracked surface when she found it warm and dry. She shivered as a pleasurable sensation assailed her.

* * *

Later they lay side by side on the warm rock, gazing idly up at the clear sky. Their hands were linked and they could feel the heat from each other's bodies. They had hung up their clothes to dry on the thorny bushes. In the meantime they were both prisoners in each other's custody.

"How did you know I was coming up here?" Ombima said at last after the languid moment had passed.

She turned over lazily and stretched out with a satiated sigh. "I just knew." She was looking at him through her slanted eyelashes, her dark eyes clouded.

"How?" insisted Ombima, curious. He had a strange urge to smoke.

"I saw you passing by." She let her hand linger on his chest. "You were smoking a cigarette, and I thought it was strange because I have never known you to smoke. I figured you could be up to some mischief," she blinked wickedly at him, "and I decided to follow."

A huge black bird rose out of the valley and flitted across the open firmament. It was slowly swept by the current in the direction of the ridges in the distant Tiriki country. It's shadow passed over their sprawled forms, and there was an eerie feel about it. It felt like a magic spell had just been cast.

"You know what we are doing is wrong, Madam," Ombima now said.

"Yes I know. And please don't call me Madam."

"I can't call you otherwise," answered Ombima seriously. "And anyway, whatever I call you, this is wrong, and it *must* stop. It could also be dangerous," he added as an afterthought.

"How so?" she was scratching an itchy spot on her thigh where an insect had bitten her.

"*How so?* What if your husband found out?"

"What if he did?" There was a look of girlish heedlessness on her face, as if she did not care.

"You know Andimi would be furious if he ever got wind of what is happening between us. I am endangering my life being with you."

She gave him a long look, as if she was turning round and round inside her head what he had just said. "You are right," she said. "He *would*." She propped herself up on one elbow and started drawing lines around his belly button with a long fingernail. "He *would* get furious indeed—if he found out."

"What do you mean, Madam?" The circling motion she was idly making on his skin with her fingernail were tickling, and he found, to his chagrin, that he was getting excited again.

"What I mean is," she was speaking directly into his ear, "he wouldn't possibly find out. Not unless you told him yourself, that is."

"But you can't be so sure..." Ombima started to protest. But she placed her fingertip gently on his lips.

"*Shhhh*! I know what I am doing, Ombima. Do you think I was born yesterday?"

"You are out of your mind, I still say!" He rested again on his back, his face screwed up. "As for what you are doing right now, if I may say, it is sleeping with someone's husband, that's what."

"And you know what?" She raised herself on one hip at this point and threw her arm across his bony chest, at the same time as she ran her fingertips up the length of his thigh. "Sooner than you know, you may become my husband too."

"Please stop this," he protested, trying to throw her hand off his chest. But she only laughed and arched her body next to his, covering his lips with her own. Her tongue pushed against his teeth, and it was moist and warm. "Please stop, Madam," he pleaded

"Say you will marry me, Ombima," she said suddenly, pausing in her kiss, the way someone would when something important they had planned earlier springs up.

Ombima froze still on his back, not quite sure he had heard right. "You want me to—"

"Marry me." She was poised above him, the setting sun's rays haloing her profile. Her eyes were deep wells of beauty, rounded and surprisingly sincere, pinning him down with their naked candor. He looked at her hair, still wet from the tumble in the stream. He looked at her graceful neck, ringed with tiny stretch lines like a child's. He looked lower at her breasts, full and proud, hanging over him, mocking. She could not possibly be real. There was this unearthly radiance about her, every curve and hollow on her body intoned in shadow, like she had been kissed all over by an artist's tentative brush. He had never seen her in this way before, not even that time they had made love for the first time in her moonlit garden. There was a childlike daintiness about her this evening that he had never seen before. He wondered if she had drugged his senses with her magic, so that he was now seeing her through a kind of screen. She looked almost unreal.

"I asked you a question, Ombima," she tilted her head to one side and the fading sunlight caught her jawline. There was a point on her cheek that was in shadow, as if the artist had meant to shade it partially with his brush. There was a slight cleft in her lower lip that was swollen with a rush of blood. Perhaps it was a childhood scar. He had never seen even Sayo, who had shared his life for a long time, in this light.

"Eh? Ombima, won't you speak up?" She flicked up his jaw with her long fingernail and rested her lips very blushingly on his. "Don't you like me?"

With an incredible force of will, Ombima rose up on one elbow, pushing her gently but firmly off him. He crawled up to the branch where he had hung up his clothes to dry and started dressing, trying not to think about anything. He slowly slipped his shirt over his head, and then he pulled on the old corduroy trousers that had ripped in one knee where a thorn had caught it in their downhill tussle. As he dressed, he looked at the valley below.

The landscape was now bathed in a deeper shade of orange. He could see a tiny spot far in the distance that could have been a man moving among the banana trees. Out there somewhere a cow lowed, the way they do when they want to be milked. Its calf called back in response. The beat of the drums still sounded and the light wind brought the sound of singing. One of the singers surely must have seen them on the hilltop.

He turned back to Madam Tabitha. She was sitting up with her feet drawn, head buried in her arms, which were wrapped around her raised knees. She still had not dressed.

Touched by her posture, he went over and placed his hand on her shoulder. "Madam, what is the matter?"

She raised her head slowly and when she looked at him, her expression, which had just a moment ago been so full of life and mischief, now looked clouded and pensive. Her eyes were ringed in dark lines and as he watched, her dark pupils suddenly dilated and a slow tear squeezed out, rolling down her cheek.

"Madam..." He sat down beside her and placed his hand on her shoulder, rocking her soothingly. "What is it? Please don't cry."

The tears rolled freely down her face and he thought he had never seen her look so downcast in all the years he had known her. She had always been the tough schoolmistress, so much in control. But now this...

He got up and fetched her clothes from the tree branch. Gathering up the dress into a ring, he gently slipped it over her head.

"Please stop crying, Madam," he rocked her gently as he might a child. "Do tell me what makes you this way."

She leaned back in the curve of his embrace and rested her head on his shoulder, letting him brush away the tears from her face. She looked at him, a very somber expression emanated from deep within. She looked at him for a while, and then shifted her gaze slowly to some distant point in the horizon far across the deep valley that was now washed in a purplish spray. She pursed her lips and spoke in a very low voice, thick with emotion.

"I don't know if this is right, but I'll tell you anyway," she paused to swallow something that clogged her throat. "Perhaps it took my meeting you to realize, but I finally know that I am a trapped person, Ombima." She spoke slowly, her voice laden with deep sadness that only she could have harbored over a long time.

He stared at her, waiting for her to continue. She looked calm, but her eyes, still gazing into the distance, burned with a fierce fire. "Do tell me, Madam," he urged when he saw that it was difficult for her, feeling her sadness as if she was a part of him. She sniffed and blew her nose in the hem of her dress.

"I will," she said passionately. "I *will*, Ombima. Because I gather it is good for the soul."

He waited as she composed herself, conscious of the fact that he was about to travel to a very tender spot in her heart that had been accessed by no one else.

"I am a person trapped in a marriage to a person who doesn't care about me at all," she said calmly, but forcefully. She seemed determined to say what she had to say. "And I think now I must be honest enough with myself to admit it. I cannot hide from it forever, the truth. And the truth, Ombima, is that I am living a loveless marriage, which I endured since that fateful day many years ago when I was foolish enough to let myself into it. I am paying, Ombima," she swallowed yet again, painfully, "I am paying for the mistake I made."

She remained silent for a while before continuing. "Initially, I thought it was true," she said after she had collected her thoughts. "I thought it was true that my husband actually felt love for me. And, you know, they were so rosy, those days he was courting me. The man would come to our home and sit at the veranda with my elder brothers and I would serve them the evening tea." Her brow was knit in concentration as she journeyed into the past. "At first he was just a friend with my brothers. They would sit for hours on end, talking about many happenings in the village and laugh late into the evening. He was like any other boy who came visiting.

"And then I looked at him one day and he looked back at me and I realized I was wrong all along. That day it seemed like something passed between us. I noticed him in a totally different way for the first time. It was like a note had been struck between us. I was young then, just new out of high school. I had never experienced real love before, you know, the one between a grown man and a grown woman. We of course talked about a great deal of things in school, but to say the truth, I had never quite experienced anything like what the other girls said. And so you can see why he easily swept me off my weak feet, what with his strikingly good looks and suave manner, not to mention his perfected smoothness of tongue! What more need a girl ask for?"

She paused to swallow the lump in her throat. "Before I knew it, I was serving him in a special cup that was normally reserved for my father's best friends, polishing his side of the table especially keenly after they'd had their tea, you know, those little things we all do unconsciously, but which really betray the turmoil that is the true feeling deep inside our hearts. I even wanted to sit there and just listen to him talk with my brothers. He was such a charmer in those days. But then, my elder brothers wouldn't let me because they needed to talk 'manly' things that a girl who had come out of school just the other day shouldn't be party to. I was really in love with a man for the first time, Ombima."

She paused yet again to swallow that painful lump that would not go away. Then she continued, "In the space of a few days, I had fallen headlong into something with which I had no prior experience, and had now tied myself up in knots over this man of whom I knew very little. All of a sudden, I could not go to sleep as usual for thinking about him, and every time I tried to close my eyes I would see his face swimming in the darkness, or I would hear his voice somewhere in the room. I was confused. I could only think of the following day and hope that he would turn up so that I could serve him tea and listen against the keyhole as he told jokes with my brothers. How I liked the sound of his voice, so steady and soothing.

"But you see, Andimi was a businessman, and what I didn't know then was that he was seeking to get close to my father for reasons only he knew. In those days, the man you see now didn't have much really, still struggling to get a fledgling milk business in Kiritu going. And, indeed what I liked about him was that he didn't make a secret of it. The man was open like a book, or at least that's what I thought. And he had a genuine love for me too.

"We started seeing each other and, I even suspect, my father found out about it. But you see, he was so taken in by Andimi's charm. He pretended to know nothing. The same with my brothers." She paused and took a deep breath.

"All of a sudden I was swept up into a world that I had never known existed. He was my fearless warrior with a brand of honor on his heart, and I would move the world to be his woman. I discovered pleasure and an intimacy like I had never known existed between a man and a woman. He taught me many things too that I had never known before, and just brought a new breath into my life. I was a naïve woman in love and it was all that I lived for. It was more pleasurable than any friendship I had been in before, more filling than any food that had gone down my throat. I discovered what loving I had stored up inside me, and I knew the joy unimaginable of showering it all on a person I cared for."

She looked out toward the distant hills and her eyes, for a fleeting moment, were like flaming wells. The golden sun hung poised above the jagged line of hills, as if hesitant to cross the boundary. Its fiery rays reflected on her face and set her cheeks and the point of her nose aglow.

"Marriage followed only naturally, the both of us being so much at ease in each other's company like that. It had reached a point where we displayed our feelings for each other openly, without fear or embarrassment."

What she said next was in a dragged flat tone that had no enthusiasm, as if she was reciting an unpleasant fact of her life.

"We got married and our first child soon came. Then the second. My husband was all heaven, his delight written on his face, carried with him wherever he went. I went with him to parties hosted by his friends and we also hosted quite a lot in the new house my father had built for us for our wedding present. My husband leaned on my father for business connections, which was of vital importance to him in his new business in school stationery and uniforms that had suddenly grown out of the small milk business. He was like a machine, my husband, working late into the night everyday. I suppose he was the last person to go to bed in the whole village. Some days he was away from home for a week, or sometimes he was home but I couldn't talk to him because he was terribly busy.

"At first I excused him and attributed it to the fact that we were young and needed to work hard to make it on our own. I heeded my mother's advice on the wedding day that marriage is not all bliss, but lots of hard work as well. That a woman would have to preserve for the better part of the marriage in order that it might work. I was willing to give it time. I believed that we would get rich eventually, even richer than my father, and that then he would scale the crest he would have been working hard for and, finding nothing else beyond, would turn back to me and that he would rediscover the love we had awoken in each other during our courtship... and... he would shower it all on me.

"How wrong I was! I simply wasn't given much attention in that house. Mostly he was tired and weary, and I had to prepare his bath water like the dutiful wife and soothe him after a long working day. He hardly ever came to our bed, I mean in the way of a husband and wife. But I understood! I comforted myself and concentrated on taking care of the children, putting all my miseries into ensuring that they at least had a decent upbringing. And, oh, how I went at the task! That was until they went away to school."

A tear slowly trickled down her cheek and Ombima did not attempt to brush it away, nor to interrupt her.

"And then one day I realized that the happiness I craved for was not to be. He was never going to come back. His business was all that mattered to him. I needed a friend, Ombima. I needed someone to talk to. Suddenly my eyes were opened to what living was. This was not what I had bargained for. Money and riches were not everything to me as a person. I needed... *love.*"

There was such pain in the words she could no longer continue speaking. The lump in her throat was so big it was choking her, and so she looked away toward the valley and the open scrubland beyond. He could hardly look at her himself. It was as if she had opened the dressing on a deep laceration in her flesh and allowed him a glimpse of the wound's raw redness. And now she could not find the strength to put back the bandages.

A crimson haze came and hung over the periphery and put out the glow of the sunken sun. The evening sky turned a dark beet color and a long stratus cloud appeared, stretching right across the darkening firmament. A sliver of moon prepared to make its appearance in the eastern sky and in the grasses the crickets and other night insects took up their call. A warm current blew uphill and caressed the weather worn rocks with its lingering kiss. Far above the slumbering hills in the distance, the first star, a twinkling little dot, appeared. Soon the night bodies lit up the warm night with their milky twilight.

"It's getting late, Madam. Let's go back home," said Ombima, getting to his feet. He gave her his hand and she took it hesitantly, her soft fingers curling onto his.

Slowly they made their way downhill, Ombima pausing now and then to help her climb down a steep rock. The village path was deserted, save for the children who would sing and howl all night, judging from the excited noise they made. From the ridges beyond the village in the direction of Matsigulu, a drummer was busy tuning his drums for the nightlong fete to welcome Christmas.

Chapter Fourteen

EARLIER THAT EVENING, Sayo was preparing to go home after they had broken off the last song, *Kare mu'madiku yago*. She could still hear the words ring clearly in her ears, as well as the undulating voices of the village women as they wove in and out of the song, straining to give it the best they had, even when it was mostly just simple flat chords all through. And Sayo could not blame them, either. She could still recall with nostalgia how her own mother used to sing the same song, watching them practice in her maiden village church. So passionately did they do it on those sun splashed breezy evenings, perfectly heralding the good things that were soon to come. She too wished that they could go on and on practicing the songs because this time around they should not allow the women from Imonyero to scoop the first prize like they had done the previous Christmas. But then it was late and she knew that she must let the women go back home to cook for their households. After all, who wanted beatings in the village at this time of the year?

As she put back the hymnal and Bible in her old leather carrying bag, she wanted to give it to her son Aradi to carry for her. She also needed him to go on ahead and ensure that the cattle were driven in and properly tethered in their pens for the night, while she followed slowly in her woman's leisurely walk.

Her husband was acting rather distant lately, and she did not want a pointless, avoidable argument after such a fine day. She thought she had seen the boy around with his friend Kesenwa, hammering on the big drums the older boys used in the youth choir. But now that he was needed, as usual, the boy was nowhere to be seen. He was always running off, this Aradi of hers. One moment he was right here having a good cackle at the top of his voice among peers and the next he was gone. She searched the yard behind the church and only found a handful of the younger children struggling to carry the drums the other boys had left inside, fighting over the smooth sticks so that they may have the last strike.

Giving up, Sayo slung the bag under her arm and drew her old jersey closer about her shoulders, adjusting the faded head-scarf she wore over her freshly clean shaven head, as custom demanded. She felt a bit chilly, but she was happy inside for the commendable way the village women had picked up the song. Usually, they were quite troublesome. It was difficult first just getting them together, and then making them memorize the verses and, last of all harmonizing their voices. Almost all of them were wont to sing it, if it should be a popular one, the same way they did in the Sunday service; droning on through to the last verse, hanging onto the last syllable in the line as if they were not in a hurry to get into the next stanza, hardly making an effort to alter the pitch of their voices. They sang more the way they talked. There was that Eside, wife of the termite trapper, who was especially hard to get to come in the evenings, and yet the old lady had such a melodious voice. Sayo made a mental note to pass by her compound next evening, resolving to physically drag her out if she had to. All the same, she was not worried much because the song they had to perform was common enough, and all it needed was just a bit of polishing here and there. As Sayo was turning out of the church entrance, Rebecca hurried up to join her. "Wait for me, Sayo. I am afraid of walking alone in the evening," she could still run too, for her age.

"The children will see you running Rebecca, *bayaa*!" said Sayo with a good laugh. Rebecca had sung especially well this evening, a gleam in her eyes all the while that Sayo did not know if it was some good fortune that had befallen her or what.

"So, give me the news," she said panting, "I hear Eregwa is going to bring a case against Ngayira the day after tomorrow at the chief's *baraza*. That it was the woman who killed his newborn calf... is it true?"

This story had been doing its rounds in the village. That on the day the brewer's grade cow had delivered, Ngayira the witch, not normally known to wander into that part of the village, had been seen carrying a basket, collecting cow dung just outside Eregwa's compound, ostensibly to use to smear her hut. Everyone knew that the old woman had a powerful evil eye, that she would just as much as glance at a newly born child and the next day the mother would be rushing to the health center in Mbale because the little bundle of joy would be covered all over in warts. It was strange because the woman had actually been seen by a number of people. Why, of all the days, had she chosen just that day to go and collect cow dung in that part of the village? That was the big question.

"I've heard the news too," Sayo said, slowing her stride to keep pace with Rebecca. "And I'm not surprised either. I've never trusted that woman all the days I've been married in this village. I hope the chief gives her a flogging."

"*Mwana*," said Rebecca sympathetically, "just when Eregwa was going to say goodbye to the problem of milk after all those years tending to the cow, and then the demon does this to him."

"Well, what do you do," said Sayo with a shrug. "God gives and He takes away, you know."

"That's true," said Rebecca, thinking how this had come to Sayo, particularly now.

They walked on in silence for a while, each lost in their own thoughts. Day was fast being overtaken by night, the dying sun's rays lancing through the trees on either side of the road, spraying the darkening village a startling gold. Goats bleated their protest as the children in the compounds chased them and the last amorous cockerel did its final run for the day before the unwilling hen could dash into the safety of the kitchen hut.

Down the path the lazy, newly married women dashed to the well, hoping that it wouldn't be dark before they got there.

Passing by Andimi's compound, Sayo and Rebecca saw lights come on in the windows as someone inside drew the blinds to keep out the night. Madam Tabitha stood just inside the gate, talking to another woman whom she had been escorting out. She called out a greeting and Sayo and Rebecca chorused back.

"You are from the choir?" she asked, coming over.

"Yes. You were not there, Madam, why?" Sayo asked, seeing that she was in a dress that looked unusually disarrayed, meaning she had been around, probably working in her garden. Tabitha smiled apologetically and said, "Oh, I really have no excuse to give. I was just lazy today."

"Well, you had better not be tomorrow, or I'll strike you off the team." Sayo felt humbled by her elevated position as choir mistress and yet she knew she had to be firm, even with Madam. "You are one of our best sopranos, you know. You can't afford to miss like this."

"Oh, I'm sorry, Sayo. I'll be there tomorrow."

"That's better."

As Sayo and Rebecca made to walk on, Madam suddenly remembered something. She said to Sayo, "Oh, and before I forget, could someone come over tomorrow for the help *Mzee* promised? I don't have it on me now, or I would give it to you."

"Oh, that! I'll ask Ombima to come. Thank you very much, Madam," said Sayo, quite touched that she had remembered.

"Don't say it, Sayo. You know that we should all help each other. Say hello to everyone for me, then."

As Sayo and Rebecca walked on down the road, Rebecca, who was still staring at the brightly lit house through the gaps in the fence, said, "Some people have all the luck, Sayo."

"Why so?" Sayo asked, not getting Rebecca's point because she was still thinking about the promise that had been made to them, wondering how much money they would be given.

"Imagine living in a house like that all to yourself," said Rebecca, mesmerized at the immensity of the building. "It can house a whole village!"

"Hey, mind where you are going, woman," said Sayo following Rebecca's gaze. "Don't lose yourself dreaming about things that are well beyond your reach."

"I guess you are right," said the older woman with a shrug. "She's a lucky woman all the same, and I can't blame myself envying her good fortune. At least she doesn't have to wake up at cockcrow and go out to work for other people like I do. I wish I had a husband like that who would provide me with everything I needed. How I would shower him with all my love!"

Sayo shook with laughter, not so much at the older woman's words as at the way she said them, her lined face aglow, tiny eyes bright and focused in her dream, as if it could happen to her, even at her age.

"You should look at yourself, Rebecca," she said, struggling to stifle the laughter.

"Why? You think there's something the matter with me?" asked the older woman, surprised, pausing to hold out the hem of her old dress. "Look, Sayo, I'm woman enough as Madam is—see for yourself." She made a stiff legged pirouette that sent Sayo roaring with laughter. "You see... I'm not quite spent as you might think!"

"I'll give it to you for one thing," said Sayo, walking on because she knew they would probably be there half an hour if she should stop to watch Rebecca demonstrate. "You certainly don't take your fate lying down. You are a proud old woman, Rebecca."

This visibly touched the other woman and she dropped her gaze shyly, her eyes shining in the dark with what might have been tears. "And," Sayo added with a casual sideways glance, "*he's* sure got reason to lose himself in that way too. The old boy's heart seems to me to be in a good place!"

191

"Hey, what are you talking about now?" asked Rebecca, suspicious all of a sudden.

"Oh, you know well what I'm saying," said Sayo with a don't-you-fool-me ogle. "Come on, it's an open secret, my dear. I could see the way Ang'ote was watching over you the other day during the funeral, even if I was bereaved. The old boy sure doesn't know to keep it a secret. It's almost as if you are a little chick that someone must keep away from buzzards hovering above all the time!"

"Now, now Sayo, I really don't like the things you say, hear?" The older woman was visibly embarrassed, not taking the comment lightly at all.

"Oh, *pole*, Rebecca," Sayo said soothingly. "I didn't know. I honestly didn't mean to pry."

Rebecca's gaze remained fixed to the ground and she did not say a word. They passed the *duka* and saw Indimuli preparing to close for the day. He waved, and Sayo waved back.

Soon after, they came to the little turning that Rebecca was to take home and Sayo paused to say goodnight. The older woman, for her part, responded rather gruffly and walked on, still bristling. Sayo, puzzled, went on home down the dark path, surprised how easy it was to touch someone's tender spot.

* * *

Ang'ote came calling early the following day. He found Ombima sitting underneath the guava tree in front of the house having his breakfast. Being a Sunday, one could afford to breakfast late in the day. Across the compound underneath the mango tree was some washing Sayo had been doing but abandoned for some other duty in the house. It was a bright, clear morning full of promise, only there was no money for one to go off to drink beer somewhere.

"Good day to you, my friend, Ombima. I can see you are eating," Ang'ote beamed into the compound, his sweaty face brightening at the sight of food.

"Yes, my friend. *Karibu!* Please come and join me," said Ombima. "I was starved just now for some company. You know that good food, however well prepared, is never enjoyable when one is eating alone."

"Yes indeed."

Ombima called to Aradi to bring a chair for the visitor. Ang'ote carried a *panga*, which he placed down against the tree trunk, its sharp edge glinting in the sun. It had just been honed.

"I can see you are off on some business," said Ombima, glancing at the *panga*.

"Yes, indeed. I'm going to the valley to look for some poles, and I meant to pass by here to see if you were idle. I was hoping you would accompany me."

"As you can see, I am quite busy. Maybe some other time."

They laughed heartily. Aradi brought a folding chair and Ang'ote sat down, washing his hands in the rusty metal trough by the stool that served as a table.

"Hey, and bring a cup for Ang'ote, will you?" called Ombima as the boy started to disappear in the direction of the bananas.

"I don't think I'll be having any tea," said Ang'ote, shaking his head.

"Why?" Ombima asked, mildly surprised.

Ang'ote scratched the side of his bearded face and said, "I just had some. In fact, this very minute."

"I see," said Ombima, smiling knowingly. "So you choose to behave like some of these women who say that, and then end up drinking a whole pot in the end when they are persuaded. I know you far too well, my friend."

Aradi, who was still within earshot, could not stifle his laughter at the expression on Ang'ote's face.

"Bring him a cup all the same, son," said Ombima laughing. "There's a lot of tea in this pot for one stomach to finish on its own." Ang'ote, for his part, was already busy attacking the roasted groundnuts in the bowl beside the teapot, scooping a handful and aiming them straight into the back of his mouth.

"Don't you remove the skins first?" Ombima asked

"Oh no," he paused, with the hand that had been going to his open mouth suspended in the air. "What for? It's women who indulge in that unnecessary exercise." It was as if Ombima had made a most absurd observation. "And guess what? They don't have any idea just what it is they are throwing away. As a matter of fact, a groundnut's sweetness is in its skin, and so when you peel the nut, you are actually throwing away its flavor. Also, it is in the skin that the *vitamwanzi* are stored," he added as an afterthought.

"*Vitamins*, Ang'ote," said Ombima, making a dip into the bowl.

"Whatever. As long as you get what I am saying. You know I never went to school like you did, my friend."

They ate in silence for a while, the only conversation being the cracking of their jaws as they crushed the nuts.

"*Hmmm*! These groundnuts are so sweet! Where did you get them, Ombima?"

"They came from Jivaswa. Some of my wife's people live there."

"I see," said Ang'ote, angling his head so he could toss another handful down his throat. "I hear things are so cheap on the market in Jivaswa. I've never been there myself."

"Yes, indeed they are." Ombima helped himself to some more tea.

"*Huh*?" Ang'ote spoke as he swallowed a big ball that had formed in his mouth. "That the sweet potatoes there are so big a man can't finish one in a single meal, is it?"

"Who is that asking about Jivaswa? Is it you, Ang'ote?" Sayo had heard the talk and she came out to greet the visitor.

She had grown thinner in the last few days, with tiny dark sacks showing beneath her eyes.

"Yes, it is me, Mama Aradi. What have you saved for me in the kitchen? You know I haven't eaten anything for the past two days."

"Really? These days you hardly ever work, anyway, pretending you are busy preparing your choir for the Christmas competitions. And so I really think you don't deserve to eat at all."

Ang'ote laughed off her taunt as he usually did whenever anyone took a jibe at him.

"I heard you talk about Jivaswa, Ang'ote," she said.

"You weren't mistaken, Mama Aradi. I was just asking my friend here about the place. I am planning to visit one of these days."

"It is women who normally go to the market, Ang'ote," supplied Ombima.

"Yes, indeed," said Sayo enjoying the direction the conversation was taking.

"You are right, the two of you," Ang'ote concurred, tilting the bowl to collect the last burned nuts at the bottom. "You are right, and I'm no fool to venture in their place." They waited as he swallowed, knowing there was more coming. "But you perhaps don't know the other half. I might just be taking there my newfound sweetheart so that when we are eventually married, she knows where to go to do shopping for our children."

Sayo shook with laughter, knowing full well whom Ang'ote was talking about. Of late, the two of them had been seen together quite a lot, although the elderly lady still had some reservations. But it was obvious how deeply they cared for each other, and the village grapevine was abuzz with the talk. It was good to hear Ang'ote talk about it so calmly.

But for some reason, Ombima found that he was uneasy with the topic. He called Aradi to fetch an axe and stood up, rolling back the sleeves of his old shirt. Sayo went back to her washing under the mango tree.

As they left the compound for the valley, Ang'ote paused to call over his shoulder to the boy, "*Eeeei!* And tell your mother I'll be hanging around, Aradi, will you? She should keep that in mind when she prepares the midday meal."

Sayo, who had overheard him, called from across the compound, "I'm sorry I've got just enough for my family, Ang'ote. In any case," she added thoughtfully, "I've never been entertained to a meal in your house, anyway." She was holding Ombima's corduroy trousers, which he had worn the day before, out of the white suds in the trough. It had unusual green stains on it, as if he had been romping in the grass down in the valley like some child. She had been working on it just before she left the washing a while ago, and had intended to ask Ombima about the stain. Now with Ang'ote there, she could not.

The two men went in the direction of the valley enjoying a good laugh at her parting remark. As they crept their way through the profuse green bush that overgrew the narrow winding path a short distance from the compound, Ombima said, "You are really going to get married, Ang'ote?"

Ang'ote slashed at a hanging tendril with his *panga* and laughed. "No, my friend. I was only pulling the wool over Sayo's eyes." He screwed up his face. "I intend to myself. My heart is hungry for some company. But then, like I told you, the woman just won't hear of it."

"But it's only you haven't tried hard enough to persuade her, Ang'ote," said Ombima, shifting the axe to his left shoulder. "I know Rebecca will finally say yes."

"Is it? You don't know how hard I've tried, mister. Rebecca just won't hear of it!"

"You know, Ang'ote, I believe that no woman is impossible. It only takes a bit of tact and persistence, my friend. Most of them eventually cave in. She might just be testing to see if you really love her from the heart."

"You are right, my friend. But then, you just don't know this woman. When Rebecca says 'no' she means 'no.' There's just no way anyone can make her change her mind."

Ombima scratched at a speck at the corner of his eye and kicked at the dust. A cheeky look hovered on his face. "But the woman does turn up once in a while to clean up your fireplace, doesn't she?" There was a glint in Ombima's eye.

Ang'ote laughed, his gaze lifting above the trees to somewhere in the distance, "Of course, yes. But then..."

"Then why are you complaining? If you asked me, I'd say you just take what you get and be content with it."

"And it is fine for you to say so, because you know yours is always there for you, rain or sun. You know a man needs a woman to keep him company, especially so when age is catching up."

"Like it is doing you?"

The poles they sought grew deep in the valley where the undergrowth was thick and unyielding and the creepers clinging and tenacious. They had to cut a path through because normally no one ventured this deep into the valley. The poles at the valley's fringe were twisted and much warped, and no good for any job other than as firewood.

"Talking about poles, what is it you are planning to put up, Ang'ote?" Ombima paused to extract his trouser legging from a trailing thorn.

"Oh, I just want to construct a little shelter for my chickens, a small lean-to behind my house, really."

"You own chickens, Ang'ote? I've never seen any all this while I've been to your compound."

"*Ohoo*. And you thought I was a useless old drunk who spent his shilling as soon as he made it, didn't you?" It was too dark in there to see what his face looked like as he told the lie, but Ombima could very well imagine. "Well, for your information, I own four chickens. And the fact that you haven't laid your eyes on them doesn't mean they are not there. You know, you are even welcome to judge for yourself if I'm lying on Christmas day when I'll slaughter the big cockerel in the brood. I plan to throw a big feast for all my friends. After all, what good does it do a man to have wealth that he does not enjoy?"

Ombima laughed, though he wondered if there might just be a grain of truth to it after all. To imagine that Ang'ote the spendthrift had kept a secret all this time...

They worked a long while, hacking at the creepers with their machetes and hauling until they had harvested a good number of long straight poles. They stopped to rest in a clearing by the stream that snaked its way silently through the dense woods. Instinctively, Ombima reached into his back pocket and pulled out a pack of cigarettes that was much crumpled because he had been sitting on it. He searched inside and took out a bent stick, which was squashed almost flat.

"*Che!* Since when did you start smoking, Ombima?" Ang'ote was surprised, watching him intently, shiny dark eyes shifting as if he was not sure of what he had seen. Ombima produced a match and went through the ritual of lighting up, all the while his friend following his movements with amused interest.

"I started smoking only yesterday," he said when the cigarette had finally lit. He took a long drag and exhaled slowly, guiding the long jet through his parted lips as if it was the most natural thing.

"I see," said Ang'ote, still surprised. "And just what decided you? You never appeared the smoking type to me, if I must say."

Ombima worked his way down the stick in silence for a while, debating with himself, eyes drawn to slits from the smoke. In the end he decided there was no harm in coming out with it. He had been meaning to since the previous night, anyway. His conscience nagged him to share his new indulgence with his only true friend of many years, and with whom they had been party to so many secrets. "Tell me something Ang'ote," he said, taking a deep breath and flicking the grey ash at the end of the stick onto the grass. "Do you keep a secret?"

For a moment Ang'ote appeared puzzled, not knowing where his friend was driving. And then he said, "Of course you know I do, Ombima. You know well you can trust me with your secret because I am your friend." He appeared a bit hurt that Ombima had expressed doubt in the easy confidence that they had built between them over the years.

"Well, you had better," said Ombima after a bit of meditation. "Because I intend to tell you a most personal secret."

"*Ehe?*" Ang'ote moved closer on his seat of leaves. "You have got my attention." His wide-open eyes were almost popping out with speculation. "And just what secret is that?"

Ombima cleared his throat and took another long drag at the cigarette, tossing the spent butt into the swirling stream. When the smoke was ejected, he turned around so he was looking Ang'ote straight in the eye. "Just you promise no one will hear a breath of this, Ang'ote. It might be dangerous."

"Oh, you have my word," said Ang'ote impatiently, hardly able to forecast just what it might be.

Ombima, satisfied that he could take the leap, took a swallow and lifted his eyes slowly away from his friend's anxious face. "Ang'ote, I am moving with Andimi's wife," he said as calmly as he could, as if he meant not to be in the least distracted by the heavy guilt in his utterance.

Ang'ote watched him for a while, mouth hanging agape as the news slowly sunk in. And then the hilt of it hit him and with a jolt, he said, "You are *what*?!" his eyes were popping right out "You are moving—I mean..."

"I mean she and I are lovers, if I must put it to you so bluntly." Ombima was staring calmly into the stream, his gaze fixed on a point in the water where the current eddied round in ripples, as if the water was disappearing into a hole somewhere in the silty bed.

"M-madam," he stammered. "It is *Madam* you mean?" Ang'ote looked like someone who had just seen the tall old dead tree outside his compound sprout a fresh green branch.

"Yes. *Madam*, is just who I mean." Now that Ombima had finally uttered the words, the immensity of it all suddenly descended on him, the way a huge rock might settle in the soft mud at the bottom of the river. The implication of just what could come out of the revelation to his friend caught up with him. And so, glancing sideways at Ang'ote, he reminded him, "You promised, remember?"

It took some time for the message to sink fully. And then the other man licked his lips which had suddenly gone dry, and said, "*Aye, aye.* You really caught me by surprise there, my friend Ombima." He looked down at his dusty big toe that he was wriggling in the grass and shifted his weight from the support of his right hand to the left. He gazed across the stream at the cone shaped treetops, rustling softly in the morning wind.

"*Phee-e-eew!*" a thin whistle escaped his lips, his throat momentarily dry for words.

"Ang'ote, it is true," Ombima said when he saw that his friend was not going to say anything. "You don't believe it, do you?"

At long last Ang'ote regained himself. "Hey, I do. I really do believe it." He turned to look at his friend. "That was quite a shocking one," he said, letting out his breathe slowly.

"You don't imagine it could be true?" There was a tinge of sadness in Ombima's voice.

"Oh, for sure I don't. I mean..." Yet again Ang'ote stared at his friend, and found that the words escaped him.

"Go ahead," Ombima persuaded him.

"Well I just can't imagine it," said Ang'ote, trying unsuccessfully to level his gaze with his friend's. "You and Madam... lovers..."

"We've done it twice now." Ombima decided that now that he had let the big cat out of the bag, he might as well let all the claws out with it. "Once in her garden, just a couple of weeks ago, and once on a hilltop in Kisangula, atop a flat rock. This last was just yesterday evening."

"*Pheeeew*! I think you are a devil, Ombima," said Ang'ote, still wearing that look he had assumed when the news had first been broken.

"And the sticky part of it is that the lady is now crazy in love with me. She actually wants me to marry her. That, in a nutshell, is the crux of this whole matter. And so, my friend, to cut a long story short, I am asking you for advice."

Ang'ote drew up his knees and let his head hang between his legs, staring fixedly at the ground. Then he shook his head slowly from left to right, taking in everything he had heard. "You mean, you've done it with... Madam? I mean, there's something the matter with that. I just can't picture *you*."

"It's true, Ang'ote."

"I know. It's just the picture that I'm trying to get to come clearly inside my head. And, you know what, Ombima? I think you are mad."

"Mad?" Ombima was astounded.

"Yes, just that. Out of your mind. You know, look at me, Ombima, come on."

Ombima turned to look at his friend, wondering what could possibly be going on inside his head.

"Yes, that's better." In Ang'ote's eyes there now was a fiery look that Ombima had never seen, and which was almost manic. "Now, tell me one thing in honesty, Ombima," he said, licking his dry slightly quivering lips. "Just who do *you* think you are?"

"Who do I think I am?" Ombima was clearly puzzled by the question. Ang'ote, on his part, looked as if he was getting worked up, his sweating lips trembling even more in his halting speech, voice unsteady. Ombima had no idea where this could be leading.

"Yes. Just who do you think you are, Ombima? *Eh*? Please tell me that," he inched forward so he could stab his finger in Ombima's face. "You take a good look at yourself and tell me that. Go on!"

Ombima leaned back, surprised at the intensity of the other man's agitation.

"You won't, *eh*?" said Ang'ote, heaving. "Well, let me tell you just what it is, if you are afraid." He took hold of a fistful of grass at his feet and tore it out of the earth, throwing it into the swirling stream, the way someone who is angry would do. "I'll tell you. You, Ombima, are a *nobody*. A *nobody*, hear?" he repeated for emphasis.

"Now, now, Ang'ote," Ombima started to rise to his feet, not at all happy with what his friend had called him. "You are insulting me, I say."

But Ang'ote was unmoved by the man's agitation and went on, his breath wheezing through his stained teeth. "You are just that, Ombima—a nobody. Just look at you."

"Ang'ote!" Ombima poised on his toes, looming over his friend, ready to take a swing at him.

"Yes. That's good," said Ang'ote, cowing away, a bemused look on his face. His eyes were shiny with mirth, shifting all over on Ombima's enraged face as if he was satisfied at some achievement. "That's good. I just wanted you to realize it." His nostrils still flared wildly. "At least now I can see I have your ear."

They both sat back down, seething like a couple of cockerels. "That's good. Now, listen to me carefully, Ombima." There was a new sternness about Ang'ote's face. He might have been a school master looming above a cowering errant pupil. "You have made a mistake, my friend, and a grave one at that. You cannot be lovers with a woman of such stature as Andimi's wife and expect life to remain the same as it was before. No, you can't my friend. That is the hard fact, and I'll put it to you bluntly, whatever you think of me, because I am your friend. I can't see you about to step on a puff adder and remain silent. No, I can't. I must warn you," he paused, swallowing before resuming.

"What you've just told me, if it's indeed true—God forbid!—then you've done a very dangerous thing." Ang'ote's eyes now locked with Ombima's. He now wore the face of an

aggrieved patriarch issuing a condemnation. "Very dangerous, my friend. And you know what I would advise you?" He
held his index finger in a way Ombima had never seen him do
before, and it scared him. "Leave that woman alone. Steer clear
of her completely. She might just be like that creature people of
Mombasa talk of that is half pretty woman and half fish, which
leads lustful fishermen, unsuspectingly, to their death underwa-
ter. If you think I am lying to you, Ombima, then just remember
these words I say to you. They might come true in the future.
And it's not as if I am throwing the blame on you—no, that I am
not, my friend. God knows the woman is beautiful!" He paused,
a strange glint in the depths of his eyes, jaw hanging as if in
laughter. "Yes, Madam is beautiful. And, honestly, I wouldn't be
so sure how to react myself if I were in your shoes. But then, as
they say, it is those on the outside who see more clearly. Please
give thought to what I have said," he concluded, rubbing his
hands in a cleaning gesture like the final speaker would use in
an elder's court.

Ombima remained silent for a while after Ang'ote had
spoken. And then he raised his head slowly and, locking stares
with his friend said, "Do I get the remotest feeling that you
might be jealous, Ang'ote?"

"Jealous!?" There was a look of utter astonishment on the
other man's face.

"Yes, jealous." The expression on Ombima's face was still
calm.

"But why should I be?"

"Yes! Why should you be? I don't know. Maybe you tell me."

"You are out of your mind, Ombima. Just why should I be
jealous? *Eh?* Why should I be jealous of a fool like you, making
a bad joke of yourself?"

"I wonder. Perhaps you wanted for it to be *you*, the fellow
making happy the rich man's wife?"

"You are disgusting, Ombima. You are totally sickening!"

"It is you who is sickening, Ang'ote. You can't stand the fact that something good is happening to me," Ombima fumed challengingly.

"Something good?" Ang'ote asked incredulously. "What is good about vileness?"

There was disbelief written on Ang'ote's sweaty face, as if he was just witnessing his worst fear. In the long run, he just hung his head and muttered between his knees, at a loss for what further to say.

Eventually it was Ombima who broke the uncomfortable silence. "Let's get on our way home, Ang'ote," he said getting to his feet.

"A good idea," said the other uncomfortably. "There's a lot of work still ahead of us."

They set themselves to the difficult task of hauling the long poles out of the valley and up the path back home. And as the two friends worked side by side in the hot midday sun, one broke the silence that hung over them and said from underneath his cuff, "Is that where you learned to smoke cigarettes?" To which the other laughed, rather uneasily.

Chapter Fifteen

LATER THAT EVENING the drummers calling closer the impending Christmas holiday had tired themselves out and retired home. Rebecca, still a bit discreet about their relationship, had just snuck in the night into Ang'ote's compound after having ascertained that her grandchildren were safely in bed.

An old oil lamp was burning in the hut, and in its yellow light Ang'ote was reclining on his creaky wooden bed. She was bending over his foot, which was resting in her lap, squinting her eyes in the dim light, trying to make out the tiny black head of the evasive chigger she was trying to pull out of his corny big toe. She was using one of her grandchildren's safety pins, which she had brought over with her. She kept wetting a finger with spittle and dabbing at the spot to soften the tough skin. In the poor light, her face was deeply lined and her hair, freed of the old nylon scarf that she always wore, was going grey all over. But even then, she looked strangely vibrant, even youthful.

"There's talk that Mudeya-Ngoko is going to work in Andimi's shop in Chavakali, have you heard?" Ang'ote was saying.

"I'm hearing it from you now," said Rebecca, wiping the pin on her *lesso* and then pausing, ready to plunge it into the tough skin. "*Ehe?* Tell me. Who says?"

"I heard it said around. Miroya was discussing it with her husband in the shop."

"*Oooo.* Then that will certainly be a good boost for him."

"Indeed it will." Ang'ote arched his back to scratch his buttock where a bedbug had just bitten him. "I wonder if he'll get a big ratio of *mahengere* and tea there as well. I hear the workers there must go to a hotel where *mahengere* is measured in a plate just about the size of a palm."

Rebecca laughed, pausing with the pin in mid-air.

"All the same, I wonder who will take over the running of *Mzee*'s farms," he finally said.

"Maybe they'll appoint someone from among us," said Rebecca, examining something on the tip of the needle she had fished out of the wound, which turned out to be just a scrap of corny skin. She cleaned the pin on her *lesso* again.

"I hope so..." said Ang'ote with a thoughtful look on his face.

"*Ehe?*" Rebecca looked up from her task. "Do I hear something turning in your mind?"

Ang'ote, in the scrutiny of her full glare, leaned back on his elbows and looked away shyly. "That's right, Rebecca." He paused a while, as if gathering his scattered thoughts. "I want to be the one to take over the running of the farms," he said in a low, calm voice.

"*Ho-hooo*... Someone listen to this madness!" When Rebecca laughed she shed almost half her age and became a young woman again. "You do make me laugh sometimes, Ang'ote. Just how can someone like you dream of ever having a job like that?"

"And just why might I not?" Ang'ote rose from his slouched position so he could face her. "*Eh?* Why not?"

"Why not?" Rebecca asked, a trifle surprised that he should be asking the question at all. "You are illiterate, that's why."

Of all people, only Rebecca had the capacity to give Ang'ote a dressing down without the fellow hitting back. Maybe it was in the way she said it. Right then, Ang'ote reclined back to his earlier position on the bed, a look of hurt on his face, mouth shut.

"There, there, I'm sorry, Ang'ote," she hastened to add, moving up to sit beside him on the bed in order that she might put her arm around his shoulder. "Now, I didn't mean it quite that way, honest."

She understood the immense pride that made up his character, and which also enabled him to trounce over most of his shortcomings in life. And she seemed to know too just where to poke to set the brickwork crumbling.

There was just no way he could resist her petting any longer and soon his weather scoured face crumbled into a cackle of amusement.

"There, there. That's my man," she said, resuming her place on the stool.

"You know, Rebecca, one of these days—"

"—you are going to do what?" She met his stern look with a similar one of her own.

"I'm going to marry you," he said, gazing fixedly into the depths of her rounded dark eyes that had seen many happenings, both joyful and sad, and which still shone richly with life and hope.

For a while she concentrated on tearing into the skin of his toe with the sharp pin point, skillfully skirting the subject he had just brought up. "You know, Ang'ote, you must learn in life to accept yourself for what you are," she said at last. "If at all you are incapable of something, then just accept it that way, because that's just how it was meant to be. I'm sure you'll get more out of life if you learn to be honest with yourself."

"Oh, you are starting to sound like my late mother," said Ang'ote sulkily. "That *kanywere* you talk of is no more educated than I am! And yet he has managed on the job," he added irritably. "What Mudeya-Ngoko can do, I'm certain I can do just as well!"

Lowering her gaze back to what she had been doing, Rebecca shrugged and said, "Well, go ahead then. I wasn't trying to stop you."

"And I will, too. Just you wait, you will see!" There was that childish resolve on his face that she had seen before when he once told her of his decision to rally all the farm workers to demand a pay raise out of the immovable Andimi, a venture that had not even gone beyond his threshold early the following morning when he had awoken much sobered up. So well did she understand his changing moods she could now tell them off, more the way she would feel each of the hard calluses inflicted by the hoe handle in the toughened palms of her hands, each in its familiar old place.

"Besides," added Ang'ote, still agitated, "people who reason the way you do hardly ever die rich. Why? Simply because they can never dare to do anything beyond the familiar!"

"You are right."

In the comfortable silence in the hut after the mutually unresolved but surrendered little argument, a rat scuttled somewhere amidst the broken pots heaped in the corner, its horny claws scratching restlessly against the pot bottoms that had not a dry morsel left. Rebecca wetted her finger with spittle yet again and applied it to the tough skin. Then she picked up the safety pin and, biting her lower lip between her teeth, she made a deep incision that drew a sharp cry from Ang'ote, who had all along been trying his best to brave the little poking of the sharp needle that was poised delicately between a pleasant tickling and acute pain.

"*Ooooi*, Rebecca!" he cried. "Now, you did that deliberately, I swear!"

It took some convincing before he could put his foot back in her lap and allow her to carry on, and only after she promised to be much gentler with the sharp pin. He then sat back against the sooty wall and closed his eyes, enjoying the near pleasant sensation in the now pulsating big toe.

And then he sprung up suddenly, his eyes shining. "Rebecca, how in the world did I forget to tell you this!" There was open excitement on his face now, eyes wide like he had just remembered a very important thing he had planned to confide in her. "I had meant to tell you this, listen..." Rebecca rested her safety pin, knowing whatever he had to say was pretty interesting if the look on his face was anything to go by.

Then he told her all that Ombima had confided in him earlier that day concerning his affair with Madam Tabitha.

All the while he spoke, her face remained blank, her wise dark eyes shifting occasionally with every interesting turn in the account. For Ang'ote's part, he told it well like he had been told, and even better, filling up where his imagination told him Ombima had omitted some details. He was greatly enjoying the astonishment that crept into her face as the story unwound bit by bit.

And then, when he was done, he sat back and crossed his wiry hands over his bare chest and declared, more the way a logger might after felling a particularly stubborn tree, "And that, Rebecca, is the story of Madam's boy, Ombima, going about looking so saintly policing the big man's garden for thieves when he is the worse thief for stealing *that* fruit of the tree most forbidden."

Rebecca sat back and linked her hands in her lap, her task momentarily forgotten. Licking her dry lips, a serious expression on her face, she said, "And you know what, Ang'ote? I don't believe a word of what you say. You have told many a lie to me before, but this…"

Ang'ote got up. "There! Exactly the way I reacted just this afternoon when he told me. I tell you, I didn't believe a word of it at first. But you know what? You should have seen the look on Ombima's face when he revealed it to me. The fellow was serious as our local pastor, I tell you."

"Well…" There was that calm way in which Rebecca normally took in something he told her, trying to filter the information for the bits she should reject and those that she thought were incredible, knowing well his penchant for spinning a long tale out of a simple enough happening. But in this instance, something told her Ang'ote was not spinning one of his yarns for her.

"So, what do you say?" asked Ang'ote, looking anxiously at her.

"I think it is the most surprising thing I've heard this December," she said slowly, her brow knit in thought. "*If* at all it is true."

"It is true, I tell you," said Ang'ote with a nod. "No wonder the fair Madam seemed of late to go out of her way to assign duties that should otherwise have gone to the more trustworthy Mudeya-Ngoko to Ombima. She was really just sprucing him up. Although I must admit I hardly ever suspected a thing myself."

"You are right," said Rebecca, nodding slowly. "But then... Oh, my I just can't picture the two of them."

"Exactly the same with me!" exclaimed Ang'ote, excited by just how on par they both seemed to be, as if they thought along the same plane. "It beats my imagination completely—she, so clean and stately, a person of status and he, so... so *ordinary*, a common worker of the open fields. The two, if you ask me, just don't mix. It is like oil and water."

"You are right too," said Rebecca, her eyes figuring. "I wonder what it is she saw in Ombima, of all the people," she offered, a look of amusement playing on her face.

"I wonder too," concurred Ang'ote, musing. "Or maybe the fellow knows his job well," he added snidely. "That, for all his common field hand attributes, the fellow could also be a sturdy enough bullock—that which passes dung lying down on its belly, *he-hee heeei!*" He broke off, laughing derisively. "That he really knows what it takes to make the good madam happy, could it be?"

"Could be," said Rebecca, tickled too by Ang'ote's words.

"Or it is just that common adage about *ugali* and choice beef every day that eventually gets the eater craving for cheap old *sukuma-wiki* for a change?" added Ang'ote, his harbor not yet exhausted.

"And you think Ombima is *sukuma-wiki*?" queried Rebecca, not quite agreeing with him.

"I don't see him otherwise," said Ang'ote. "I mean, I don't seriously see anything so unique about him that would make a woman of standing like Madam want to bend down so low."

Rebecca regarded him with a squint for a while, then said, "Ang'ote, why do I get this feeling you are jealous of your friend, *Eh*? That you are irked by his good fortune, if I may call it that? That you even probably wish it had been you in his place?" This last was delivered in the manner of a challenge.

But then Ang'ote did not rise to it. He was shocked to know that he hated both Rebecca and Ombima all of a sudden. Both of them pretended to be his friends and yet they persisted in thinking the same negative things about him.

"You are jealous, *eh*, Ang'ote?" Rebecca persisted in the tense silence that followed.

"Just you shut up and take that chigger out of my foot woman, will you?" he snapped back. He then reclined against the wall and refused to make any further comment.

Later, as they sat eating, he broached the subject again. He had been thinking and an idea had occurred to him. "Rebecca, there's something I've been thinking about," he said lightly.

"Yes?" she paused with a fish bone she was preparing to clean held in her hand. They were dipping balls of *ugali* into a large common bowl full of fish stew, in which pieces of sun dried tilapia floated.

"We were planning to build a new house, weren't we?" Ang'ote asked.

"*You* were planning to build a new house, yes. What about it?"

"Well whichever way you view it. The two of us were planning to move into a new house. Now, what do you say if we can persuade Andimi to loan us some money to purchase the iron sheets we need?"

"I don't know exactly what you have in mind, Ang'ote, but please just keep in mind that I am not party to your plans," she said, a warning look creeping into her eyes.

Ang'ote took his time, phrasing and rephrasing his words. In the meantime, he explored the fish stew with his fingers and hooked out what looked like a chunk of boiled squirrel meat. He tested its softness between thumb and forefinger and, deciding it couldn't possibly be unpalatable, hinged open his great jaws and tossed it down his throat, swallowing like he usually did without chewing.

"Rebecca," he said, wiping his sweaty brow because there had been too much pepper in the piece he had just ate. "I think I've got an idea just how I can get close enough to Andimi to make him loan me some money."

She was listening keenly, anticipating some wicked scheme to come out of him.

"Look at me, Rebecca, please," he said with some earnestness. "What I am about to tell you could be a bit shocking to you."

She did like he asked, knowing her suspicion had proved right, because no one had ever got close enough to Andimi to the extent they could borrow money off him, however diligent at work they might be. Not even Mudeya-Ngoko. And as she listened Rebecca knew that whatever she did or said, it would not deter Ang'ote from his chosen path. Her many years with their numerous hardships had taught Rebecca to recognize the evil bite of jealousy and the depravity it injected in a man. And so she just listened as he told her what his plan was.

Later, as they lay in the darkness underneath Ang'ote's worn old blanket, she begged him, "Please don't do it, Ang'ote."

"But why, my love? Don't you want us to be rich too, like everyone else?" There was the pained note of a convinced zealot in his straining voice.

"I mean, it is wicked, and you don't know what might come of it. In any case, riches that are acquired in that way hardly ever last."

Enraged, Ang'ote sat up in bed. "Just why do you have to harp on all the time about justice and righteous living, and

God knows what else, Rebecca, *eh*? Why do you drag me back with your stupid, old woman's fears every time I set my mind on a certain course, *eh*? Why? Why is it you've got to approve of every little thing I do, tell me why?"

The darkness was crackly with static. Rebecca moved farther away from him on the bed, pinning herself against the wall. She was afraid of his rage. But more, she was afraid of the cold steeliness in his voice. While earlier she had thought that people who had a love for music deep in their hearts could only live the kind of virtues the songs extolled, the kind of deeds that reflected their calm musical nature, this came as a sobering shock to her. This here was a totally different face of the gentle musician that she loved. Rebecca realized that both God and His once-upon-a-time angel, Satan, used the same mud in molding their beings.

In the end she decided that it was only better if she spoke her mind.

"Ang'ote, for all the things I might willingly do for you, I cannot be party to what you plan to do," she said in a calm composed voice. "No, I cannot," she was shaking her head in the dark, her voice trailing away to a whisper. "I just can't live with it."

"But why, my love?" Ang'ote's tone was gentler. He momentarily acknowledged he had just injured her self worth, and so naturally brought out the poet-musician in him to make amends. "Why, my precious flower that blooms for me even in my darkest hour, tell me why please." He moved closer and enclosed her in his arms, squeezing as gently as he could.

"I just can't," she whispered in a frightened little voice. Suddenly, his arms had taken on the embrace of an ogre.

"I want to assure you that I don't mean any harm at all, my love." He spoke directly into her ear. "I only want a better life for the both of us. I only want to get us out of this squalor and be rid of some of our endless problems. I assure you I mean well, my love," he cooed in a gentle voice that normally came out at that moment when the song had completely possessed him so he was one with it, rocking her slowly on the weak termite infested bed. But now that cooing sounded to her the same as the *manani* songs her grandmother sang to her as a child.

"I understand," she said in a frightened voice. "And I so much want for this life we lead to change. But then, why must you do it this way?"

He slipped his hand underneath her thin dress and rested his face in her soft grey hair. "I'll be as cautious in everything I do as I can, my love. I promise," he said. "Please look at it this way: here I am, so deep in love with you. And yet I cannot have enough with which to assuage my pride, *eh*? I cannot have enough to make you happy. Why must it be so, my love?"

"But *I am happy*," she whispered passionately. "I am happy the way I am, I tell you. I am happy enough for what little we have, and indeed that's why I am here with you right now. I don't need anything more to make me happier, Ang'ote. Certainly nothing that makes others unhappy."

"I know that already," he said, holding her even closer. "And indeed that's why you will always remain someone special to me. But then, like I said, I also want to give you something in return, however little. I want to give you a little token for all your trust and confidence in me, my love. I only want to give you a little 'thank you.' And surely you must understand my predicament. It is my innermost desire to afford you the pleasurable things that other people enjoy, and which have eluded the both of us all our lives. It is my desire that I take you out to Mbale to purchase whatever your heart desires without your having to look over your shoulder, worrying what we'll eat tomorrow. I'd like to take you to the *shoho* in Kakamega. Just how do you suppose I feel inside when I see my friends take their loved ones there? It rends my heart into pieces that all I can do is just sit and watch. Am I not man enough as they are? Please answer me in honesty. Were the good things in life meant only for other people and not you and me? No, I don't think so, my love."

A soft breeze rustled the tall cypress trees outside and in the distance a sleepless hound bayed.

"I loved you just the way you were," whispered Rebecca. But the wind blowing in the ruffled thatch at the apex of the old hut whooshed her words away.

Chapter Sixteen

ONE SUNDAY MORNING, a few days before Christmas day, Ombima had a pointless argument with his wife. It all started in the morning when he realized that things were going to go a little too fast for him that day. He knew days like this, when everything just seemed to go wrong.

It started as he was letting the two cows out in the morning. The tether on one of them got entangled on a nail sticking off the post-and-rail enclosure and he stayed back to fix it. Meanwhile the other cow wandered out the open door and headed in the direction of the banana trees. By the time he got the entangled cow freed, the other had worked its way through the new cabbage patch his wife had been struggling to establish. Sayo, when she realized that the munching noise outside that disturbed her as she prepared the morning meal was the cow ravaging her patch, shouted herself hoarse. And then Ombima, needing to wash his face, went into the bath shelter behind the house and found some dirty water in the broken pot that served for a trough, or so he thought. He poured it away and fetched some clean water from the pot in the kitchen. It turned out he had poured out Aradi's medicine.

"That was the boy's mix for fever that I had preserved there in order that I may reheat it for him today!" fumed Sayo. "Don't you know the child has a fever? Or can't you tell the smell of medicine? Now you'll have to go to the valley to fetch some more of the fever leaves."

Shaving with his newly honed razor outside, he was distracted by a crow perching on a banana leaf just above an elderly hen, which was scratching the ground for food for her ravenous brood. Looking up to shoo the bird away, the razor slipped and he cut himself badly on the side of the chin. He went into the house to find a piece of cloth with which to wipe the wound and, groping about on the bed in the dark bedroom, he found a soft piece of cloth thrown among the rumpled beddings, which he duly applied to the wound. But it turned out to be Sayo's white headscarf, the special one that she would match with her white church dress for the coming Christmas ceremony. It happened to have fallen from the clothesline hanging above the bed.

"Someone look at this madness!" The veins in Sayo's neck stood out like buttresses holding up her head. "The cloth I bought just the other day at the market, and the only white scarf that I have, covered all over in *blood*. And yet I had washed and pressed it only yesterday. Now what shall I wear to the choir? Ombima, tell me. Have you gone mad?"

Aradi was standing a little distance away pretending to be busy at play, while really he was listening in on the tirade. Ombima did not wait long enough to have breakfast. Going into the house, he came out shortly pulling on his shirt and left the compound, headed down the path to Eregwa's. He meant to pass by Ang'ote's place to ask him to accompany him for a beer. Word had gone round the village that the brewer had prepared a special brew for the Christmas season. But just as he branched off the wide path that led on to the *duka*, he bumped into Madam Tabitha.

His breath caught in his chest at the sight of her this early in the day and he stopped dead in his tracks. She was coming from the direction of the stream where her husband owned a farm under napier grass. She was in the company of the new boy who tended to the cattle, no doubt allocating him his work for the day.

At the sight of him, she waved the boy to walk on, and stopped. "How is your morning, Ombima?" she said, her eyes lighting up, extending a hand that was adorned with a thick bangle fashioned out of real ivory.

"Fine, Madam," said Ombima, suddenly feeling as if his throat was lined with a gauze of coarse steel wool. He shook her proffered hand and was certain she could feel him trembling.

"How did you sleep last night?"

He wondered for a while if she meant it in jest.

"Just fine, Madam."

She was standing very close to him, and he could feel her breath on his skin. She was gazing up at him and her darting eyes easily noticed the welt on his chin where the razor had slashed him.

"What is this gash?" she asked, touching it most tenderly with her fingertip. "You weren't in a fight with Sayo this early in the day, were you?" She was holding her head angled to one side, and there was that knowing look in her eyes, as if to say she wasn't exactly a stranger to such.

"I only cut myself with a razor, Madam," he said.

Just then someone was heard coming up the path from the direction of the stream whistling some church tune. The mood between them changed at once, but not before Madam Tabitha said, "Three days from now will be the climax of the night celebrations, Ombima. The drummers will come out and people will sing and dance all through the night to welcome Christmas. Come with me. I'll be waiting for you in the hedgerow just outside my compound. I'd like to go to the rock that night."

There was such charge in her words. And then, before Ombima could say anything in response, she was gone round the bend and up the path.

Ombima continued down the trail to Ang'ote's compound and almost bumped into Andwang'a, out already, laden with his knives and other ironware, knowing today was drinking day and that the school teachers would only be too easy on buying one a drink at the prospect of trading in something.

"Hey, look where you are going, mister!"

The look Andwang'a gave him was sour. "I almost got this blade here right into your abdomen." He was holding a hideous looking hunting knife with a saw tooth blade that glinted in the sun. "I don't want to start my good fortune for the day with an accident," he snarled when he saw Ombima was not the slightest bit interested in his wares. Still giving him a nasty look, he walked down the path, resuming his off-key whistling.

Ombima turned into Ang'ote's compound, his thoughts still whirling from the meeting he'd just had with Madam. Ang'ote was standing outside, grooming himself in a cracked flyblown mirror.

"I was just now wondering who would give me company to Eregwa's," he beamed when he saw Ombima. "I hear the old man has prepared real good stuff today in keeping with his tradition around Christmas."

"Actually, I meant to talk to you too," said Ombima, resting himself on the fallen log by the doorway on which Ang'ote usually received his few visitors. "The mother of my children this morning is like a nest of wasps, I tell you. I must have woken up on the wrong side of the bed."

"It's usually that way in marriage sometimes, my friend," Ang'ote said, as if he had prior experience of the matter himself. "You see, that's why sometimes I never regret this bachelor life I choose to live. I've had my fun while it lasted, you can be sure."

"You are right in that aspect," acquiesced Ombima. "But then, as a matter of fact, I don't particularly envy you."

There was a fresh pile of posts and rails against the wall of the leaning hut close to where Ombima was seated. "I can see you are making headway, Ang'ote," said Ombima, wandering over.

"Oh, it's only a drop in the ocean, my friend," said Ang'ote dismissively. "It's not even half the work."

"I see," said Ombima, fingering the tender spot on his chin. "I wonder what type of chicken house this will be."

Ang'ote paused, the piece of mirror held in front of him. Then he shrugged as if to say, I wonder too, but instead said,

"Give it time and you'll see." Then he seemed to remember something. "Ombima, I was thinking of clearing up some of the bush behind my house and reviving my bananas. Could you lend me your big hoe sometime next week, after Christmas?"

"Of course you may have it anytime you want, my friend." Ombima turned to his friend who was busy trying to run a wooden comb that had a few teeth missing through his crinkly hair. "I wonder who has convinced you to revive it at last. You never quite cared about bananas and vegetables before."

Ang'ote laughed into the mirror and gave no reply.

"They call it love," said Ombima lightly. "It makes a man of God out of an avowed atheist. You never used to comb your hair, Ang'ote."

"Oh, shut up," said Ang'ote, still smiling.

When Ang'ote had dressed up, they left in the direction of Eregwa's compound. And it seemed like they were just in time, for even from this far they could hear the merriment already in progress.

"So, how's the little affair with Madam going?" said Ang'ote casually as they walked down the dusty path, winking knowingly at his friend.

"Oh, *that*," Ombima passed a hand through his hair and gazed toward the hills in the distance shrouded in blue. "It's actually getting out of control, to be honest." He recalled the accidental meeting with her just a moment back and the reaction she had excited in him. "It's going rather fast for me, I must admit."

"*Ehe?*" prompted Ang'ote, interested. "Give me the news. I thought you were in control of the whole thing."

Ombima told him about the meeting he had just had with her, and the appointment she had given him for the night preceding Christmas.

"*Phe-e-ew!*" said Ang'ote on hearing the last bit. "You know what, Ombima? Now I am really starting to get jealous, like you said. I am starting to wish it were me in your shoes."

"Is it? I am afraid I must disappoint you."

"But why? I mean, if it were me plowing such a *shamba*, I would simply... fly! I mean, I'd feel great, because it is a big achievement for ordinary folk like you and me." There was a look of bewilderment on Ang'ote's sweaty face.

"Maybe you are right," said Ombima pensively. "Indeed I thought so too at first. It was pretty exciting, if I must say—and it still is! But then, I don't know. I'm starting to have some doubts. I don't know why I get this feeling all the time as if I am gradually being herded into a corner, as if my life is changing, you know what I mean?"

"Say, Ombima," Ang'ote patted him on the shoulder. "Don't tell me you are starting to have a chicken's heart... not this early, *bwana*! I never knew you to run away from a woman before. More so a pretty one!" The words were meant to sound encouraging. "You were always a fine old cockerel, my friend. What is it that has taken over you?" Ang'ote could hardly believe what he was hearing. "Just think about it," he added earnestly, "the woman could make you rich as you have never before imagined. Think of the money and the gifts she would avail to you if this love should really grow in her heart. *Think*, Ombima!"

Ombima, for some reason, could not find the words to answer his friend. The matter, all of a sudden, seemed so much more complicated than it had appeared at first. And so he relapsed into silence, troubled by his thoughts.

* * *

The ceremony for taking back the shadow of the deceased child, which was due shortly after Christmas, was going to be expensive. This was mainly because Sayo had exhausted almost all her resources during the funeral, and now there was hardly anything left. She knew that the church people and other guests would need to be fed, and certainly she was not going to feed them dry tea. There was still a little maize left for *ugali*, but what to serve with the *ugali* was the problem. If only she could find about two kilos of meat, then she was certain she would manage. She could make them a mix of many vegetables from the farm, provided there was a little meat in it to make it tasty. After all, who wasn't aware the dry season was hard on everyone?

It was while she was thinking about this ceremony that she remembered she still had to collect the money promised them by Andimi. And just in time because *that* would certainly save them the worry. What ways the good Lord uses to help his people! She had meant to send Ombima, but then he was rarely at home in the evenings these days. Just that morning he had stormed off without even having breakfast after messing up all over.

Seeing it was still early, she went in to get her headscarf, which she could not forget, at least not now while her head was still as bald as an egg. She would pass by Rebecca and ask her to give her company to Madam's house. Sayo hadn't seen Rebecca since the evening of the choir practice, and yet she was so used to her lately. Perhaps they might even have a talk about the women's *chama* they had been planning to start in the village to help them save the little money they earned and, hopefully, invest into a profitable self help project that they would agree on.

As she approached Rebecca's compound, Sayo thought she heard noises, as if an argument was going on. She wondered who could be picking on Rebecca, a woman who wouldn't harm a fly.

Rebecca was standing close to the fence with her hands on her hips, her grandchildren hiding behind a flower bush, listening. She was still in her farm clothes, her old *lesso* around her waist, feet covered in mud. On the other side of the fence was her neighbor, Kanaiza, holding a piece of cassava stem that had blunt stubs like fingers at the ground end where the fat tubers had been detached. She looked rather agitated.

Apparently, while she had been away working on her maize farm, someone had stolen into her kitchen yard and uprooted all the cassava she had wanted to prepare for lunch the following week. She had strong cause to believe it was Rebecca's grandchildren because they were the immediate neighbors.

"You tell me how a thief can come from the path and cross all these gardens and settle on mine, *eh*? Sayo, it is good you've come. Perhaps you can shed some light on this!" the woman said when she saw Sayo approach. "I tell you, this woman here shelters a gang of nifty little thieves in this house. One day they are going to turn into a real menace in this village, just you mark what I say!"

"Yes, indeed. As if your own were little angels." Rebecca was on the verge of tears, her eyes bloodshot with emotion. "Many people have lost their crop in this village, including me. And yet we don't go and shout it off on the hilltops for the whole world to hear. We bear our losses in silence. And yet you, Kanaiza, are like a mad woman whenever something of yours disappears. One would imagine you were more special than the rest of us who carry a pregnancy and birth the hard way!"

"Enough, enough, women," said Sayo, stepping between them. "Oh, swallow some of your dirty words, will you? It is still day and the whole village is listening in. Can't we talk this over in a more sensible way?" She shepherded Rebecca away from the fence into the house. When she emerged the other woman was still standing there, gesturing angrily with the cassava stem.

"Tell her that this matter doesn't end here! I'll wait for my husband to come back from the valley, and then we'll decide if we should take it further with the elders. I'm really fed up with this!"

"*Bayaa*, Kanaiza, hold on to your tongue," Sayo said. "These things happen, and you've been living well as neighbors a long while, so why should you break apart now? In any case, we don't even have evidence about anyone here. For all we know, the thief might have come from Kigama! And so, I beg you to go inside and let the matter settle some. You might be blaming the old lady's grandchildren for nothing, you see."

In the long run, Sayo persuaded Kanaiza to give it up for the time and even got her inside her house. But not before the other woman observed for the whole world to hear that she did not mind if one chose to harbor all the children of her children— even if they be in their hundreds—as long as they did not feed off other people's farms.

When Sayo went back inside, Rebecca was seated by the hearth with some of her grandchildren playing in the ashes close by. She was holding her head in her hands.

"You know, sometimes I really wonder if I should just send these children away to their mothers," she said when Sayo sat down. "It seems like no one likes them around here. I wonder what they ever did to them."

"Take heart, my friend," said Sayo edging closer. I know it's hard enough on you just keep keeping them fed. Perhaps they are just jealous that you are managing to do so single handedly."

"Oh, it really takes a heart of stone to live among such people," the older woman lamented, adjusting her headscarf on her grey head. "The things they say sometimes! Whenever someone's property disappears, it is always this house. I tell you, Sayo, it is starting to get unbearable!"

"Take heart, I say," said Sayo, patting her on the shoulder. "It will pass someday, be sure of it. God does not sleep, you know."

There was some porridge in the pot on the fire, which Rebecca offered her visitor, bringing down a calabash from the rack above the hearth. But Sayo declined. "I've got to see Madam about the money they promised us at the funeral and I was hoping you might come with me, if you have a moment to spare."

"Really, just now I was thinking of coming by your compound before this woman interrupted my plans. I was wondering about the shadow ceremony for the child."

Sayo was glad that her friend was taking her mind off the argument.

"I was thinking you could do with some bananas to help you host the church people. I've got a ripe one down in my garden. I know you squeezed yourself dry during the funeral—I know about them." A pensive look flipped over her furrowed face as she reflected on the death of her own husband many years back. Sayo was touched by the generosity of the offer, as well as the older woman's perception of her situation. But then, there was just no way she could accept the banana, not when Rebecca had so many mouths to feed.

"Thank you, Rebecca, but no. Let the children eat it. I know Madam will give me enough support. It's really most kind of you."

"Well, if you say so," said the other woman, shrugging. "But, just in case you need it, I will reserve it until after the ceremony—that is, if someone's child doesn't do me in as I wait!" She rose to her feet with a chuckle. "Give me a moment then, I'll just wash my feet and change out of these clothes."

She called to the eldest of the children and gave him instructions about what they would cook for the evening meal and then she stepped out into the little yard at back.

They found Madam in the company of one of her workers tending to passion fruit in the garden. "Oh, you'll probably not die soon, Sayo," she said coming over to greet them. "Just now I was thinking about you, and here you are!" They shook hands, and then she dispatched the boy she had been working with to fetch stools from the kitchen.

"Ah, so it's you who has been giving me hiccups since I left Rebecca's place, *eh*?" said Sayo, laughing.

"Really, it had a purpose. I've just met Oresha and she was mentioning to me about the *chama*. It seems like the women in Kisangula and Inyali are already into these things, and it's only us who are being left behind!"

"Indeed, we must do something," said Rebecca, sitting herself in the shade on the stool the boy had brought. "We must pull together to improve our lot."

"*Mwana*," Madam said in agreement, leaning against a trellis. "We certainly can't afford to have the children of this village become famous for theft of bananas and cassava because we are unable to educate them."

"True!" Sayo and Rebecca laughed approvingly at the observation, the latter rather uneasily, recalling her argument of just a while back.

"Did I hear someone mention *chama*?" asked the housemaid Midecha, joining them. She carried a tray with a teapot, some mugs, and a bowl of boiled sweet potatoes. "Rebecca, I heard your voice from a mile away. *Eh*, you are so lost, you and Sayo—I can't remember the last time you came by!"

"Is it?" said Rebecca, shaking hands. "But it is only the other day that I came to work!"

"You see—*work*. You didn't come to visit us."

"Indeed, Midecha is right," said Madam, reaching for a potato, which she proceeded to peel slowly.

Rebecca and Midecha came from the same maiden village in the hills in the south, and naturally they found that they were close. Indeed it was Rebecca who had shown Midecha the path to the well when she had been married in the village, and generally shown her the way about the new village. Rebecca too had been by her side when her husband had died after a snake bit him while he was out gathering weaving twine in the valley four years ago.

"I am sorry, my friend, I was committed," Rebecca now said, washing her hands in the bowl provided. "You know the duties of a woman are endless!"

"Especially so when she has to do it alone," added Midecha, a suggestive tone in her voice. "One wonders why it should always be the woman to take care of the family while the menfolk are somewhere having a good time with their money!"

"Oh, it is the curse we have to bear, I guess," said Madam, taking a bite of her potato, savoring the rich purple firmness inside. "It is a woman's curse, ever since the days of Hawa in the Bible."

"You speak the truth, Madam," said Sayo, reaching for her mug. "My Ombima back home is a fine example. We will work hard putting together our savings for something we want to do, and then one day the *mugoma* just decides it is spending time. And, mark you, there is nothing quite like a man who's set his mind on doing something—I tell you! In just a day, everything we had put together for a year will be gone!"

"It is the roots Eregwa brews into his beer, I think," said Midecha, laughing. "I remember mine when he was still around, he would drink until he pissed on himself! You know, one day I really had enough of him and I rolled up my sleeves and dared him with fire in my eyes and, you know what? The *muroji* took off into the night, straight into the pouring rain! I had never seen him look so scared, howling at our neighbor to come and save him from sure death! I think he spent the rest of the night in a tree."

The women laughed, trying to picture Midecha with her fists sticking up and Solongo, the late weaver, scared witless.

"You know, they are really quite scared all of them," said Madam, drying her eyes. "It is only that they conceal it so well. And that male showoff when they are angered is just that—a show. All it takes is a pin prick and then you'll see the coward underneath!"

"True... *eh!*" Sayo felt her side, tender from laughing so hard. Midecha looked admiringly at Madam, recalling the morning of the funeral and how she made *Mzee* change his plans.

Slowly a pile of potato peelings grew on the grass as they busied themselves eating. And then Rebecca paused, "*Mwana,* where did you get these potatoes?"

"They came from my garden here," Madam said proudly. "The seed vine came from far, though. *Mzee* brought it with him from Matsigulu."

"I knew it," said Rebecca, pouring more tea. "I haven't seen any quite so big around the village. They are like the ones from the market in Jivaswa."

"You mean like that one in the story which a man was made to carry to the land of *manani* as punishment?"

"Indeed. Jivaswa has always been famous for extraordinary things. I bet the people there use sorcery when they go to the farm. Surely they don't do it the same way we do."

"Oh, it is you who is in the dark, Rebecca," said Sayo with a wink. "I heard they use the droppings of an ant-bear for fertilizer, that's why. You know, those scary bears are still found in the many caves in the hills there."

"I've heard that too," Madam said. "I'll have to find someone from there and ask them if they can fetch some for me."

"Is it?" Midecha paused from pouring. "And you might just as well forget it, Madam. A *muroji* will go to the grave with his secret!"

They were in a good mood and talked about many things, and the afternoon slowly rolled on. Soon they finished the huge pot of tea. It was as the shadows were starting to lengthen that Sayo and Rebecca rose to take their leave.

"Ah, so soon!" Madam said, holding her palm cupped over her eyes to look into the blazing horizon. "It is just now that the two of you got here!"

"And the sun too was overhead just now," observed Rebecca, securing her *lesso* around her waist. "As you can see it is preparing to drop into the hills in *Imadiori*."

"Indeed, you are right." Madam excused herself and disappeared into the house. She reappeared with a manila envelope, which she handed to Sayo. "We really feel for you and Ombima, Sayo," she said as she walked them to the gate. "She was truly a sweet child."

"Oh, thank you so much, Madam. God will take care of everything, I trust. Why, you have made the burden half as light!" Sayo bowed low as she took the envelope, thanking the good fortune for taking care of the hosting ceremony ahead of her.

"It is nothing really, Sayo," Madam said. "I believe you would do the same for me."

The three parted a little down the path, with a promise to visit each other again soon. Rebecca branched off soon after Madam had left to go see about her grandchildren. And as Sayo watched her disappear through the trees, she got the feeling she was hurrying to finish off her chores before night fell, when she would sneak back this way to visit her lover. The two were getting rather inseparable lately, Sayo reflected.

Then her mind went back to her own life and she once again thought about her husband. The way he was behaving, forgetting things, disappearing for long hours in the evenings, smoking cigarettes... and lately he had not reached across the bed toward her. Sayo decided that the child's death must have affected Ombima much more than they realized.

Chapter Seventeen

THE VILLAGE WAS aglow with the Christmas mood. The walls of the houses all over reflected brightly, newly plastered in brilliant white clay that the children had brought from the valley. Some were covered in patterns of all designs made using a mix of soot and the juice extracted out of pumpkin leaves, which the children had applied with their fingers. Some had used fresh bananas as chalk to write Christmas messages above their doorways.

Everywhere one looked children ran about, busy in the last preparations for the big day they had all been waiting for. They ran with messages inviting friends and relatives to a big feast the following day. Some were sent to the *duka* to do last-minute purchases, maybe an additional bag of wheat flour, or a measure of frying oil, or a packet of baking powder for raising the *maandazi* to desirable shapes. At such a time no child refused to be sent. They were all excited, and as they trooped to and from the *duka* for their piecemeal purchases, it became such that Miroya had to abandon her other domestic chores and join her husband at the counter.

On the drying lines in the compounds hung strings of laundry the women had brought from the stream earlier in the day, where they had beat them against the streamside rocks until the fabric almost ripped. White and yellow linen danced in the wind, trailing from the sagging lines like many brightly colored flags. On the thatch roofs, those who had shoes had washed them and placed them there to dry, the leather slowly stiffening and curling in the sun so that when the time finally came, the wearer would have to brave a tight fit because the leather would have shrunk. The baskets in which the children would carry bottles of soda, biscuits, and pieces of sugarcane to the choir competitions in Kisangula were hung upside down on poles driven into the earth to dry. The few women who had iron boxes gave terse whispered instructions to their children to tell any visitors that Mama was not home, because everyone would want to borrow the iron to straighten their Christmas clothes.

The young men who had arrived from Nairobi announced their presence with blaring radios they had brought with them from the city, their sophisticated *Kisuaheli* spilling over the hedge around their compound loud and raucous, as if they meant to intimidate the village youth who had never set foot in the city.

Those in whose households such a relation from Nairobi had arrived were easily recognized by the ear-to-ear grins they wore, delighted at the presents they had received. Those who did not know anybody in the city were not to be left out either. They dipped in their huge metal trunks stowed away underneath their beds in the inner rooms, which contained the family heirlooms, and brought out their treasured items. They beat the old shoes for dust and measured the not-quite-long-enough flannel trousers against their leg and, ascertaining them still in condition enough to do yet another occasion, went about getting them as clean as their delicate condition would allow. All the farms were deserted, at least for today, and no one did any meaningful work other than wash and scrub. There was merriment in the air, everything happy and free, save for only one: the big cockerel that would be slaughtered the following day, which was now restrained in a tiny reed hutch behind the main house, gazing lingeringly at a few scattered grains through the slats on its confining walls.

The whole village was pulsating in the joy and excitement—and even the little tension—of Christmas.

For the third day, Eregwa's compound was abuzz with humanity, drunks from all the villages in the neighborhood crawling the cramped space of the brewer's compound like bees on a matured hive. Ombima and Ang'ote made straight for the back of the house where the brew was being served.

* * *

The day passed slowly and strenuously, perhaps because of all the anxiety. For Ombima, time seemed to remain suspended as if in a haze. He did not know why he did not seem to get drunk, despite the barrels of beer he drunk. And yet all around him everyone was sleepy-eyed, their knees unable to keep them upright with every *gorogoro* of beer they downed. As for the drinkers they descended on Eregwa's compound in droves, especially as the sun climbed up into the sky. Soon all the beer was finished. And so, disappointed, they left for the neighboring village across the valley where it was said someone else had brewed.

By evening, Ang'ote was very drunk. As he and Ombima made their way back home through the dense valley he broke into song. Those few from their village who accompanied them soon caught up with them and joined in Ang'ote's song, which progressively turned into a drunken chant. When they reached Ombima's gate, Ang'ote said he was going to look for drummers—real drummers—and put up the greatest dance Maragoli had ever seen. But Ombima, who was hardly drunk, heard all these—the singing and the bravado from a distance. He had been nervous all day.

And so as the sun went down Ombima sat outside his compound watching, a distant look in his eyes because his thoughts were far away. There was no one around, all having gone to the final choir practice, the women knowing they would only have to reheat the soup pot to go with the *ugali* at supper. In any case, it was not to say the menfolk would be getting home any earlier either. With all the drinking the men would most certainly stumble in during the small hours of the night.

The drumbeats and voices raised in song filled the air from all round. It made those who were not participating feel like they were missing out.

* * *

Ombima's unease was such that he could barely sit still. Through his hut's open front door the night insects slowly came buzzing in, drawn by the dancing flame of the tin lamp on the table. He watched a fat brown moth circle the flame, its motion getting faster and faster as it burned with a passion that only the flame could assuage. Then it tired and dropped on the table where a giant black beetle lay upside down, its claw-like feet circling feebly in the air like a newborn baby's, unable to get back upright. In the open field outside, the fireflies swam in a fiery display, particularly bunched above the spot where Saliku's grave was. Ombima saw these and was filled with premonitory thoughts. Sayo still had not come back, and neither had Aradi.

Unable to stand the loneliness any further, he blew out the lamp, locked up, and left the compound. He strode casually down the village path, pausing to light a cigarette from a crumpled pack that by now had become a constant companion.

He became quite tense as he approached the entrance to Andimi's compound. He hoped Madam had not been serious. He hoped she had gone off to the choir to join the other village women and forgotten about it. But as he went past the high gate, he heard a rustle in the trimmed hedge and saw her emerge through a gap in the cypress fence.

"You've kept me waiting," she said in that accusatory voice that he was well used to by now. She was dressed in a long silken gown that covered the whole length of her, draping her plump body in that exciting way she had appeared the first time they had met in her fruit garden. She was adjusting a velvet shawl around her shoulders, as if she was about to embark upon a long journey.

Looking at her, standing there suddenly in front of him on the deserted path, Madam looked to Ombima like a character out of the stories he had often heard Sayo tell the children as she prepared the evening meal. There was always a wounded heroine. That's the image Madam Tabitha now conjured in Ombima's mind—a wounded heroine. And this particular evening, with all the magic of Christmas in the air, Ombima empathized with her.

"Come on, let's go!" Madam Tabitha whispered with urgency, coming up so she walked close by his side. "I can't wait to get to the rock. I wonder what it will feel like up there when the new moon shows itself."

Ombima caught the heady perfume in her hair that had captivated him on that first night they had met. Tonight it seemed even stronger, dulling all the good sense left in him. He glanced back over his shoulder at the huge stone house rising above the trees in the manicured gardens. There was a light burning in one of the wide glass windows, but otherwise it looked like some huge harmless mammoth of limestone and baked tile that might even be dead. Nevertheless, Ombima got this creepy feeling that those dark windows just might have eyes that watched everything.

Madam Tabitha seemed to see what he was thinking and whispered, "Don't worry about him, he's not there. And there is no chance of him coming either. He has left on a trip to Nakuru, to see about a business he's trying to establish there. He won't be coming back until tomorrow," she added, as if Ombima had actually asked about him.

She linked her soft hand in his and urged him on up the path, the warmth of her flesh pressing into his side and electrifying him out of his senses. Her strong presence somehow drove all the fear out of him, relaxing his tense tissues the way a soothing balm might relieve a cramped muscle. Even then, deep in the recesses of his mind, a vague uneasiness lingered.

They walked on down the path, arm in arm, finding instant peace in each other's company. They were quiet, as if fearful of the sharp ears all the inanimate objects around them seemed to have. The voices of the choir sounded muffled and distant, coming from inside the church building where the singers had been driven by the evening chill. Only an occasional dog barked, but otherwise, no one was around on the path. It felt eerie just the two of them walking in the deserted village that lulled underneath the blanket of night. At one point Madam, mesmerized by the magic of the night, found a rock by the side of the path and sat down and refused to budge. She was staring wide-eyed at the millions of stars arrayed above. Ombima sat down too and they just stayed there gazing, lost for words. It was a long while that they just sat there touching, savoring the closeness of the other. And then they remembered the merry makers and they rose.

It was as they neared the gravel road close to Kisangula that they heard the sound of drumming. And there was no doubt it was a huge gathering because their voices, strained in the passion of the song, carried through the maize fields like the march of a whole army. These voices were coming from the direction of Simboyi, and they rose and faded on the night breeze, tantalizing everyone still inside their houses.

"Quick, Ombima, let's go!" Madam said. All of a sudden the earlier plan of going up to the hill was forgotten. "Let's go join them! Come on!" She tore off through the maize fields in the direction from which the singing came, loping over bushes like a little girl, incensed by the mounting excitement. Ombima ran after her, creating a path where the bushes would part. He knew the path that cut through the fields and joined the gravel road at Simboyi but for some reason, he just couldn't figure it out. Everything looked different in the moonlight. And in any case, Madam was paces ahead of him and there was nothing to do but follow.

The frenzied drumming rent the moonlit night as the drummers got closer. Weaving in between the belly-filling beat of the long drums was the unmistakable piercing voice of Ang'ote who had just joined the singers and taken over as soloist from the young men. He called out the lead verses with the masterly experience of age and practice, while the throngs of young people chanted back in unison, their footfalls, which caused the earth to shake as they neared, like a legion of infantrymen marching to battle. Madam Tabitha and Ombima ran on, impatient to join the revelry.

The night revelers had come together, young and old, from all the surrounding ridges and assembled on the road. It was a dense column of humanity that Ivona had not witnessed on any other day of the year. Not even the crowd that had gathered at the inauguration of the new chief had been anything close to this.

They spanned the whole breadth of the road with some running through the bushes alongside, all thronging forward like one great army of safari ants. They had broken off twigs and branches from the roadside trees, which they now waved above their heads like fly whisks, the enormous thumping of a thousand feet kicking up a cloud of dust so thick only those on the flanks of the swirling mass were visible. The rest were drowned in the thick yellow dust easily seen from a mile away.

There were the young, their bodies lithe and lanky, muscles stiff and firm. There were also the middle-aged women with full breasts jigging under their loose bodices, their farm-toughened calf muscles shaking to the stomping of bare oiled feet while their men watched from the sidelines, in their keen eye visible the heartwarming pride that they had selected well after all. There were old men in throng too, tired bones rattling to the irresistible invigorating rhythm that they had danced to more energetically in their day. They were all there because the drumbeats made the old bones lighter and the weakening heart younger. There were children in the crowd too, their bright eyes wide with excitement, thrilled at the one chance in the year to do adult things without a condescending, parental presence watching over them. There were married couples and secret lovers dancing side by side, just like there were hangers-on who did not have a companion but who went along with the stream, glad that they could get close to a mate they admired and steal their warmth, or even hold them in the pretext that they were drunk of the dance, confident that no one would tell who they were because in the pale moonlight, everyone else looked the same.

They were unified by the invigorating beat of the drum. It strung them together, young and old, tall and short, like a string through thousands of beads. It throbbed through them as through one body, their song echoing throughout the stone hills of Maragoli.

Ombima searched for Madam Tabitha in the crowd. All of a sudden he was afraid that he was going to lose her and that if he did, that he would not find her again. The drums beat to a frenzy and the swollen crowd inched on, a giant swirl that swept everything along and which was so large nothing would stand in its way, not even the new chief's *serikali*.

Ang'ote, the soloist, hooked into a fresh tune:

Mpenzi wangu wacha lala,
Utaenda asubuhi…

My love, please stay,
You'll leave with the dawn…

And the frenzied crowd picked it up:

Saa hii ni usiku,
Na njiani kuna wakora…

Right now it's late,
You'll be attacked by the wayside rogues…

The women shrieked. They ululated. They were stirred by the lyrics of the popular song. Those among them who were married remembered with nostalgia when their men had first turned up at their father's compound with a proposal. For the young maidens, a madness clawed at their lonely hearts and they inched their way toward the flanks where the young men could dance pressed against them, stimulated by the touch of a stranger.

A thousand feet stamped the yellow gravel and a rumbling like thunder roused those in the houses and brought them outside to join in the merriment. The high note that the song had ascended to incensed the drummers and they struck harder on their long drums, which were so heavy they had to lean back to support them on their hips. Rivulets of sweat broke through their hairline and soon they were glistening all over, their bodies like pieces of polished ebony smothered in oil. Their assistants, seeing they were thirsty for a smoke, placed a cigarette in their mouths and lit it for them.

Ombima saw a gleaming face bobbing above the crowd and elbowed his way forward.

"Madam!" he cried into her ear, grasping her elbow. But she only threw her arm around his shoulder and forced him to dance with her, jabbering incoherently above the din, her eyes wild with excitement. She wriggled her body and rolled her hips to the tantalizing beat, sweating freely so her flowing dress stuck to her back and thighs. She had lost the shawl that had been draped on her shoulders, and now the valley between her bared breasts showed beneath her deep neckline.

Ang'ote must have tired for another soloist picked up:

Amusavi, kuba indumba...
Amusavi, please beat your drum...

To which the frenzied crowd roared back:

Amajungu gasieve ku!
So that the rats may do a jig!

The children in the crowd rallied back in a chorus, tickled by the childish rhyme. In the moonlight, their teeth were like a thousand cornrows, their eyes shiny with tears of joy. The air was no longer fresh but warm, charged with the vigorous activity, pungent with the smell of human sweat and dust. Occasionally, a whiff of warm marijuana smoke was caught on the air, sweet and grassy and distinct. And as the balmy night rolled on, the crowd surged forth, headed for the market of Kiritu just round the bend.

* * *

One of the people who had been drawn out by the noise and revelry was Andimi. Earlier that evening, as the sun's last rays faded and the night sky had started to come alive with a million twinkling little stars, his car had come slowly down the village path, unusually dusty from the long journey he had to make in the late afternoon.

Everything had been going well, just as planned, and indeed Andimi had gotten off on his journey to Nakuru. The business he needed to conduct there was of vital importance, and he wished that everything would go well. And then he had gotten to Kisumu and stopped to fuel his car and check the wheels, a little cautious because this was a rather long journey for his modest Peugeot. He had been meaning to get a better car now that he had to travel quite far from home. Maybe a Mercedes, which would enable him leave the Peugeot to his wife to use around the village. In any case, the Peugeot hardly fit his status these days. Indeed he was aware that his friends said things behind his back whenever he attended serious functions. A man of means needed to travel well.

It was while they had been checking the car that Andimi had suddenly remembered an old Asian friend of his who lived in the Tom Mboya area with whom he had conducted business while he supplied school uniforms, and whom he had not seen for a long time. He wondered if he still lived in his old residence along Kibos Road. Andimi decided to drop in after the car was ready and say hello to him. A man needed to keep in touch with old friends because he might never tell when they might turn useful.

It was at his friend's house that he had got news that the Asian realtor he sought in Nakuru, coincidentally a family friend of his host's, had left town just the previous day to join his family in Nairobi for the Christmas festivities.

At first Andimi was disappointed by the news, being such a stickler to the rules. He believed that every little thing that one indulged in should be according to a preplanned schedule, and that appointments, especially business ones, should be honored at all costs. But then, realizing there was not much he could do in this season that could amount to as much as a ten-cent sale, he decided that it was just as well the fellow had skipped the appointment. He could join his wife in the festivities and spend some time with her. He realized, with a slight pang of guilt, that of late he had been spending even less and less time in his house, always on the move chasing business. Perhaps it was time he made up to his wife and everyone else, he told himself, suddenly assailed by a magnanimous sense of goodness.

It was a long bumpy ride home, but he did not mind. It might just be for the better that he was taking a while off to relax. He arrived in the village to a household of servants only.

Midecha answered the door and relieved him of his brief-case and coat.

"You didn't go off to the choir practice like everyone else?" he asked as he loosened his tie, glad that she was there, because right then a cup of good *tangawizi* tea like only she knew how to make was just what he needed to help him unwind.

"No, *Mzee*. My old frog's voice would only make it worse," she said laughing. "They are better off without me, I am sure. What can I get you, *Mzee*?"

"Right now," Andimi crossed the airy lounge and sank into his favorite cane chair in the adjoining patio with a sigh, "a cup of good strong tea would feel like heaven!"

"In a moment, *Mzee*." She padded off down the hall, a warm contented smile on her dark face. It was as if she knew she was the best, something there was no doubt about.

He kicked off his shoes and swung his feet onto the stone balustrade, enjoying the cool breeze that just then swept up from the pink-splashed valley below. He loved this perch up here above the trees. It always made him feel very pleased with all that he had achieved in the world of business, which had been up and down and down and up to say the least.

The maid brought in the tea and set it on a carved coffee table he had bought from an old Malindi Arab in the year he had established his first Day & Night Boarding Hotel in the seedier part of the town. As the maid went about pouring, Andimi caught himself wondering about her.

Midecha was quite the opposite of his wife, Tabitha. Where Tabitha would have brought out warm milk in a jug and tea in a pot for him to mix his own cup, Midecha did everything in the kitchen in the traditional way. And she brewed a perfectly balanced cup. It was as if her fingers were measuring cups and scales, while Tabitha would have fussed about with all sorts of kitchen tools. Andimi, now that he thought about it, realized with a faint smile that he was quite comfortable with the maid's village ways. Her little bowing acts when presenting meals and her general lack of sophistication. They made her feel like an old tree that is going to wood, but which cannot be chopped down as yet because there is a bucket-shaped seat at the foot of its warped old trunk that holds pleasant memories.

He took a sip of the tea and leaned back in his chair, crossing his hands behind his head. The breeze blew the treetops and brought with it the faint scent of the moonflower in the garden. It was not a bad idea to have come back home after all.

As he sat there, taking all this in, thoughts about his children briefly entered his head. Esendi, the first and bright one whom he hoped would make a fine doctor when she completed her medical studies. Perhaps she would find work in a big hospital in Nairobi and become a famous cardiologist, and bring honor to his name. That one had followed his every wish, and he had never found cause for complaint in her.

And then there was Damaris and Mmbone. Well, to be quite honest with himself, he was not exactly thrilled about having a systems analyst and a newsroom editor in the family. In any case, he did not quite comprehend what these careers entailed. What exactly they did he was not sure of. He was convinced that people like them did not quite make heads turn in a crowd. Perhaps he might just persuade the girls otherwise next time he visited. He was certain, though, that it must have been on their mother's advice that the two had made those choices. He could still recall how vigorously she had defended the girls, saying a child had the right to what she wanted. No wonder she was stuck at the village school, never bothering to better herself. It was for their own good that he had insisted the children go for their studies abroad, so he told himself. Andimi's children had to be able to stand shoulder to shoulder with the children of those who mattered in the district, at whatever cost.

But then there was the last, and his most loved child, Cindy. Now here, in the deep privacy of his thoughts, Andimi's resolve wavered. It was indeed with a heavy heart that he had seen this one off, even though not a soul of the few clanspeople who had gone to see her off at the airport had known this. This girl never ceased to amaze him with her fascination with machines. Even at the age of four she was already hanging onto his arm wanting to know what he was doing tinkering behind the hood of the old Peugeot whenever they stalled in the middle of the road. At the end of her five-year mechanical engineering course, he would see to it that she came to work in Kakamega or Kisumu, at least somewhere close to home. He silently vowed that he would push his weight around to achieve that. And the girl had scored good grades for it too. So much brain for such a small girl. How he wished she had been a boy.

He started to wish they were home for Christmas. At least Cindy should have been home. Now that he ruminated on it, he realized just how quiet the house had become, especially after her departure the previous year. Right now the walls would be ringing with her laughter as she harassed the servants about this last-minute decoration for Christmas that hadn't quite gone the way she wanted, or something rare she especially wanted for dinner on Christmas Eve. Indeed some achievements in life came at a price, sometimes a pretty heavy one at that.

Just then Midecha appeared on the patio to announce a visitor, interrupting Andimi's reverie. Thinking it was probably just one of those farmhands coming to ask for a little money to spend during Christmas, Andimi bellowed to let them in, rather irritated that whoever it was should be disturbing his evening calm, but also realizing that his wife was not around to take care of such nuisance.

Ang'ote was led through the airy living room that he had only seen through the windows, all royalty with cushioned seats and dark varnished surfaces that looked even more breathtaking at close range, to the back patio where the wealthy man was having his tea. He knew that he was drunk, and that he should rightfully have gone round to the back of the house and awaited the wealthy man to come down to him there after he was through with his tea, instead of walking up to the front door like that. He was even remotely surprised that he had been let into the big house at all. But then, he was not about to turn back because this was something pretty important for his personal development and was quite certain that the wealthy man would want to take time to listen to him.

Ang'ote had seen the green Peugeot turn the bend in the path from the village *duka* while he had been leading the band of drunken stragglers to go search for drummers. It was strange because he realized it was what he had really been hoping for, even as he told his friend Ombima about the greatest dance Maragoli had ever seen. He had abandoned his friends in a hurry, his eyes shining, just as the red taillights of the little car turned into the open high iron gates. There could never be a more opportune moment, he thought, even as the image of Rebecca flitted briefly through his mind, especially since he had spied Madam Tabitha headed in the direction of the church a moment earlier.

Andimi looked up from his tea, his dark eyebrows curling slightly upward when he saw who the visitor was. He placed the cup gingerly on the antique coffee table and turned around slowly in his padded cane chair.

Below him the manicured gardens rolled on and on, a multiple splash of color among which the insects trafficked in a collective buzz.

"*Ah*, Ang'ote!" The surprise on Andimi's face was barely concealed.

"Good day to you, *Mzee*," said Ang'ote, stepping through the connecting sliding doors that he had never dreamt he would cross. Midecha, seeing the uncertain look on her master's face, hovered nearby, no longer so sure she had done the right thing bringing Ang'ote here. Ang'ote looked all the farmhand that he was, and worse—tattered old woolen coat and faded brown trousers rolled up to the knees and patched on the seat—though mercifully concealed underneath the long tails of the coat that was a size too big. As he crossed over, the nails in the soles of his worn *akala* shoes rang out against the polished wooden floor as if loudly punctuating the fact that he was entering a place far beyond the realm of people of his ilk.

"How was your day?" said Andimi, getting to his feet and wearing a cheerful smile that only he could slip on at any time at will, and which made it hard to know exactly what he was thinking. He even held out a hand, which Ang'ote shook eagerly, the drink in his head making him feel like a king.

"Oh, very good, *Mzee*," Ang'ote answered brightly, his brown teeth bared in a wide grin.

"Well..." Andimi was never one for small talk, and indeed he looked very much like a pretender whenever he had to. "So, I see you are gearing yourselves up for Christmas?"

"Indeed, we are." Ang'ote was faintly amused, seeing the wealthy man didn't know exactly what to do. He took his time, letting him squirm a little. In the meantime, he indulged himself, partaking of the vista of the distant hills seen through the tall trees at the fringe of the valley that had made such a restful companion to the wealthy man's evening tea before he had interrupted. In the recesses of his drunken mind Ang'ote wondered why some people had so much and others so little. Maybe some were just created lesser beings...

"Well, aren't you going to sit down?" Andimi asked when he saw that his unusual visitor wasn't going to speak up. The smile was no longer there and he was now weary of the man. "I was just having my tea."

"Thank you," said Ang'ote, selecting a seat across from Andimi's and sinking into the padded softness, all ease and calm. He almost laughed out aloud for the thrill.

Andimi, now getting wearier, having gotten over the shock of seeing the small man, cleared his throat and asked Midecha to fetch another cup. There was an awkward silence as they waited, during which Andimi spooned sugar into his dainty china cup and made a ruckus of stirring, clearing his throat with a coarse raspy sound all the while, as if something real viscous was stuck in there.

Midecha came and poured Ang'ote his tea. Her fluttering gaze hardly left the table as she did so, her lips sucked in dutifully. It was as if she was wondering what madness had gotten into the little man.

"How many spoons?" she asked faintly, holding the sugar bowl. And for a while there Ang'ote was tempted to say, "ten." It was such pleasure to be attended to by the lady, who normally wouldn't let the laborers any further than the threshold of her immaculately kept kitchen whenever they went to ask for some of the cold drinking water from the master's magic icebox. Ang'ote cleared his throat and said, "Two will do, thank you."

After she had retreated—not without an acid sideways glance cast furtively his way—Ang'ote took a sip of his tea, then another, and sat back in the comfort of the cane chair, finally discovering the secret behind the good health of the wealthy man and his wife.

"Well, what brings you here, Ang'ote?" Andimi asked. He had seen that the waiting game was going to extend into the night if he allowed it. He turned around and glowered at Ang'ote with that fixed stare that said, it-had-better-be-good-enough-too, little man.

Oh, so now I have your full attention, big man. Ang'ote drew back his feet from under the table and looked at his dusty toes, searching for an apt word. Then he suddenly looked up, straight into the wealthy man's glowering eye, and said simply, "Gossip, *Mzee*."

Andimi took a while digesting what he had heard, and then his eyebrow rose all too slowly, yet again caught by surprise by the little man's manner. "Gossip, you say? What about?"

Ang'ote decided it was time to quit the game. And so, licking his lips, he said calmly, "About Madam, *Mzee*."

Andimi placed his cup slowly on the table and pushed his seat forward, licking his lips slowly. And as their gazes met Ang'ote was aware that he was staring into eyes that could do a common village layabout with some ideas on his mind far worse than a little harm. *Well, it was about time...* he told himself, not flinching in the wealthy man's stare. In any case, he had better be out with it soon enough and be off to the celebrations. And so—taking a deep breath—he returned the wealthy man's stabbing gaze, still bolstered by the beer he had taken, and proceeded to spill the saucy beans that he had been keeping down his throat all this while, detail by graphic detail.

As the mischievous farmhand with a heavy secret left in a hurry through the airy lounge a moment later, his *akala* shoes still echoing irritably against the polished wooden floor, Andimi got slowly to his feet. Suddenly, there was a strange look in his dark eyes.

* * *

The revelers were tired, most of the zing with which they had commenced the dance having ebbed. Now they dragged their feet in the dust and waved their heavy arms above their heads, the singing waning to just a few struggling croaks as they made their way slowly uphill. Those who were too flushed out leaned against their equally exhausted companions and made them drag an additional load uphill. Even the drummers no longer struck their drums with as much vigor. As if by general consent, the song ceased and the soloist allowed everyone a moment of respite in order that they may revitalize themselves for the stretch still ahead.

They had gone all the way to Kiritu, singing and dancing. No one knew where the revelry would take them next, only that it would go until daybreak. The young men wanted to go all the way to Matsigulu and even Mbale, but the elderly were wary.

In the silence, the singers lit cigarettes and passed them round. One young man produced a jerrycan of water and doused the lead drummer to refresh him. In response the short slim fellow flashed a toothy grin around as he brushed the water from his face. It was obviously something routine.

In the lull, Ombima saw Madam Tabitha sitting among a group of young women, her dress gathered between her dusty legs, face glistening with sweat. He looked at her inquiringly, wordlessly asking if she was tired. And she, judging what was on his mind from his raised eyebrows, turned her head sideways indicating that she would go on. Ombima smiled, happy in his silent communication.

At first he had been hesitant about joining in the revelry. But surprisingly, now that he had done the whole lap to Kiritu, he was no longer unsure. All of a sudden he felt invigorated, and all that rang in his ears was the sonorous beat of the long drums in which twined the thin ring of the metal triangle. He had gradually soaked in the spirit of the dance until he became a part of it, throbbing along with the rhythm. Later, he would see that it had been his first day of complete happiness since Saliku died.

A glowing butt was passed in their direction and Tabitha grabbed it and took it to her lips. She inhaled the cigarette for a while. And then she spat out suddenly when the thick smoke hit her at the back of the throat and she broke into a coughing fit.

"That is not an ordinary cigarette!" Ombima said, alarmed, taking the piece from between her fingers. He threw it away into the bushes, an admonishing look spreading on his face. "Never take things from strangers, isn't that what you say to your pupils?" he said, sitting down next to her. "We are mixed up with all sorts of people in this crowd, just you remember that. The cover of night brings all sorts of people!"

"Oh, do you have to be so patronizing?" Madam asked, laughing, glad that they were happy, the two of them out here tonight, melted into the concealing blanket of nighttime strangers.

He wanted to laugh freely like she was doing, but was afraid that the people around might think him insane.

She was leaning heavily on his arm as the *gengere* gong was struck and the trudging crowd resumed the dance and moved toward Kisangula. She felt heavy on his shoulder, and he was about to complain. But then, without warning, she straightened and grabbed hold of his arm and started dragging him away from the crowd into the bushes by the roadside. Someone close by laughed. But Ombima was too stoned on all the fun around to care.

She dragged him further away from the crowd till they were just the two of them on the warm moonlit night. It was only then that he realized she was leading him up into the hills, and that down beneath, the voices of the revelers receded down the road in the direction of Simboyi.

"What are you doing, Madam? Where are you taking me?" Ombima asked, his voice suggesting he already knew the answer.

"I am so happy tonight," she said in response. "I want us to be just the two of us."

He stumbled on a loose rock just after she had spoken and almost lost his balance, grabbing at a banana tree that had freshly been planted by the path side to mark the ceremony of the coming day at the school. But just as he steadied himself, she lost balance herself and the next instant she came crashing fully into him, sweeping him onto his back, felling the banana tree.

"Look what you've done!" Ombima said, struggling to push her off him. But she only laughed and held on. They rolled in the dewy grass for a while before her back came to rest against a small rock, stopping their progress. Tabitha was laughing all the while, the fun of the moment pulsing through her veins.

In the shadows down the path along which they had come something shifted and the faint sound of dried twigs crushing was heard. But then they were too far gone into each other to hear a thing.

"Let's go up to the rock," she was saying, hanging onto his arm. And there was nothing he could do, seeing as she was set on leading him there tonight. And so he followed, his heart palpitating in the excitement of their senseless escapade. Side by side they made their way across the school field, which was awash in the silvery light of the new moon overhead.

On one side of the field the school's wooden desks had been brought out of the classrooms and arranged in rows underneath the shade of the tall *misinya* trees close to the main assembly. On these desks would sit the guests who would grace the ceremony. A little dais of tree branches had been erected at the front for the judges.

The school's night watchman, a little old man wrapped up in a frayed woolen trench coat, was sitting sprawled on one of these desks, his jaw hanging slack, a stream of saliva dripping out of his mouth. On the desk in front of him was the huge club he always carried to the job, together with a crooked old bow and a couple of poisoned arrows. The old man was steadily snoring, too drunk on the beer he had consumed at Eregwa's compound earlier that day to stay awake on the job.

The two lovers, oblivious of the presence of the sleeping guard, made their way across the field and climbed into the line of rocks at the other end, disappearing out of sight.

Ombima felt tight in the head. He did not know if it was the beer he had drunk earlier in the day that had suddenly gone to his head or maybe the folly of what they were doing. All he knew was that he was dazzled by the bright light of the moon that made objects sway in his vision.

Madam Tabitha knelt in front of him on the rock, shrugging off one shoulder of her sweat-dampened dress. In the moonlight, her rounded face looked pale and silvery, her eyes glowing seductively from their shadowed pits.

He watched her shrug out of her dress and slowly come toward him, her nude body traced in the metallic moonlight like a goddess cut out of marble.

"Don't worry, Ombima. We are going to get married tomorrow," she was saying as she sat beside him, cutting out the light of the overhead moon as he too began to undress. "Wouldn't it be a lovely thing to do on Christmas day?"

A long shadow cut across the flat rock and the next minute Ombima saw a thickset, dark figure looming up above her smoothly sculpted profile. Whoever's head it was lowered and his shoulders tensed into an intimidating posture. Ombima quickly shoved Madam Tabitha aside and pushed himself into a sitting posture. Simultaneously the hunched figure darted across the flat rock, making directly for him.

Madam Tabitha crashed heavily onto her elbow and cursed aloud. At the same time she spun around and saw the presence that had caused the commotion. The dark figure was wielding some kind of weapon that glinted coldly in the moonlight, and there was no doubt about his intent. She reared back in fright and screamed.

Ombima was up on one knee, reaching for his clothes strewn among hers on the rock. He heard a thin whizzing sound like an object flying through the air and before he could tell what it was, something cold and hard struck him on the side of the head.

He started to fall, his head spinning with the impact of the sudden blow. As he fell, he struggled to keep his gaze focused on the burly figure that was looming menacingly above him, his thick shoulders framed in what looked like sackcloth that was loosely draped about him, and which hung open on either side.

From the edge of his vision, he saw Madam Tabitha rise to her feet and launch herself at the figure, screaming her head off. There was a dull thump as she was swept aside and the next moment Ombima was seized by the neck, and was staring eye to eye with the dark intruder.

"You snake!" spat a low thin voice vaguely familiar to Ombima and laden with hate. "How dare you?"

Suddenly, Ombima was flung back and as he fell, his head struck a sharp edge of the rock and he felt his brains explode all over inside his skull, followed by a sharp pain and a warm wetness that spread slowly on the skin at the back of his head, soaking into his hair.

He rolled onto his side in an instinctive effort to save himself and slipped over the edge of the hanging rock. He started rolling downhill through the thorny bramble like a log, banging against outcropping rocks. In his fear, every thought told him to make sure he got as far away from his attacker as he could, no matter what.

But down the hill the hooded attacker came, no doubt intent on getting his hands on him, seeking to mete out justice for what misdeed only he knew.

Ombima broke his fall and braced himself to face his attacker, seeing there was nowhere to run.

"I want your eyes," the attacker was whispering through clenched teeth, the thin voice incensed like a madman's. "I want your eyes, you snake!" he spat out. "Why did you covet what was rightfully mine? Eh? Why did you break my leg? Well, this is your unlucky day, and you must pay, my man!" The voice was very cold, condemning. It sent a shiver up Ombima's spine. "I want your eyes, my man. That is your punishment for stealing from me. NOW!"

Ombima shook with fright, watching the slow approach of the hooded figure. He tried to grab a rock with which to defend himself, now convinced that he was facing a madman, but then all his groping fingers gouged out of the earth were just clumps of loose dirt and wet grass. Seeing the figure was almost upon him and that he still had nothing with which to defend himself, he braced himself and hurled the clods of dirt into the man's face.

The advancing attacker stopped short and raised his hands to brush the dirt out of his face, at the same time as he uttered a low curse that was charged with rage. In the suspended moment Ombima thought of breaking for it downhill, if only to save himself. But he hesitated too long. The next minute the attacker uttered a bone-chilling cry and flung himself bodily at Ombima, his clawed hand going for his face. Ombima felt a tearing pain as a deep rent was made in his face with the claw-like fingers. This was followed by a sharp thump right into the back of his skull. He cried out in sudden convulsions.

For a terrified while the two of them grappled among the thorny bramble. Then Ombima managed to toss his heavy attacker away and sprang to his feet. He tried to find his bearings, but then a slab of rancid warm wetness was hanging over the painful left side of his face, leaving him with sight in only one eye. He swooned back, almost losing his foot, and dropped to one knee.

Twisting his face around, he looked uphill and saw Tabitha racing downhill. At the same time, far behind her, he heard a sharp sound of a whistle, accompanied with cries of "Help! Thieves! Thieves!"

Shortly after, a haggard figure in a shabby old woolen coat scaled the flat rock, in his extended hands held what looked like a bow that was being stretched as far as the string would go. Tabitha ran down, cutting off the view of the new arrival, her frightened screams piercing the night that had suddenly gone chilly.

Ombima wanted to rise to shove her out of the way of the danger that he knew lurked behind her, but when he tried to move, the same *thwack!* sound that he had heard before sounded close to his ear, and the next minute he was falling into a deep hole that was swimming with a million stars.

* * *

The school watchman stood above the two naked bodies holding his broken bow by his side, and the dizziness that had earlier driven him to sleep on duty lifted slowly, the way a cloud of mist might rise above the treetops when the dawn breaks. One of the bodies had an arrow shaft sticking out of it, and the other was curled up, trapped underneath the other's weight. The night guard saw the lower body move—very slightly—and thought it might even be alive.

Then he became aware of the other man at the scene and the thought crossed his dazed mind that he should ask him, whoever he was, to give him a hand in order that they might lift the heavy body he had shot off the other trapped underneath.

But when the watchman looked closely at the face of the other man, who was standing with his rounded shoulders sloped as if he was also dazed himself, he suddenly gave a cry, jumping back.

"Hey, I know you, don't I?" cried the old man, trying to shake the thick fuzz out of his brain. "I say, I know you! Don't you come from Ivona, mister? Don't you own the big shop in Chavakali that sells fertilizer?"

Meanwhile, as the watchman struggled with his memory, the night revelers were heard coming closer, their voices rising above the silver-topped trees as they sang:

Tura ichova, tura ichova,
Pastor, tura ichova cheriza avageni!
Tura ichova
Pastor, tura ichova cheriza avageni...

Open the door, come out,
Our pastor, come on out and salute the guests!
Come on out,
Pastor, come on out and show yourself...

Chapter Eighteen

ANDIMI WAS GLAD to be back home. It had been a long forty-eight hours that he had spent in the damp cells in the police station at Vihiga. In this period, squatted on his laurels beside common criminals he would never in his life have dreamt of sharing a roof with, he had received an education. He experienced the generosity of men at the very deep end of survival where a crusty slice of bread can be heaven compared to a whole loaf on a shop shelf in freedom outside, and how that morsel could be split equally among all, regardless who they were. He had also come face to face with the meanness of man, where a steel-toed boot could readily dispense terror to a backside that was sitting in the wrong place at the slightest provocation. He also learned to answer to a call at the snap of a finger and, most important, he had come face to face with the frightening reality of losing power completely, such that in the space of an instant, every little thing he did—even the presumed privileges of sitting down and standing up—would be at the behest of another man. It was this that had frightened him most.

He now sat thinking over this long period of his life, a cup of coffee steaming away at arm's length. He was sitting on the raised patio in his favorite cane chair gazing out at the undulating treetops as night slowly fell across the distant hills, hardly conscious of the vista because his mind was miles away. He had just taken a long warm herbal bath prepared by Midecha, and it had eased him somehow, although the tenseness was still inside. Midecha had been wonderful, coming to the cells twice a day, bringing him food. It was her who had so efficiently handled the guests who streamed to tell him *pole*, a good number of them just there to see what he looked like after the ordeal. Honestly, now that he reflected on it, he didn't know how he would have coped without her.

It had been a long tussle that his lawyers had put up for him and it was with relief that the magistrate had finally agreed to bail. And the boys had pulled the good job even further and muscled him into his car through the crowd that had been waiting outside the courtroom. It seemed like his perception had changed about so many people because until now, he had thought that the lawyers' only interest was in fleecing as much money as they could out of his businesses. He was grateful that his children had not been around to see him dragged through all this. *That* would certainly have broken him. Maybe it hadn't been such a bad idea to send them away for their education after all. His only hope now was that the old man who had been guarding the school that fateful night would be found and made to confess so as to set the record straight.

Midecha coming to announce his evening meal interrupted his reverie. She served *ugali* and *ngege* in pepper stew, just as he liked. He looked up at her dark soft face, honorably rounded as middle age took over, and a most strange feeling came over him. Most of the staff had clocked out and now there was only the boy who took care of the cattle still to lock them up and let the dogs out for the night. Andimi slowly lifted his hand and rested it on her plump soft one. She was so much different from Tabitha, he now realized. "Midecha," he said softly, "please sit down. I need to talk to you."

There was mild surprise in her round eyes given she had been waiting, anticipating to be let off for the day, so as to get back to her room at the back of the kitchen to see her children to bed. She hardly saw them these days, being on and off to the courts in Vihiga.

There was another cane chair close by in which Madam had sat some evenings when there was work she had carried home from school. Midecha sat down in it and crossed her hands in her lap over her spotlessly clean apron, waiting.

"Move closer," said Andimi, gazing out toward the fiery hills in the distance. She pulled her chair closer, a little tense. Once more he rested his hand on hers and in the softest voice she had ever heard him use, he said, "How would you like to come take care of me here, Midecha? I mean, permanently?"

There was utter surprise on her face this time around. At the same time, it dawned on her that it had not been quite out of the blue. Nevertheless, she found herself rising to her feet, her breath sucking in.

"*Mzee...*" she started to say, but the words somehow dried on her lips. He was watching her keenly, a strange look that she had never seen in his eyes, which had gone very soft all over her.

"I'm sorry, I didn't mean to surprise you," he said getting up. His lips had curled at the corners, although the smile didn't reach his intense dark eyes.

"No, it is alright," said Midecha, looking out toward the fiery vista, a splash of fire touching her dark face. "I was only... well, not expecting anything like that, that's what I meant."

"So," he moved up to where she was and rested his hand on her shoulder, "does that mean yes?"

For a while the confusion played on her face, and then she turned to face him in perhaps the boldest gesture since she had started working for him. She studied his eyes, although not for long because hers soon dropped to the floor.

"At least think about it," he implored, stepping back. "You can take as long as you like."

"Yes, *Mzee*," Midecha said, surprised at the man. Then she picked up the forgotten cup of coffee and, bowing in the same way as she had done countless other times, she turned and left through the sliding doors.

As she trudged her weary feet back to her quarters at the back of the house, Midecha's head was in a spin. She was wondering at the hardheartedness of the man. Even before the grass on Madam's grave could sprout, the blood in his veins was already yearning for a replacement. Midecha loved her work, true. But she realized she would have to leave.

"Good night, my new love," whispered Andimi to himself as his unperceiving mind took in the fading vista of the setting sun, before it grotesquely settled on his new life with Midecha.

* * *

The day Andimi arrived in the village was the same day Sayo left. She woke up Aradi unusually early that day and asked him to take his porridge. They were going on a journey, so she said, although she did not tell him where. After his father had been taken to the hospital, there had been a change in her that now held Aradi back. She did not talk much and preferred to pass the day sitting in the shade of the tree outside the home. Sometimes she picked grain, or wove a mat, or sung, or just sat. Close by was Saliku's grave, now becoming overgrown with grass. Aradi had been going silently about his duties, preparing most of the meals and doing the washing that needed to be done.

He hoped there was something he could do to help her pull out of her mood because it made him sad to see her so.

Today, his mother had changed. She got up early and by the time Aradi awoke, she had already made breakfast. It looked as if she was her old self again. He also saw she had brought out his Christmas clothes and shoes. Maybe they were going to visit his father at the hospital. He was suddenly excited.

He went outside. It would be a welcome change, he thought, as he watched steam rise from the tall grass fast encroaching on the back door, now that there was no cow to eat it.

Some old men had come and taken away the black cow to the market in Mudete on the day Father had been admitted to the hospital to raise the money the hospital demanded. And only two days ago they had returned for the grey one, leaving the compound without a cow. Lately it had been so quiet, with only him and his mother in the compound. A few women from the church came by to sit with his mother under the tree and talk, but even those were coming less and less now. Only Rebecca made a point of passing by every evening, and Aradi wished she knew how warm she made the house with her chat and laughter. Kesenwa came too sometimes, but then he had to leave to attend to his father's cattle and Aradi found himself alone. Then he thought about Saliku and her friend, Mideva, who had gone to a new school in Kericho, as if she too had died. It was certainly good to be going somewhere, even if only for a while.

Aradi went back indoors and changed from his patched old shorts, now thrilled at the thought of putting on the stiff new khaki ones that came out only on very special occasions. He whistled softly as he got into the ironed shirt that smelled of the white *marashi* balls his mother kept at the bottom of the clothes trunk to keep it smelling good and to keep cockroaches away. It was only as he put on his shoes that he realized he had forgotten to wash his face ran out to the bath shelter at the back where there was water in the bottom of the earthen trough.

As he was slurping up his porridge, his mother emerged from the inner room. She was dressed in her best dress too, the one she had worn to the show. She brought out what looked like a bundle of clothes wrapped up in her *lesso* and this struck Aradi as a bit odd, as she usually packed like this only when going away for more than two days, like when she went visiting grandmother in Masana. He wondered if she had packed his clothes as well.

Realizing it was him who was holding them up, he hurried up with his porridge and sprang up.

"I am ready, Mama."

"Good. Take this here for me, will you?" She handed him a package that contained some food, which he slung onto his shoulder. She picked up the bigger bundle and raised it to her head the way she carried things from the market. "Now let's get on our way before the sun is hot overhead."

The dew was still heavy on the path-side grass and the frogs down by the valley croaked. It was only when they met a man coming in the opposite direction close to Chugi and his mother barely stopped to greet him that Aradi begun to realize they were going on an unusual journey.

* * *

Shira umudoga garaha, shira umudoga garaha...
Gase urasena umwana...

It was the same dirge that Ang'ote had sung so passionately at the funeral, and he was going to sing it again. It irritated Rebecca, and she wanted to ask him to stop, but at the same time, it was better than the deafening silence inside the hut.

Rebecca sat at the fireplace, fanning the fire to prepare a throat remedy. She had hardly eaten the meal she had so carefully prepared for him that evening, the remains of which steamed away in the pot by the fire. There was a constriction in her throat that made it hard to swallow anything, even saliva, which was making her very uncomfortable. Soon her voice would fade away too, she knew. It must be the water they had drunk at Madam's maiden village when she and Oresha had gone to report the bad news.

Ang'ote, on his part, seemed quite at peace with himself. He was sitting up on the new bed he had bought, leaning against the sooty wall. The bed was threefold what the old one had been. He had dumped the old termite-infested cot in the banana trees to rot away together with the lumpy, bug-infested mattress. Now he had a stiff, new foam mattress on which he would dream a thousand dreams in the company of his love, in the comfort of the new cotton sheets that still smelled of the mill.

There was a light on in the hut, a decent Dietz lantern with a huge clear globe that shone like the one in Indimuli's shop. So brightly did it shine not a single rat had shown its face, Ang'ote observed with amusement. In the corner of the brightly lit hut the new tin sheets the pick up truck had brought from Mbale were stacked leaning against the wall, shining like mirrors. The *fundi* had already taken the measurements and the work on the new house would start the following day. *Mzee* had said to hurry it up because he had a journey to make the coming week.

Everything was ready. The boys from the village who would be working with the *fundi* had been told to come early in the morning. They were not to worry about even a cup of tea because everything would be provided. Now it remained only for the night to mature into day and the work would begin.

Ang'ote had a self-satisfied smile on his face as he reached for his old one-string fiddle up in the thatch. It was a dark sooty color from hanging up there, and he blew on it to get the dust off. It was quite a while since he had last played it.

He tightened the string of the little bow and rubbed it into a wad of tree wax on the side of the hollowed resonator. He turned the tuning peg at the end of the slender arm until he struck a chord that he was looking for. Then he made himself comfortable on the bed, crossing his legs and drawing his feet in the way children do. A dreamy look came to his face as he slowly played the fiddle and launched into the song:

Shira umudoga garaha, shira umudoga garaha,
Gase urasena umwana...

He paused to allow the lyre time to weave into the tune. It was a slightly different style in which he was singing this song that momentarily captivated Rebecca. She stopped making the fire to listen. She had hardly spoken a word to him in two days, and he had at last given up trying to start a conversation, seeing he was going to get nowhere.

He rubbed the little bow against the string and plucked it at the same time with his left hand so it vibrated in a most unusual way, weaving into the song. It was a long wavering note that rose and fell with his mourning. It was like nothing Rebecca had ever heard before.

Shira umudoga… garaha!
Bayaye-bo! Ondego!

The little bow twisted to a higher note and grieved on that impossibly high level for a while, straining. And then it dropped almost suddenly back to the former note where it scoured and rubbed most mournfully, the result was like a bucketful of water doused over a roaring fire.

Bayaye-bo! Ondego!
Bayaye-bo! Ondego!

Rebecca had never heard the song sung quite in that way. It was as if both Ang'ote and his fiddle were singing, one leading and the other responding. It was amazing, but painfully annoying all at the same time.

Once Ang'ote cut out his instrument and propelled his unaccompanied voice up to a pitch higher than the one he had started with and left it there, exploring, taunting, until he could no longer keep his breath. And then he let go and wove his way back down in a flutter like a wounded bird falling suddenly out of the sky. As he gulped more air, the lyre picked up and deftly climbed back to where he had been, perfectly simulating the timbre of his voice in every progressive step. Under different circumstances, this could have been sheer wizardry.

But that was before they both went up the same path together, goading each other like goddesses of the rare arts, leaning on the other whenever they faltered until they both exploded in a crashing climax that saw tears come to Ang'ote's eyes:

Drive the car slowly, drive the car slowly,
For you could knock down a child...

Drive the car... slowly!
Bayaye-bo! Ondego!

And Rebecca, starved for breath, buried her face in her lap and whimpered. She was weeping too, just like he was.

"Please stop singing that song, Ang'ote," she burst out at last. Her voice was coarse. It was the first time she had spoken to him in two straight days.

"Why, my love?" Ang'ote asked, lowering the lyre from his shoulder, a look of mild surprise on his face.

"I don't like it, I just don't." She sniffed and dried her eyes on the corner of her *lesso*.

"I'm sorry, I didn't know."

Ang'ote slowly put aside the lyre and rubbed his moist eyes. He watched her prepare the fire, for a moment lost for words. Then he found his thoughts wandering to the new house they were going to put up starting tomorrow. It was all that occupied his thoughts of late. He had already prepared the bundle of sticks, sharpened at one end, which the *fundi* would use when measuring the house on the ground. They were placed neatly against the wall in the far corner. Beside them was the coil of new manila string he had bought in Mbale for the job, together with twenty kilos of nails in a sack. He hoped that they would be enough for the job. There were the tools for the job, which he had forgotten to buy in his haste, but somehow, that did not worry him much. He would borrow Rebecca's old axe for any chopping work they might need to do. As for the machetes, he would go to Mariko down the path. Makambi, the weaver, would provide one too. The rest, the *fundi's* assistants would bring along—after all, he was going to pay them, wasn't he? As for the rest of the labor, he was certain it would be no problem. The young men would come in their numbers.

So, if all that was in order, then what could be the problem? He looked at his bride… yes, *bride*. That is what she was. They were getting married tomorrow. It was almost unbelievable.

Rebecca was bent over the fire, stirring the liquid in the pot. She took some dried *imbindi* roots from a bundle on the floor she had brought from Oresha's compound and broke them in little pieces into the pot, stirring slowly. She then searched the bundle for some dried *abachi* leaves, which she added to the mixture. Already the steam rising from the pot was becoming pungent. She broke some more twigs into the fire and covered the pot with an old metal plate. The rest of the bundle she tied up neatly with a string of banana fiber and stacked it away.

Ang'ote watched her working. She was so silent, he wondered why. There was the new dress he had bought her in Mbale, which was still neatly folded in the paper bag on the bed. She had not tried it on yet. He was anxious to see what she would look like in it, but then he did not want to hurry her. Perhaps she was just a little nervous because it was new?

While the pot boiled, Rebecca went to wash the dishes that had been waiting for her the whole day. She had taken off her headscarf and in the light of the tin lamp her hair was a dull grey, her brow lined. But her eyes, as usual, were dark and bright. There was something on her mind but Ang'ote did not know what. But it clouded her timeless beauty. He knew that because he knew when she was troubled. What was it? Was she simply overawed at so much wealth so suddenly? Or, and he shuddered just to think about this, could she be doubtful of his love?

He watched her, seated in partial darkness out of reach of the wavering light. She gathered up her old dress between her knees and sat on the low kitchen stool facing the wall, her lips sucked in, strong hands scrubbing deftly. The light heightened the features on her face, high cheekbones and arched eyebrows, cleft chin going soft underneath with age. There was this rugged tenderness about her that defied the long hours out in the open sun. She was the one special woman that he would move the world for, Ang'ote realized with a shudder. And, as usual, when this feeling came to him, he wanted to reach across and touch her, if only to reassure himself that she was there with him. He wished to sing her a special song he had composed to celebrate their love tonight, a song he had secretly been working on late into the night the whole of the past week. And he was waiting for the most opportune moment that evening. Especially tonight, he had to sing the song to her. It was significant because it would be their last day of... freedom. The thought of the word *freedom* brought a snide laugh to the back of his throat. What freedom had he really had in the life he had been living?

All of a sudden, Rebecca rose to her feet, the dishes she had been washing still in the old pan full of soapy water.

"Ang'ote, I am leaving," she announced, picking up her headscarf draped on the sooty shelf on the wall. "I am going home."

There was a note in her voice he had never heard before. Ang'ote sprang to his feet, knocking over his prized fiddle.

"What? Wait, my love, what?"

But Rebecca was already moving out the door, throwing her *lesso* about her shoulders and adjusting her headscarf. She was walking fast, determinedly, and there were tears in her eyes as she bent in the ring of light to get beneath the low eave.

Ang'ote looked about him, bewildered. Her throat medicine still simmered away on the fire, and her gift parcel was on the bed, still unopened. There was disbelief on his face, as if he had not really heard what she had said. And then it hit him that it was indeed true, she had left. With a sense of urgency, he grabbed for his club behind the door and dived under the bed for his old *akala* sandals. There was not time enough to secure the door as he hurried out into the dark night after her.

"Rebecca, please wait!" he shouted, a tight edge to his voice. She walked fast on down the path, hugging her *lesso* to herself and did not turn around. Ang'ote kicked up a trot, almost tripping his foot on some root on the dark path. His breath hissed out of his clenched teeth, his heart beating in his ears. It was a very dark night and he could just barely see her hurrying on the path ahead. The bright moon of just the day before had disappeared suddenly, whipped up by a mass of clouds that had come blowing from the hills in Ivugwi. Now the night was dark and chilly, no longer ringing with the drums of Christmas time. The rains would come early this season.

Rebecca's compound was not very far from Ang'ote's, but by the time he got there, he was out of breath, panting hard. As he turned into the entrance he saw Rebecca getting into the old hut and a moment later, the lance of light died as the door was pushed shut. Ang'ote hastened and knocked on the door.

"Rebecca, please open," he called, frightened. "Don't lock me out, please open the door."

There was no answer from the other side. He crouched and looked through a chink in the weather worn door. She was seated at the table on which a tin lamp burned, black smoke rising in a straight column toward the old thatch that was decorated with tendrils of soot as thick as fingers. She leaned forward on the table, her face buried in the crook of her arm, her worn *lesso* thrown over her head. Around the table the children were asleep, curled up on the old mats in the best positions where they could get the most comfort out of the few shared blankets, snoring softly in their sleep. There were some more in the inner room, sleeping side by side with the cow. On the few folded chairs stacked against the wall were the few chickens she owned, perched on the dirtied wooden slats.

Ang'ote knocked on the door again, almost giving in to despair.

"Please go away," said Rebecca, not looking up. Ang'ote knocked harder, persistently, until she rose from the chair.

She stood in the doorway, framed in the lamplight with her *lesso* thrown over her head. In the faint light that reached her dark bright eyes she looked tired, even a little aged. Ang'ote felt all the words he had meant to say dry up on his lips. He retreated into the shadows and waited.

At last she stepped outside and drew the door closed softly behind her, careful that she should not disturb her grandchildren too much.

"Come," she whispered, moving into the shade of the scarred fruit tree that grew close to the hut and which would never bring forth its fruit because the children were forever breaking off its branches in their play. She stood beneath the tree with her arms crossed over her chest and Ang'ote went closer, dropping the club he had been carrying. He drew even closer, mesmerized by the faint shine in her eyes. But when he went to embrace her, she held out her hand and said, "Don't, please don't."

Ang'ote stopped dead. Something invisible, like a gust of intangible wind, hit him smack in the face. She stood still, her shaded eyes like deep wells with no bottom. It was a while before he finally found his voice.

"Rebecca," he said breathlessly, "Are you deserting me? Don't tell me it's what you are trying to say." He could hardly believe the ring of frightening truth even in his own words.

"Yes, that's what I'm saying, Ang'ote," she said in a calm, sure voice, the sort of tone she might adopt with an errant grandchild. "I can no longer love you."

It confirmed Ang'ote's worst fear, hitting him with a suddenness that sapped away all the strength in him.

"You are not... you *cannot*..." he hung on, disbelieving, trying to see into her eyes to discern any minute clue that the words were not true, but failing because of the poor light.

"Yes, I am, Ang'ote. I am sorry, but we can no longer see each other."

"But *why*?" cried Ang'ote, a painful lump pushing up his throat.

"I just can't. I can't explain. But I just can't. I am sorry, Ang'ote." She had hardly moved, but as she said the last part, her voice wavered and faded, a slight shudder shaking her frail shoulders. "You must find someone else."

"Oh, I see," said Ang'ote, taking a step back. "Someone else, indeed!" Now there was spite in his voice. He paused to look at her up and down, tears of pain welling up behind his eyes, which had suddenly turned fiery in the dark. "Oh, I guess I should have known better."

There was a grating at the back of his voice that alarmed Rebecca and she said, "What is it, Ang'ote? What should you have known?"

"Oh, I guess it doesn't matter now," he said with a shrug.

Rebecca moved closer, suddenly feeling some urge to hold him, just like he had felt a moment back. It took all her will to restrain herself. "What doesn't matter, Ang'ote?" she asked, uncertainty lacing her voice.

"I should have known that you were never going to start this new life with me. It was there all long—all those times you pretended to persuade me—oh, how I wish I had seen through you, *you old woman!*"

"Stop!" Rebecca's voice rang with authority that she had never used before with him. "Stop what you are saying. You know it's not true." There was hurt as well as shock in her voice.

"Oh yes, it is," said Ang'ote, unfazed. "You were never meant for me, really. I should have known."

"Yes, you are right," said Rebecca, sadly. "You deserve a better woman, Ang'ote. A *younger* woman. You don't need me."

"Oh, just shut up, old woman!" he snapped, turning his face the other way. "Just stop, will you? I don't want you lecturing me anymore."

"But I am right and you will agree with me. This new life you will be leading was never for me. I just can't picture myself..."

"Yes, you can't live that life," he said with conviction. "I should have listened to my friends—they indeed tried to warn me."

"*Friend*, you mean?" said Rebecca, moving round to stand in front of him so she could peer into his face. "*Friend*, you really mean, Ang'ote? *Eh?* Where is that friend, now? Tell me. Where is Ombima? And where, too, is Madam, *eh?* Aren't you now saying you are going to live your life of luxury with the eyes of your so-called 'friend' on your hands? Eh? With the blood of Madam reflecting in your iron sheets? Is that what you are saying, Ang'ote? Well, one just hopes you are going to be happy as the new Mudeya-Ngoko!"

"Shut up, old woman! I will find cause to give you a beating, I say!" Ang'ote's voice had risen such that one of the grandchildren sleeping inside awoke. He came to stand in the doorway, rubbing his eyes, gazing out into the night, wondering who was with his grandmother outside. Soon another child joined him, peeking through the gap beside his brother.

"Go home now," said Rebecca, the earlier firmness back in her voice, casting a nervous glance at the spectators standing in the doorway.

"Oh, and I will too, old woman," said Ang'ote, inching back into the shadows, searching the ground for the club with his hands. "I will, indeed. And you will never have to worry about me, I promise you. Now, you go back in to your grandchildren, I can see they need you more."

And with that his hands closed around the smooth handle of the club and he turned on his heel, hurrying off into the night.

Rebecca waited a while by the barren old fruit tree, a hundred thoughts coursing through her head. One of the grandchildren ventured out and came to stand by her, tugging at her skirt. She turned away and shepherded them back into the house, closing the door softly behind her, shutting out the night.

As she lay in her hard bed after putting the grandchildren back in their places, Rebecca thought about Sayo. She admired the younger woman and her capacity for goodness. She had left the village that morning to go back to her people in Masana, where she would remain with the boy until the required separation had been made and the home cleansed. God give us more of such characters, prayed Rebecca as she fell asleep, that the world may smell of some goodness.

Chapter Nineteen

THE RAINS HAD come and washed the country clean, the red soils first sucking in the rain drops like a hungry child, then running in rivulets that carried away the dirt and dust of the dry season, before giving birth to a fresh greenness. Aradi had been walking the whole morning and was feeling thirsty, but he knew that if he told his father, he would insist that they go to a hotel where they would end up ordering some food, spending all the money they had collected that day. What was more, Aradi did not like going to hotels because he disliked the way people looked at them, with him leading his father by hand. Often they would turn when his father's white cane went *tap! tap!* on the floor, and stop what they had been doing to see how the blind man would find his chair.

Aradi wondered why they just couldn't leave them alone. After all, what was so strange about a blind man?

It was a hot, windy day and the market in Mbale was teeming with people doing their Easter time shopping. It was the end of the third month and, in the town's main street, many people walked up and down, keen on buying one thing or another to mark the crucifixion of Jesus Christ. The shoppers were attracted by the huge discount signs the Asian traders had pasted on their windows, the village women drawn by the petty items the traders pasted to their two-kilogram bags of sugar and rice: a pencil for their schoolchildren, a teaspoon or a plastic comb for their daughter who had recently joined secondary school.

In the main market square a young man with a megaphone was saying "*Ee,* Mama! Buy your husband this shirt here that came from London for Easter. Don't put your house to shame by letting him walk around the village in a tattered old shirt!" Those *mitumba* traders who could not afford a megaphone simply hollered out their wares, ringing tiny bells and whistling shrilly at anyone who cared to listen.

Aradi cut his way through this din, leading his father who kept stopping to ask after something he had overheard or to allow someone to put an offering in the little tin he jingled. They needed to hurry. His father had an appointment with the doctor that afternoon and Aradi was worried that they would miss him, and that if they did, it would have to wait until after the Easter holiday. And yet his father would not go to sleep last night for the tingly pain he kept complaining about deep in his head.

Even then, Aradi could not blame him for stopping now and then. Today the people seemed especially generous with their loose change. Perhaps they would raise enough to buy a packet of wheat flour and a kilo of meat for their Sunday meal tomorrow. Mother had left to go seek work in the village but Aradi was doubtful that she would bring back enough for all that they needed. It made Aradi think of the Easter season when they had been all together with Saliku, before his father lost his sight. Life had been good.

Father had been asking a lot about his old friend Ang'ote of late, and Aradi was at pains to explain that Ang'ote just might have left the village for good. It was now near three months since Ang'ote had disappeared, and there had been no word of him. There were those who claimed to have seen him last. That he was carrying his old fiddle slung on his shoulder and a little bundle wrapped up in an old *lesso* like Aradi and his mother had carried on their journey back to his mother's village. That was before a team of elders from Ivona had come to take them back. Ang'ote had been headed in the direction of Mbale. At first they had all thought that he had left on a journey somewhere and would be back, but then with the passing of time, hope had slowly died. The rains had come and it was planting season and there had been no one to farm his tiny maize *shamba*. Eventually his kinsmen had come to take over his property and keep it maintained for him. Mudeya-Ngoko, on Andimi's instructions, had mobilized the other workers and they had put up the new house for him one sunny Sunday, although they had left the *kesegese* at the top of the house undone, hoping that one day he would come back to do it himself. Meanwhile the young men from the neighborhood were free to use the house as a *siimba* while they awaited his return.

Aradi's father, somehow when he was told, thought it was all a big joke. He still believed that Ang'ote would be here, even if only to prepare his singers for the Easter chorals. And that was the big problem with him.

As usual, there were crowds in the hospital grounds, some lying on the lawns resting in the shade after long hours of haggling in the hot sun of the marketplace, and others sitting on the benches waiting for the doctor. There was a white Land Rover parked outside the hospital, similar to the one that had come to the village to give children polio jabs. Perhaps they were going to another village close by, thought Aradi.

He led his father down the now familiar corridor to the bench outside the doctor's door where some patients were already seated waiting. They were mostly elderly people in the company of their relations dozing away the hours leaning on their walking sticks, and who hardly bothered to look up to see who the new arrival was. Aradi's father took his seat and adjusted his hat over his brow, resting his chin on the cane. There was a strange expression of contentment on his face today, as if for once his troubles no longer mattered. And Aradi was pleased for him.

Aradi begged Ombima for permission to go to the toilets and his father sleepily grunted his assent. He could go walk around if he cared, for the queue was moving pretty slowly, anyway. Aradi, glad at the chance to indulge in some play, ran off in the direction of the toilets at the back of the building.

* * *

As he sat there waiting, Ombima soon got the urge to smoke. Lately he had been feeling that way, especially when his son was not with him and he had nothing to do. It helped ease the restlessness inside him. Forgetting where he was, he reached into the folds of his worn coat and took out the little tobacco tin he had taken to carrying around together with a bundle of old yellowed newspaper. He had learned to roll his cigarettes on his own mostly because his wife did not approve of the habit, and he could not ask the boy to do it for him.

The moment he opened the lid on the little flat tin that had once carried hair pomade the old man seated next to him stirred and said, "I can smell tobacco. Who is it taking snuff at this time of day?"

He was addressing his grandson who had accompanied him to the hospital. But of course he had forgotten that the boy had shortly run off to play.

Ombima, careful that he shouldn't disturb the other patients, turned to the old man who had spoken, "Does it bother you if I smoke?"

"Oh, not at all, my friend!" said the old man cheerfully. "You can do whatever you please. You know, I believe a man should enjoy all that gives him pleasure in this life while he still can. I learned that after I lost my sight. But, of course, like all wisdom, it came rather too late!" The old man broke off in a hearty cackle that soon progressed into bouts of chesty coughing and he had to break it off, breathing heavily through his teeth.

Ombima, who had just torn off a neat piece of newspaper ready to roll the cigarette paused and turned to his compatriot, alarmed.

"I am sorry, my friend, that was some serious coughing there."

"Oh, don't say it!" said the old man with a wave of the hand, as if it irritated him to be reminded of his condition. "It is nothing, I say." He took a swipe at the clear drool staining his bushy moustache, wiping his hand on a soiled handkerchief that was tied to his coat button for the purpose. "It is nothing. It should have killed me a long time ago. But look at me, I'm still here with you my children, breathing the air of this world as the sun travels from Ivugwi to Imadiori, and back again tomorrow."

"So did I hear you say you are blind?" asked Ombima, wetting the cigarette with spittle to make it form a more compact roll.

"Yes, why?" The older man's eyebrows rose above his absent eyes, wrinkled face brightening underneath his slanted old tweed cap.

"You see, I am blind too," said Ombima with an immense sense of discovery.

"Is it?" The old man was visibly surprised. "But you sound so young, how then did it happen?"

"Oh, you thought it was only old men who got blind?"

A younger woman seated next to the old man, and who was waiting to have a bandaged wound on her foot examined was listening with interest as the two blind men conversed. She was, in fact, wondering just what it was like to see the world through the eyes of a blind man.

But just then, as the younger blind man raised his cigarette to his lips and fished out an old box of matches, a nurse who had been passing by came and snatched away the cigarette. "You cannot do *that* here, you! Don't you know where you are?" she spat at the patient in a sharp reprimanding voice. "One wonders just what sense there is left in some of you *shamba* people. Or do you imagine that just because you are blind and old you can do whatever you want?"

There was a moment of shocked silence in which Ombima paused with his match ready to light the missing cigarette. And then the old man, obviously used to this kind of treatment, snarled, "And just where should he have gone to smoke, you mannerless child, *eh*? Walked his way to the field outside? One would think the helpless would have some peace left in this world!" He broke off with a wheezy laugh, which encouraged the rest of the stunned patients to join in, tickled by the old man's ghastly wit.

"What is the world coming to?" said someone else far down the hall. "Is this what they call modern living—when a child of just the other day can talk in that way to an elder, and still have the dignity to feel right about it?" He shook his head, tut-tutting to himself. "Oh, the children of today!"

The door squealed open and a man with his hand in a sling stepped out. The same nurse who had reprimanded Ombima appeared to call in the next patient, jostling them in as if every bit of time wasted was the doctor's money gone down the drain.

"Just you let her give me that treatment, I will teach her a few lessons with my *bakora*!" vowed the same man who had spoken just a moment back.

Ombima, who was still silent, was jerked to his senses by the hand of the blind old man falling on his shoulder.

"Don't let it worry you, my friend," said the old man, "It is just a passing cloud. Where was it you said you came from?"

"I come from Ivona, far across the hills close to Tiriki country," Ombima said.

"Oh, I know where Ivona is, son. Do you think I don't know Maragoliland? Or is it you think I was born blind?" Yet again he interjected his speech with a wheezy laugh. "I know Ivona, alright. Doesn't one pass through your village on the way to the cattle market in Mudete? You see, I even have relations there, although I really wouldn't call them that. Our daughter was married to a nasty man from your village called Savatia. He was mean as a *fisi*!"

"That Savatia of Mukangula's, you mean?" asked Ombima. "He died a long time ago. He was drowned in a swollen river coming back from a beer ceremony in Mago."

"It was probably free beer too!" spat out the old man. "The man was too cheap to buy anything, even for himself. Let him rest wherever he went!"

Ombima was surprised at such bitterness in the old man who had appeared rather civil just a moment back. But just as he was going to ask about it, the doctor's door squealed open yet again and the same nurse appeared, shouting at the old man to get in, unless he wanted to spend Easter Monday with his ailments.

The old man got to his feet, cursing. "Someone seen my grandson?" he asked as he took a wobbly step, tapping the floor.

And just at that moment the boy came running down the corridor, a bright look on his face. "Wait, *Guga*! I will take you." Behind him came Aradi, the same bright expression on his face.

When his father a moment back had excused Aradi, he had wandered about the hospital grounds, looking at the long straight buildings. It was then that his eyes caught a face he thought looked familiar among the people seated in the open waiting bay. Curious, he approached the bay trying to recall where he had seen the boy whose heart-shaped face became even more familiar the closer he got. As for the other boy, he sat there on the high bench, his legs swinging, a smile playing on his rather girlish face. He was chewing on a piece of sugarcane, carefully collecting the peelings in his lap to throw in the dustbin hanging on the wall.

"*Ndi?*" asked Aradi, climbing onto the bench.

And it was only when the boy said "A-ah!" that he remembered.

"Onzere, is it?" he said, extending his hand. "I've met you before—when I brought my sister here."

The boy's eyes lit up, his lips parting in a shy smile.

"Have you brought your grandfather here for his medicine again?" asked Aradi, moving closer on the bench.

Onzere nodded, swallowing the sweet juice in his mouth.

"Well, I've brought my father too," said Aradi, surprised. "You see, he is now blind!"

The blind old man paused at the doctor's door listening to his grandson explain, turning a deaf ear to the ill-mannered nurse behind him. And when Onzere had finished, the old man shook his head and said to his blind acquaintance of just a moment back, "See? Indeed the world is round, now I believe, my friend. Just now we were going to part, save for our eyes, these children here! Who would believe we would meet again under these circumstances? Indeed we shall live to see yet another tomorrow, my friend—you believe that!"

Acknowledgments

AS THEY SAY, a wall can last a hundred years. But it must have a pillar or two, however good the builder be.

I'd like to mention here a few people:

Susan Linnée, who wasted part of her breath on a breezy Sunday afternoon and prodded a journey of many steps. Also Jimmi Makotsi, this guy in rolled shirtsleeves who believes he can get perfection, even where he knows there's none ever, and who did the mule's work here. Not forgetting the affable Prof. Arthur Luvai, who had the patience to divide his attention between two drunken wannabes. Also all my friends at *Kwani?*—Binyavanga Wainaina, Billy Kahora, Parsalelo Kantai, Andia Kisia, and Annette Majanja. And it was David Kaiza who left his editorial fingerprints all over the pages.

A special mention goes to my American publisher, Shaun Randol, for rescuing the book from the garbage bin… a second time! Lastly, the countless small fry that I can't all mention here, but who said a brushing word or two that they probably didn't know mattered.

But also those few who cursed me, silently whispering that it's only crazy people who can hope to put *ugali* in their belly punching away at a plastic keyboard that doesn't sprout maize. Those, together with the nasty old KP&L—my apologies folks!—who made me write in yellow lantern light on cold Nairobi nights. To those I'm still thinking how best to curse you back. Even though they might have a point after all, because you must have a torrent to build a good bridge. And I hope this one can stand the test!

Anyway I just thought I might give it back to you. And tell all you good people, *Asande muno*. God bless.

Gazemba, S.A.
Nairobi, 2017

About the Author

BORN IN 1974 in Vihiga, Kenya, Stanley Gazemba has published three novels: *The Stone Hills of Maragoli* (Kwani?, winner of the 2003 Jomo Kenyatta Prize for fiction, published in the U.S. by The Mantle as *Forbidden Fruit*), *Khama* (DigitalBackBooks), and *Callused Hands* (Nsemia). He has also published eight children's books, of which *A Scare in the Village* (Oxford University Press) won the 2015 Jomo Kenyatta Prize for children's fiction. Gazemba's fiction has appeared in *'A' is for Ancestors*, a collection of short stories from the Caine Prize (Jacana); *Africa39: New Writing From Africa South of the Sahara* (Bloomsbury); *The Literary Review* (Fairleigh Dickinson Univ.); *Man of the House and Other New Short Stories from Kenya* (CCC Press); and *Crossing Borders* online magazine, among other publications.

A journalist by training, Gazemba has written for *The New York Times*, *The East African*, *Msanii* magazine, *Sunday Nation*, and *Saturday Nation*. Gazemba was the International Fellow at the Bread Loaf Writers' Conference in 2007.

Gazemba lives in Nairobi where he is the editor of Ketebul Music.